P9-DGC-229

Praise for CAROLYN WHEAT'S novels featuring CASS JAMESON

"A REAL WONDERFUL HEROINE."
—*Hartford Courant*

WHERE NOBODY DIES

"*Dead Man's Thoughts* was a fine first novel, and *Where Nobody Dies* is even better. Cass Jameson is good company, and Carolyn Wheat is one of the best new writers in the field." —Lawrence Block

"The author is a natural storyteller and the promise of solid talent in her debut is vividly affirmed in *Where Nobody Dies*." —*Kirkus Reviews*

DEAD MAN'S THOUGHTS

Nominated for the Mystery Writers of America's Edgar Award for Best First Novel

"Remarkable . . . a new kind of courtroom drama—achingly realistic, grimy, far removed from the rarefied atmosphere of Old Bailey or Perry Mason courtroom tales . . . Wrenching and fascinating." —*Booklist*

"Literate, witty . . . characters who have real depth and honest emotions." —*Library Journal*

FRESH KILLS

"Mounting emotional tension . . . a canny whodunit." —*Kirkus Reviews*

"She does a remarkably thorough and sensitive job of dealing with the emotionally charged issue of adoption." —*New York Times Book Review*

Berkley Prime Crime Books by Carolyn Wheat

FRESH KILLS
DEAD MAN'S THOUGHTS
WHERE NOBODY DIES
MEAN STREAK
TROUBLED WATERS

Coming in hardcover August 1998

SWORN TO DEFEND

TROUBLED WATERS

Carolyn Wheat

BERKLEY PRIME CRIME, NEW YORK

If you purchased this book without a cover, you should be aware that this book is stolen property. It was reported as "unsold and destroyed" to the publisher, and neither the author nor the publisher has received any payment for this "stripped book."

TROUBLED WATERS

A Berkley Prime Crime Book / published by arrangement with the author

PRINTING HISTORY
Berkley Prime Crime hardcover edition / August 1997
Berkley Prime Crime mass-market edition / June 1998

All rights reserved.
Copyright © 1997 by Carolyn Wheat
This book may not be reproduced in whole or in part,
by mimeograph or any other means, without permission.
For information address: The Berkley Publishing Group,
a member of Penguin Putnam, Inc.,
200 Madison Avenue, New York, NY 10016,

The Penguin Putnam Inc. World Wide Web site address is
http://www.penguinputnam.com

ISBN 0-425-16380-6

Berkley Prime Crime Books are published
by The Berkley Publishing Group,
a member of Penguin Putnam, Inc.,
200 Madison Avenue, New York, NY 10016,
The name BERKLEY PRIME CRIME and the BERKLEY PRIME CRIME
design are trademarks belonging to Berkley Publishing Corporation.

PRINTED IN THE UNITED STATES OF AMERICA

10 9 8 7 6 5 4 3 2 1

CHAPTER ONE

I thought she was dead.

I hoped she was dead.

But she was very much alive, too damned much alive, and her thin, nervous face stared at me from the front pages of every newspaper on the Court Street kiosk.

Jan was back. She'd been working at a Wal-Mart in Emporia, Kansas. One day she left work early and drove to Kansas City, where she walked into the FBI office in the federal building and turned herself in.

That night, Jan was the lead story on all three national newscasts. *Fugitive Captured: Woman who fled murder charges in 1982 lives underground for almost fifteen years.* "I never knew," says boyfriend. "She was the nicest clerk in the store," proclaims Wal-Mart manager. "I always suspected there was something," landlady announces. "She never got any mail. Not even catalogues."

Not even catalogues. Jan had fled to where not even L. L. Bean could follow.

I watched in fascination, flipping through all my channels to catch a glimpse of the exact same footage of cops marching Jan toward a waiting police van as the announcer repeated the charge: wanted for the shooting death of a federal agent in 1982.

She wore a long dress with a tiny flower print and a

stretched-out cardigan. Given the Indian summer temperatures, I assumed she was dressed to cope with the Wal-Mart air conditioning.

Face, dress, sweater all would have looked at home in a Depression photograph by Walker Evans.

I studied the face. It was the same Jan face, thin, intense, slightly mad. Darting eyes, a tendency to hang her head and gaze at the world through a curtain of limp hair. The hair was auburn, not the mouse-brown I remembered; I guessed at an over-the-counter dye job, not certain whether she'd done it as a disguise or just a middle-aged flight of fancy.

Do fugitives from justice care about covering that gray?

Once upon a long, long time ago, Jan and I had been foot soldiers in Lyndon Johnson's War on Poverty. In the summer of '69, we'd helped organize migrant farm workers into a union and gotten ourselves arrested. We'd been young, idealistic, insufficiently worried about consequences. The difference between us: I'd grown up and she hadn't.

Jan was back. On the way to court the next morning, I scooped up a copy of every paper on the newsstand. I'd need them in order to explain to the Honorable Harold "the Toop" Feldman exactly why I wasn't going to be picking a jury in his courtroom.

The Toop wore the absolutely worst hairpiece ever seen in the borough of Brooklyn, which was saying a great deal. On the outside, he resembled every pudgy, nerdy little guy who still lived in his old bedroom in his parents' house in Sheepshead Bay. But this particular nerd had graduated second in his class at Columbia Law School and clawed his way onto the bench by sheer willpower. People might laugh at Harry the Toop behind his back, but he demanded and got deferential respect in his courtroom.

He did not grant adjournments lightly. Hell, he didn't grant adjournments at all. The courthouse still buzzed over the time he'd given Kathy Malone the morning to bury her husband's mother, demanding that she show up ready to try her case after the lunch recess. She'd dabbed at her eyes with a sodden

Kleenex every few minutes, but she'd conducted a passible *voir dire*.

The Toop was not going to be pleased when I told him I absolutely, positively had to be in federal court in Ohio by two o'clock. This afternoon.

Jan was back, and that meant my brother Ron faced federal charges for the things he and Jan had done together in 1982. At the time, he and Jan had shared the same lawyer, but now, with her facing a murder charge, I wanted to be there in person, handling his case.

My Brooklyn client waited for me in the hallway outside the courtroom. He was a natty little black man of sixty-something. Pops, his neighbors called him. Sometimes he showed up in court with his twentysomething girlfriend and their four-month-old daughter, but today he'd come alone. He sported a hat with a bright green feather, which complemented his shiny, moss-colored Lawrence Welk suit. He was not unhappy to learn that his case might be put off; things didn't look good for him, and every day he spent out of jail with his wife and child was a blessing.

The judge was another matter.

"This case is ready for trial, Ms. Jameson," he said testily. "And I see no reason why it shouldn't be tried today. Whatever matters you may have pending out-of-state will just have to wait."

"This matter can't wait, Your Honor," I replied. I was uncomfortably aware that the urgency in my voice was dangerously close to the surface.

I took a deep yoga breath and willed myself to relax. Where to start? How to cut through the fog of ego that hung over the judge's bench and make him see that "the matter" I had to attend to wasn't just another case.

What you did when addressing the Toop was concentrate on his chin. You could maybe raise your eyes to encompass the nose, but you did not under any circumstances go above the eyebrows. If you did, you were in danger of seeing the Thing Itself. I aimed my words at the judicial nostrils.

"A woman named Jan Gebhardt was arrested in Kansas

yesterday," I began. "She was a fugitive from justice, having fled the jurisdiction in 1982 after the murder of a federal law enforcement officer."

"I read the papers, Counselor," Judge Feldman interjected. "Just tell me what all this has to do with you."

"I knew her in the summer of 1969," I replied. "When we were in college, we worked with migrant farm workers. Jan and I and my brother, Ron, and some other people."

"Ms. Jameson, just because you knew this woman in 1969 is no reason—"

"I understand, Judge," I cut in. "I'm not saying this very well. The reason I have to go to Ohio for her arraignment is that my brother was arrested along with Jan in 1982. The charges were held in abeyance after Jan fled, but now that she's turned herself in, they've been reinstated. He's surrendering this afternoon in the federal courthouse in Toledo." Among the many things I didn't say was that I'd had this piece of information not from my brother himself, but from my parents. It was they, not Ron, who'd begged me to go to Toledo and help out.

"I see," the judge said. His meaty hand stroked his chin.

I was aware of an unnatural silence in the courtroom. Everyone from the court officers to the front row of lawyers waiting for cases to be called to the defendants chained to chairs inside the well area seemed to hang on my words.

"Your Honor may recall that the federal agent was shot and killed during an arrest for transporting illegal aliens. Ms. Gebhardt and my brother were part of what was called the sanctuary movement. They were helping refugees from Central America." I deliberately glided over what the judge and I both knew; that sanctuary was no defense to violating the immigration laws.

"The van in which the aliens were being transported," I continued, carefully masking my feelings in legalese, "was owned by my brother. It's a specially equipped van. He's—" I stopped and drew a ragged breath, willing away thoughts of Ron facing arrest and imprisonment. "He's a quadriplegic. A Vietnam veteran."

I thought I detected a glimmer of sympathy in the judge's poached-egg eyes. Much as I hated to use Ron's condition this way, I had to pull out all the stops if I wanted the Toop to let me off the hook. "He didn't know what Jan was up to," I explained, uncomfortably aware that I was trying to convince myself as well as the judge. "He didn't know the people were illegals. But after the shooting, he was arrested along with Jan. She fled, and the charges against him were adjourned *sine die*."

This meant that the charges hung over Ron's head like the sword of Damocles. And now that Jan was being brought back for trial, the sword, which had glimmered into nothingness, had miraculously reappeared, as strong and solid as ever. Ron faced trial as a codefendant. He faced jail.

My brother faced jail. There was no way on God's earth I was going to let him do that alone, with or without Judge Feldman's permission.

He heard a few more minutes of argument. In truth, the prosecution put up only a token fight. I walked out of the courtroom a free woman. But the judge's last words hung in the air like a rain cloud.

"I'll give you two days, Counselor," he said. "And after that, I'm proceeding to trial with or without you."

In case I didn't get the full picture, he went on. "I'll assign a new lawyer, and while he prepares the case for trial, your client can enjoy the hospitality of the State of New York."

In other words, if I wasn't back in two days, Pops would go to jail.

"I'll be back," I promised.

Pops tugged at my sleeve as we left the courtroom. "What's that mean, Ms. Jameson? You ain't gonna leave me high and dry, now? You ain't gonna let old Pops go to jail?"

"No," I said firmly. "I'll be back in two days."

I believed it, too. My plan was to fly to Toledo, step into court next to Ron, play the quad card, get him out of the whole mess, and come straight home.

I swept into my office, hung my jacket on the hat stand, and walked toward the cork bulletin board in the corner. It held pink phone messages from January of last year, *New Yorker* cartoons of guys in jail commenting unfavorably on their legal representation, and, in the right-hand corner, a small collection of political buttons.

There it was, in between a NOW pin and a button from the last Legal Aid strike. A green button with a ripe red tomato in the center. Over the tomato were yellow letters that spelled out FLAC. Farm Labor Action Coalition, northwest Ohio's answer to Cesar Chavez' United Farmworkers union.

I'd spent one summer in Toledo, helping to organize that union. A summer in which I'd fallen in love, gotten high, taken political action, and seen my first dead body. A summer after which nothing was ever the same.

I removed the button carefully, trying not to damage the crumbling cork. I held it in my hand and looked down at it with wonder. Yesterday it had been a relic, a piece of the past with no possible relevance to the present. Today, Jan was back and the past had thundered into my present with a vengeance.

I stared at the button until the sun made little black spots in front of my eyes.

Stop the plane—I'm getting off!

The thought started drumming at me as we taxied along the La Guardia runway. The man in the seat ahead of mine reclined his chair as far back as it would go, in direct violation of the overhead sign, thrusting himself into my already tight space. Hell is other people, especially on airplanes.

Finally we were next in line to take off. The engines roared, the wheels accelerated, and we took the great broadjump into the sky. *Stop the plane . . . stop the plane . . . STOP THE PLANE* became a painful pounding in my inner ear.

I was never afraid to fly. Afraid to get to my destination, yes; this was not a new feeling. But flight itself was freeing. "Oh, I have slipped the surly bonds of earth." The trouble was, you had to land; the surly bonds of earth won every time.

Over the engine's roar I heard Ron's voice from the summer of '69: "Just how poisonous is this stuff, anyway?"

"A little dab'll do ya," Joel Rapaport had replied with his usual flipness.

A little dab was all it took to turn Kenny Gebhardt, Jan's cousin, from live nuisance to dead meat. The fact that he'd chosen to inhale the stuff didn't help much.

"Would you like coffee or tea, ma'am?" The real-life voice of the flight attendant brought me back to reality. I wondered just when I'd stopped answering to "miss" and edged over into "ma'am." Within seconds of ordering, a toylike bottle of vodka appeared on my tray along with a thimbleful of spiced tomato juice. I brushed away thoughts that drinking on an airplane before a court appearance wasn't a good idea; if the ghost of Kenny Gebhardt was going to occupy the seat next to me, I'd need a little spiritual sustenance.

Even tomato juice brought back memories. The last drink of the night at the old Rivoli Bar in Toledo: beer spiked with tomato juice, Wes Tannock's surefire home preventative for hangovers. Not only was it totally ineffective; it looked and tasted like you'd bled into your brew. I drank it anyway; I could have—and did—swallow anything John Wesley Tannock gave me that summer.

The story of that summer for me: I wanted Wes Tannock; I got Ted Havlicek.

We were somewhere over the great green state of Pennsylvania and I was getting as high as the plane. Pot was fine, but I was old enough that alcohol was my first drug of choice.

I gazed out the window at the tree-clustered mountains. From here, they looked like mounds of curly endive. There was something soothing about the gentle undulations of green; the throbbing in my head subsided a little as I leaned back and took in the scenery.

Wes Tannock's voice wasn't famous yet, but it already had the power and authority, the sincerity, that would put him on the political map. I saw him standing on the steps of Our Lady of Guadalupe church, the setting sun behind him, his shirt drenched with sweat, his throat as raw as Janis Joplin's.

"What do we want?" he shouted into the mike Rap had wired to huge amplifiers.

"JUSTICE," we all roared.

"When do we want it?"

The response was thunder: "NOW!"

"How will we get it?"

This time the crowd went really wild, jumping and clapping and banging tambourines and garbage can lids. *"HUEL-GA! HUEL-GA!"* We shouted it over and over again until it became a ritual chant that carried us away on a tidal wave of commitment. The strike had begun. Tomorrow's sun would rise on fields empty of the imported workers who picked the crops and kept the ketchup factory supplied with workers.

In the front of the crowd, her face washed with sweat and tears, her eyes glowing with equal parts passion for social justice and lust for Wes Tannock, stood a naive college freshman named Cassandra Jameson.

I lifted my drink; the hand that poured the rest of the vodka into the glass shook a little.

The lady next to me edged over in her seat.

Jan's voice from that long-ago summer was next. She was sobbing as she told us how four-year-old Belita Navarro had been rushed to the hospital, poisoned by the pesticides in the field the family had been working in. "God," Jan wailed, pounding her hip with a small, clenched fist, "we have to do something."

Dana Sobel's voice chimed in, thick with anticipation, "This will get their attention. All we have to do is handle it right."

Tarky, who'd grown up to be Wes Tannock's perennial campaign manager, had handled it. He'd handled it so well we all got arrested, and Ron lost the most precious thing in his life: his conscientious objector status. Because of that summer, he was drafted. Because of that summer, he went to Vietnam. Because of that summer, he came home in a wheelchair.

Oh, who the hell was I kidding? Not because of that summer. Because of me. Because big brother Ron wasn't about to let little sister Cassie play radical activist by herself. He said yes, he got involved in the conspiracy, in order to keep an eye on me.

The plane lowered itself to the ground, over checkerboard farmland cut into fields like a quilt. Red barns and white farmhouses stood like Monopoly hotels surrounded by parsley trees. Straight, black, T-square roads, sped upon by matchbox cars and trucks, sliced the countryside.

I wanted to break the window with my fist and crawl out onto the wing. Anything to keep from walking out of this aircraft and into the past. Anything to keep from standing in a courtroom next to my brother. The fear in my stomach was like a lump of cold oatmeal. I started to shake.

Oblivious to the ''Fasten Seat Belt'' signs, I undid my belt, gestured frantically to the aisle seat passenger to get out of my way, and lurched into the aisle. Brushing past the flight attendant, I put hand to mouth in a universal gesture of need, and fled to the bathroom, where two Bloody Marys hit the toilet just in time.

As I stood in the tiny metal closet, leaning against the cold glass, sweat pouring down my face, one more voice hit my ear. Like Dylan, Ted Havlicek was talking about more than the weather when he said, ''Tornado's coming. Feel the electricity in the air. Like stored-up lightning ready to strike.''

I took a deep breath, but the sense of heavy, electricity-laden air, promising severe storms ahead, didn't dissipate.

It was not for nothing that I was named Cassandra.

CHAPTER TWO

August 20, 1969

The night is hot and muggy, as only a summer night in Toledo can be. The air is a damp wool blanket, heavy and oppressive. Even the fireflies seem to glide lethargically through the darkness, hanging in the air like Japanese lanterns. On the sweeping front porch of the rambling Victorian known as the White House sit eight college students in varying poses of torpid relaxation. A half gallon of peach ice cream with one spoon passes among them, as does a joint whose tiny orange light moves as slowly as the fireflies in the night gloom. From a small transistor radio poised on the porch railing the sounds of ''Sleepwalk'' fill the night.

Joel Rapaport, known as Rap, sprawls across the creaky porch glider, his seductive salesman's smile at odds with his tie-dyed shirt and hippie headband. His arm reaches across the shoulder of his girlfriend, Dana Sobel. Dana's arms are crossed over her Grateful Dead T-shirt, her straight dark hair and eyebrows as uncompromising as her principles.

On the floor, her long bare legs crossed like a child's, sits Cassie Jameson, at nineteen the second-youngest. She looks at Rap and Dana with something close to envy; they are so sure of one another, so clearly a couple.

She sighs and glances at Wes Tannock, who has the porch swing to himself. He wears cutoff jeans and loafers without socks; one foot kicks at the porch to make the swing go back and forth. He is alone tonight; his girlfriend is at a sorority party. But alone doesn't mean available. Wes has never treated Cass as anything but Ron's little sister.

Ron Jameson leans against the porch railing, his long legs extended, poised as if to walk away any minute. His face is shrouded by his Australian bush hat, which he takes off from time to time to use as a fan.

Paul Tarkanian perches on the railing, defying gravity as he balances his bulk along the thin wooden rail. His long black hair and thick beard make Cass think he should be leading a donkey with one hand and holding a gold pan in the other.

On the floor, cross-legged, sit the two cousins, Jan and Kenny Gebhardt. The silly grin on Jan's face tells Cass that the beer in her hand is far from her first, and probably isn't the only substance in her bloodstream. Kenny, the kid, the sixteen-year-old science nerd who tags along with the older students, sits silent as usual.

One member of the group is missing: Ted Havlicek, Cass's almost-boyfriend. She tears her eyes away from the others every so often to glance along Monroe Street in hopes of seeing his pale blue Valiant chugging toward the house.

The students are foot soldiers in the war Lyndon Johnson declared on poverty. They are volunteers at Amigos Unidos Center, a social services agency for migrant farmworkers.

The migrants who work the fields of northwest Ohio come for the most part from South Texas. They are Mexican-Americans, U.S. citizens, who pile their belongings and their kids into cars every spring and drive north to hoe pickles and beets, to pick tomatoes and cherries. They live in whatever ramshackle housing the farmer provides; chicken coops and old trailers and tiny plumbingless cabins dot the countryside behind the big white farmhouses. They work for less than minimum wage, doing backbreaking labor in the fields.

"Is she still in a coma?" Dana demands. She raises her head from its resting place on Rap's shoulder and leans over to catch a glimpse of Jan's face.

Jan nods. The strand of hair she twirls in one finger finds

its way into her mouth; she brushes it back with an impatient gesture. "The doctors said she might die."

Cass Jameson leans back against the pillar, hiding her face from the cruel clarity of the streetlamp on the corner. She's supposed to be filled with righteous anger over the injury inflicted on four-year-old Belita Navarro, but all she feels so far is numb. Somewhere in the vicinity of her stomach, there is a huge, gray blob of fear, and somewhere behind her eyes are tears she doesn't want the others to see. Radicals don't cry. Radicals don't get mad—they get even. Jan and the others want to get even for Belita; Cass just wants to cry.

But then, she's the one who spent the most time with Belita. She's the one whose mornings were spent at the Migrant Ministry day care center, playing with toddlers while their parents and older siblings worked the fields. At first she resented the assignment, sullenly announcing she'd come to Lucas County to organize a union, not to baby-sit. But one afternoon with the children changed her mind. She met six-year-old girls who woke before the rest of the family to get the beans ready for breakfast. She met little boys who would be expected, when the family moved on to Michigan for the cherries, to climb to the top of the trees and shake down the highest fruit. She met children who had never had a teddy bear, never gone swimming or had a picnic with their families.

And she met Belita, whose round, solemn brown face could light up with a tiny-toothed smile. Belita, who called her *mi Casi* and laughed at her pun. Belita, who laughed when her baby brother wet himself, putting her little hand over her mouth and giggling silently. Belita, who loved playing Candy Land, even though she spoke not a word of English. She didn't understand the rules, or even that there were rules, but she loved moving the little pieces along the track to the gumdrop mountains. Cass brought real gumdrops one day, and the child was amazed to find that the colored mountains were pictures of real things you could actually eat.

Now Belita lies in a coma, near death. And all she did was play in a field near her makeshift home. A field that had been sprayed with a deadly pesticide called parathion.

Cass bites down on a lower lip that threatens to tremble into humiliating tears. She tries to tune back in to the discussion, but finds it hard to concentrate.

"Are you sure this will work?" Wes Tannock's normally self-assured baritone rises at the end of his words, which are half challenge, half doubt. He steadies the swing with his foot, preventing it from swaying with his every movement.

Rap's hand slices the air. Since his is the hand holding the joint, his gesture is punctuated by an orange streak across the face of the night. He takes a deep drag and sucks in every ounce of smoke. His answer rides the exhale: "It'll work, man. Blow those fuckers away." He passes the jay to Dana. "We've got to seize the time, that's all." Rap speaks with a lateral lisp that could make him sound like Daffy Duck. Instead, it adds spice; he never bothers to avoid sibilants.

Dana, who leans against Rap's chest in spite of the heat, holds the dwindling joint to her lips and takes a hit. She leans her head back and blows the smoke out slowly. She lifts her hand and pushes her long, black, Indian-princess hair off her neck, then passes the joint to the thin, nervous girl who sits on the floor, her back propped up against the porch rail.

Jan takes the doobie. "But what if somebody gets hurt?" she asks. The jay sits in her hand, unsmoked. "Somebody besides the farmers and the pigs, I mean."

"Hey, you're the one who got all psyched up about what happened to Belita," Rap reminds her. "You were the one who said we had to do something."

"And don't bogart that joint," Tarky adds in a low growl. His black Armenian hair is shoulder-length; he looks like a Dutch Master. He perches on the porch railing, his hairy hand reaching for the marijuana. Jan hands it over without a word, without taking a drag herself.

This is unusual; Jan passing up a chance to get high.

"You agreed to it ten minutes ago," Dana reminds her. She passes the ice cream to Cass without eating any. This is not unusual; Dana is always trying to lose weight, to coerce her stocky frame into hip-huggers.

"Besides," Cass adds, plunging the spoon deep into the

melting peach mess, "how could anyone get hurt? It's not like it was really poison or anything." She is not certain whether she's trying to convince the others, or to convince herself that what the group wants to do is the right thing.

"Yeah," Rap echoes. "Not like the stuff they used on that poor kid. You were the one who found her, Jan. You were the one who called the ambulance. So what's this fucking shit about maybe someone will get hurt? Someone's already been hurt, and it's a kid. If she comes out of the coma, she could have permanent nerve damage, remember?"

"That really sucks," Dana murmurs. Again her hand reaches for her long hair and shifts it to the other side of her neck. She puts out a hand and wiggles her fingers at Tarky, who passes her the remaining joint.

"Hey, what about my turn?" Wes says. He reaches into his jeans pocket and pulls out a hemostat. He moves the swing forward to meet Dana, who leans forward on the glider. She holds the joint between her fingers, and Wes clamps it with the medical instrument.

" 'Plunk your magic twanger, Froggy,' " Rap says, imitating Andy Devine's gravel voice. "I don't see why you can't take your roaches straight, like the rest of us."

"It burns my fingers," Wes replies. He brings the hemo to his lips and takes a deep drag.

"And it leaves those telltale burn marks," Rap adds. "We wouldn't want anyone to suspect that straight-arrow law student John Wesley Tannock might smoke dope, now would we?"

Tarky fixes Rap with a black-eyed Armenian stare, a stare that promises horrible revenge in some future incarnation. A stare that has Rap's vulpine lips stretching into an ironic smile that bares canine teeth.

"Oh, shit, not this again," Jan mutters. She puts out a thin arm and takes the hemo from Wes. She opens the clamp and takes out the roach, then hands the instrument back. She holds the remaining quarter inch of butt to her lips and sucks deeply. She closes her eyes and seems to float away on a cloud of self-absorption until the males sort out which is to lead the pack.

The radio station plays a long, dreamy Iron Butterfly tune that has Jan swaying to guitar riffs and Rap beating a tattoo on the glider with his long fingers.

A hand touches Cass's shoulder; she turns and looks up at Ted Havlicek. He motions for her to move over and she shifts herself on the porch floor to make room. Part of her is annoyed at his proprietary air, and the other part—the stronger part, she has to admit—takes pride and pleasure in being someone's girl. If she can't have Wes, she'll settle for Ted.

"So, Clark Kent," asks Rap, "they gonna put this story on the front page or what?" Rap has the bluntness of the New Yorker, but they're used to him by now, so Ted takes no offense.

"Afraid not," Ted replies. "The city editor said I'd get three graphs on page three of the local section. That's if there isn't a four-car pileup out on Secor Road. Face it, folks, an injured migrant kid isn't big news in this town."

Ted reaches into his shirt pocket and pulls out a soft pack of unfiltered cigarettes. He lights one and offers the pack to Cass, who shakes her head. Jan accepts the offer even though it wasn't made to her; she reaches across Kenny to take one and nods her thanks.

"Let me bring you up to speed," Rap offers. "We have an idea that will put what happened to that kid on the front page, but Wes here, after we've talked about it all fucking night, after we've planned and argued and reached a consensus, now, now"—he stops, faces Wes, and slams a fist into an open palm—"now we're ready to reach the final stage and Tannock here is starting to lose his nerve."

Rap's deep-set eyes, illuminated by the light from a garage across the alley, narrow with suspicion. His voice, which had been sharp and high, now goes flat as he throws out the challenge: "I'm not sensing fear here, am I, Wes? You're not starting to think this isn't going to look too good on your résumé, are you, because if you really want a job on Wall

Street when this summer's over, then you can get up right now and walk—''

Interrupting Rap in full rant is never easy, but Ron Jameson cuts in, "Let the man talk, Rap. I'm sure that's not what he's getting at."

"Let me play devil's advocate here," Wes says. He gives Ron a glance that holds no gratitude; he can't maintain his leadership role if someone else does his fighting for him. He leans forward on the porch swing, which lets out a squeak of protest. "We want to make the point that pesticides kill, right?"

Universal nods. Even Kenny, Jan's young cousin, who sits in the corner of the porch and hopes no one will remember his presence, gives Wes the compliment of an acknowledgment.

"We want to make them understand how their poisons hurt the migrants, right?" More nods. "We want to bring Belita's pain home to the people who caused it. We want to give the farmers a little taste of what they did to that kid."

"Easy, John Wesley," Tarky murmurs from his perch. "You're preaching to the choir."

Wes cuts a look at his fellow law student, then takes a breath and continues. "But we don't want to hurt anyone. Not really. So we take a can of parathion, empty the stuff out, and replace it with hot pepper oil."

"Capsicum oil," Kenny murmurs under his breath. He's a skinny sixteen-year-old wearing a tie-dyed T-shirt. Bony boy-knees and hairless legs protrude from under his cutoff jeans. He's a kid genius, a college freshman majoring in chemistry.

No one even glances at him. Rap finishes what Wes started. "We take the canister to the county fair, spray the stuff all over the farmers waiting to see who gets the blue ribbon for the fattest pig or whatever, and they all go bananas. Then we tell them it's only pepper oil, but the stuff they poison the migrants with is the real thing."

"Guerrilla theater," Cass murmurs. She realizes she's still holding the sodden carton of ice cream and passes it to her brother.

"Will there be any parathion left in the canister?" Jan asks.

Ron Jameson's voice overrides Jan's. "Just how poisonous is this stuff, anyway?"

"A little dab'll do ya," Rap replies.

Wes looks down from his porch swing throne at Kenny, who swallows hard and murmurs, "It's an organophosphate. One of the most poisonous chemicals known to man. A few drops can kill you." He warms to his topic; the only time the others listen to him is when they need scientific information. Which doesn't happen often, so his chest swells with pride as he shares his knowledge. "It comes in different strengths. The growers usually buy it in concentrate and then make an emulsion. A spray canister contains about fifty percent parathion, and—"

Jan translates her cousin's words into English. "All Belita did was run through the field after the spraying. She didn't even touch the plants. The fumes were enough to put her in a coma. The doctor at the emergency room told me that if she had touched anything, she'd have been dead in minutes."

"God," Cass says under her breath. She herself isn't sure whether it's a curse or a prayer. All she knows is that the lump in her stomach is heating up. Her tears are turning into rage, just the way Jan wants them to.

In the background, Simon and Garfunkel sing that "the words of the prophets are written on the subway walls and tenement halls." And, thinks Cass, they'll be written on the signs we'll carry when we spray that pepper oil. The words of the prophets fill her with the anger she needs to cement her purpose.

"What did that grower say when you told him what happened to her?" She knows the answer, but wants to hear it again, wants to fuel her anger with accounts of the farmers' indifference to the welfare of the people who work their crops.

"He said the fields weren't a playground and it was Belita's parents' job to keep their kid at home. He said it wasn't his fault if these people didn't understand English."

Jan's words do their intended task. The students all shake their heads in disbelief and disgust. Rap says what most are thinking: "Truth is, I'd love it if we could hit them with the real thing. Put them in a coma just like they did to Belita." His big-knuckled hands weave webs of intrigue in the night air.

"But no," he continues, "we're going to make damn sure there's no parathion left in that canister. Kenny here is the chemistry maven, so it's on him to get every bit of the stuff out of the canister and put in a neutralizing agent. So when we fill it with pepper oil there'll be no trace of poison left. Right, Kenny?"

Kenny nods. "Right." His boy-voice cracks on the word.

"There'll be no screwups like there were on the Fourth of July, right?" Rap takes the carton of ice cream from Ron. Holding the soggy cardboard carton aloft, he lifts it to his lips and drinks the melted pink mess.

"That wasn't my—" Kenny begins, but Tarky's black-eyed stare silences him.

Tarky's black brows lower like thunderclouds. He fixes Kenny with a stare intended to intimidate. "You'd better not fuck this one up, kid."

The radio has gone into a commercial. A jingle tells the listeners that if they want a used car, they'll be "on the right track at Nine Mile and Mack" in nearby Detroit.

Cass looks at the others one by one, loving the intense passion in their faces, the clear empathy they show for little Belita. They are, she is certain, on the right track.

CHAPTER
THREE

August 21, 1969

Ted Havlicek sits at his desk in the Amigos Unidos Community Action Center. He is a recent graduate of Toledo University's journalism program and acts as press liaison for the center and stringer for the local paper, the Toledo *Blade*. His desk is covered with half-finished press releases; a sign above the portable typewriter reads NO-TICE: THIS PROGRAM IS SET TO SELF-DESTRUCT DUE TO LACK OF FUNDS.

On the wall are an unframed Peter Max poster of Bob Dylan and two *Blade* stories on migrant workers with the byline underlined in red. An avocado-green radio on the desk thumps out "Duke, Duke, Duke, Duke of Earl."

"But what do you need a notebook for?" he asks the slight boy with the long, serious face. "I use them for reporting, but what do you need with one?" It isn't that he can't spare a steno pad; hell, he's already rooting around in his desk drawer for a fresh one. It's that in the depths of his journalist's soul he has to know the who, what, where, why, and how of everything that comes his way. And that includes knowing why Kenny Gebhardt wants to play reporter all of a sudden.

The kid's sixteen-year-old voice cracks as he replies, "I'm sick and tired of what's been going on around here. I want to find out who's been doing this to me."

"Doing what?" Ted's blue eyes are guileless behind his

wire-rimmed glasses. A jolt of annoyance rips through Kenny; Ted can be a real pain in the ass when he pretends not to know something everybody knows he knows.

"Setting me up. Making me look bad." Kenny shoves his hands into the pockets of his bell-bottoms. "Like the time I brought the wrong flyers to the rally. The ones in English instead of Spanish. I opened the fucking box back at the office. I checked them before I put them in the station wagon. Then when I get to the rally, they turn out to be the wrong ones. But would anybody believe me when I said I checked?" Kenny's voice rises to a boyish pitch; he drops his eyes and contemplates his worn hightop sneakers.

"They think I'm a dumb kid," he mutters. "Like I'd really pull that stunt at the radio station."

Ted stifles a smile. "Yeah," he agrees, "that was pretty stupid. We're supposed to be airing a tape in Spanish about applying for food stamps and instead all we get is Donovan singing 'Mellow Yellow' about twenty-five times."

Kenny raises his eyes and stares Ted down. "Well, I didn't do that either. I took the tape Rap gave me to the station; it's not my fault it was the wrong one."

"So how's the notebook going to help?" Ted leans back in his swivel chair and puts his elbows on the armrests. All he needs is a green eyeshade to look like a very young editor of a small-town newspaper. The long sleeves of his white shirt are rolled up and his wide, brightly colored tie is loose. But if he had to cover a story, he could knot the tie and put on the navy blue blazer and step out the door looking like a professional.

"I'm going to do what you do," Kenny replies. "I'm going to take it with me wherever I go. I'm going to write down everything I see and hear. I'm going to find out who's making me look bad."

"Kenny, nobody thinks you're sabotaging us," Ted says. "If we did, would we trust you on this parathion thing?"

On the radio, Motown has given way to acid rock as Grace Slick tells the listeners that their friends, baby, treat them like a guest.

"The only reason they want me to do the switch is that they're afraid the stuff's gonna eat right through their skin or something."

"Still, they asked you to do it. They wouldn't have done that if they didn't trust you." Ted adjusts the glasses that slide down his nose on hot, humid days. "That's got to mean something."

Kenny shrugs a skinny shoulder. "I dunno," he says. "Maybe it's just another setup. Another way things can go wrong and I can get blamed. All I know is, I'm going to be watching everybody. I'm going to find out who's screwing me around if it's the last thing I do."

Three hours later, while sitting on the porch of the White House, which sits next to the art museum, Kenny finally sees something worthy of recording in his notebook. A man in a black suit steps out of a black car and adjusts his black sunglasses before proceeding to the entrance of the museum. Kenny has seen the man before, standing in the rear of the crowd at a migrant union meeting. Rap was the one who said aloud what they were all thinking: FBI.

The Toledo Museum of Art is a miniature Parthenon on Monroe Street. Surrounded by emerald lawn and guarded by two massive copper beeches, it constitutes a tranquil bastion of culture. But what is an FBI agent doing there?

Kenny hops off the porch, smashing a purple hollyhock, and runs toward the museum. The fed is at the door; Kenny takes the shallow marble steps two at a time and gets inside just as the man takes a complimentary map from the circular desk in the middle of the rotunda. Then he turns left, toward the mummies.

Of all the crazy places to follow an FBI man, the museum strikes Kenny as just about the craziest. But the museum is right next door to the White House, the big Victorian where Wes and Tarky and Rap and Ron and Cass live. The house where the front-porch meeting happened. And even though Dana and Jan and Ted all live with their families, they hang out at the White House often enough that a meeting inside the museum would be easy to arrange without creating suspicion. And if anyone came along and saw them, anybody like Kenny himself, they could just separate and pretend they'd both come to see the El Grecos. The more Kenny thinks about it, the better the museum looks as a secret meeting place.

But where in the museum has the FBI man gone? Kenny has followed him through the Egyptian, the Greek, and the Roman rooms and is now in the medieval hall. But where is the dark-suited man with the military haircut?

It hits Kenny with a jolt: the Swiss room. Has to be! The Swiss room is a tiny little space, about the size of a cabin on a Cris-craft, off the El Greco gallery. It's wood-paneled, with bunks in the corners and a huge, gaily painted ceramic stove with steps. As a kid, Kenny spent hours standing behind the velvet rope in that room, imagining himself a Swiss child sleeping on that cozy shiplike bunk or sitting on the steps of the warm stove, listening to Grossmutter's stories of the old days in the Alps.

It's a good place, the Swiss room. A place you could stay in a long time, pretending you belonged.

A place he hates to think about someone meeting an FBI agent in.

There's one door in and out; it's perfect for a secret meeting.

But who is the federal agent meeting? And why?

Kenny steps on sneakered feet toward the huge painting that hangs right next to the Swiss room door. He pretends intense interest in the rearing horses breathing smoke, in the raised swords and the plumed helmets. His patience is rewarded by whispered voices.

"... parathion," he hears. And "county fair." But try as he might, he cannot hear more. Cannot hear what the FBI man is saying in response. Cannot even hear enough to swear whether the speaker is male or female.

He can't stay here. He can't be here when they come out. He can't be seen spying. But he has to know—which of his friends is inside the Swiss room, selling them out to the FBI?

He saunters toward the next room, the one with the Impressionists. As soon as he enters, he turns and hides behind the wall, positioning himself to see whoever comes out of the Swiss room on the heels of the FBI.

A uniformed guard walks up to him. "You're standing too close to the paintings," he says. "I'll have to ask you to step back."

Kenny reluctantly removes his gaze from the El Greco hall and says, "I wasn't touching anything." He sounds like a sullen kid, which would piss him off if he cared about anything except seeing the person who's about to walk out of the Swiss room.

"Please step back from the wall," the guard repeats. "I don't want to have to ask you to leave the museum."

Just as Kenny opens his mouth to reply, the dark-suited FBI man strolls past him. He passes the Cezannes and makes straight for the exit. Kenny's head swivels back toward the El Grecos. No one there. He races toward the Swiss room, the guard in hot pursuit.

When he reaches the little alcove, he steps inside, his heart pounding. Who will he—

The room is empty. The guard clamps a heavy hand on Kenny's shoulder and escorts him out of the museum.

Kenny sits down on the marble steps, warmed by the summer sun, and writes in his steno book everything that has just passed.

From the White House come the strains of Sgt. Pepper's Lonely Hearts Club Band. They read the news today, oh boy.

The same summer sun peers through the green canopy of the weeping beech in the little park behind the museum. The tree is a landmark; its sturdy, iron-gray trunk bears carved initials from as early as 1926, and its spreading branches conceal the two people who sit on steel-strong branches under the emerald leaves. The smell of burning hemp fills the shady nook and the sound of Cream emerges from a transistor radio hung on a strap from an upper branch.

"God, you are such a drag," the girl in the Indian-print shirt says, holding the roach to her lips and sucking deeply.

She eyes her older brother with scorn. "I mean, haven't you got any balls?"

"Cassie," Ron begins, then stops and starts again. This is the summer she refuses to be called Cassie, the summer she emerges as Mama Cass. "This isn't about balls. This isn't even about politics. It's about common sense."

"You sound like Dad," his sister replies. "Next thing you'll be telling me I ought to major in Elementary Ed so I can fall back on teaching. Or something equally bourgeois."

"Bourgeois," Ron mutters, raising his eyes to the topmost leaves. He wears his varsity T-shirt from Kent State, but the peace symbol around his neck marks him as something other than your usual jock. "What one year of college will do for you."

"All I know is that Wes is right," Cass says. She leans forward, grabbing a branch for support, moving toward her brother with catlike intensity as if willing him to see the world through her idealistic eyes. "We have to take a stand, make people listen. We have to show them the way the migrants live, the way the farmers don't care what happens to kids like Belita. We have to do it by any means necessary."

But Ron reacts to the first words instead of the last. "Wes is right," he mocks. "Wes is always right, according to you. But is he right because of what's between his ears or what's between his legs?"

The defiant, pot-smoking hippie chick of thirty seconds ago widens her brown eyes, as shocked by her brother's remark as her suburban mother would have been.

"This has nothing to do with sex," Cass replies loftily, pushing away the mental image of Wes Tannock's tanned shoulders. She finishes the last of the roach, blowing smoke through her nostrils like Bette Davis. "It's about the way the migrants live in those horrible chicken coops. It's about all the children who'll spend their lives bending over and hoeing pickles for fifty cents an hour. It's about Belita. Don't you understand, Ron? If we're not part of the solution, we're part of the problem." Now that Belita is home from the hospital, she can afford rage.

A new song from the transistor informs them that they're on the eve of destruction.

Ron Jameson leans back on the tough old tree branch and stares at the light filtering through the leaves. Sitting in this tree is like being part of the forest itself. The weeping branches bend down to the ground, covering the tree with a dense yet translucent awning. From the outside, no one could tell that two figures nestle in the low, thick branches. Inside, it's cool and enveloping and safe. Ron wants things to be safe, not so much for himself as for his impulsive, good-hearted, naive sister.

His parents will never forgive him, he'll never forgive himself, if he lets her go into this alone.

"Okay, babe," he says at last. "Tell Wes we're in. Let's go to the county fair."

"Power to the people," Cass replies with a raised fist. She sings along with the radio, gleefully agreeing that the eve of destruction is at hand.

August 24, 1969

The county fair smells of cotton candy, popcorn, and animal dung. Cass wrinkles her nose at the smell; the suburbanites of her hometown of Chagrin Falls drive to Amish country or go to the Apple Butter Festival. Manure doesn't accompany the rural pleasures she's used to.

Ron steps out of the driver's side of his tail-finned Chevy. He holds the door for Dana, who climbs awkwardly from the back seat as Little Stevie Wonder plays the harmonica on the car radio. Once out of the car, Dana looks down at her sandaled feet and realizes she's made a mistake. She takes one step, then lifts a foot to shake out a piece of gravel. "Damn," she mutters.

The station wagon pulls up alongside Ron's car. It's a huge, two-toned, green monster that can hold six people and four cardboard boxes filled with flyers. The students call it the Green Bomb; it belongs to Kenny's father, but Jan drives because Kenny only has a learner's permit. Jan slams on the brake, pulls up the emergency even though the ground is flat, and hops out of the car to the accompaniment of the Mothers of Invention.

Kenny runs around to the back, ready to start lifting the heavy canister propped up against the side wall. Ron steps over to join him.

Tarky's VW bug, which proudly bears four antiwar bumper stickers, scoots into the parking lot. He and Wes are squeezed into the tiny front seat. Behind them, Rap swings his motorcycle around in a gravel-spraying circle before pulling up alongside the little car Tarky named Eva Braun.

"The canister all ready to go?" Rap calls. He wears no helmet; his long hair is pulled back into a ponytail.

Kenny nods.

Rap puts down the kickstand and steps over to the station wagon. At six feet, he towers over Kenny. He stands a fraction too close to the boy and says, "Are you sure this thing is safe?"

Kenny nods again. "Jan and I took it out to an old quarry on Centennial Road," he says. "I opened it and we poured the parathion into a hole and covered it with stones. Then we took the canister and cleaned it out six times. Then we put in the pepper oil."

"Great," Rap says, giving Kenny a punch on the arm that will probably leave a bruise. "Let's get this fucker out of here and head for the pig stall or whatever."

"It's not the pig stall," Tarky corrects. He's the logistics expert, although he looks incongruous with his long curly hair in a headband and his hands around a clipboard. "We're going to demonstrate at the main tent in ten minutes. Ted's already there with the press. With any luck, we'll get a photo in the *Blade* and a story on local television. Plus there's a radio station doing a location spot on the midway."

"You chicks got the flyers?" Rap asks. Dana reaches in and pulls out a cardboard box. She and Cass spent the previous afternoon running the copies off the machine in Dana's father's law office.

Dana hands a pile of paper to Jan and Cass, then takes one

for herself. Cass gives a little nod of satisfaction as she looks down at the grainy photograph that fills the top half of the sheet. It is the picture of Belita that Ted managed to get printed in the *Blade*. Under it, in large bold letters, is the question: If this were *your* child, would you spray your fields with deadly poison?

Rap reaches for the nozzled tube that will spray the pepper oil on the crowd. He attaches it to the canister and lifts it out of the back of the wagon.

The chicks carry the flyers, nestling them in the crooks of their arms, the way they carried their books home from fifth grade. The guys follow behind, Rap straining under the weight of the canister. Wes, Tarky, and Ron swing megaphones from their arms. Kenny, empty-handed, trails behind the others.

Ron digs into his pocket for the admission fee at the check-point between parking lot and fair, paying for everyone and taking a roll of purple tickets. The Ferris wheel turns faster than Cass remembered; she feels sick just looking at its spinning neon presence. Screams of fear and delight fill the air, along with barrel organ music from the Gay Nineties.

They march, grim-faced, through the midway, ignoring the calls of food vendors to try the bratwurst or the saltwater taffy. The food smells add to Cass's nausea. Stage fright, she realizes as they pass the ''Made in Ohio'' tent, which promises such local delicacies as marble longhorn cheese, Catawba wine, and black popcorn. She is as nervous as if she were about to play Lady Macbeth—and didn't know her lines.

The main tent boasts a calf-judging. Boys in Future Farmers of America T-shirts stand around an antique tractor. A sign in front of the huge iron wheels says that it was made in Toledo in 1915.

Cass searches the crowd for a glimpse of Ted, wanting to get this over with before she loses either her nerve or her breakfast.

A man in a tan suit and white shirt walks up, flashes a badge, and says, ''Stop right there. You're under arrest.''

The cop says the newly minted Miranda warnings as though the words hurt his mouth. Uniformed police officers step out of God-knows-where and pull arms behind backs, snap hand-cuffs over wrists. Mothers in Bermuda shorts stop to stare. Kids with brightly colored balloons stand openmouthed as the students are marched toward waiting black-and-whites. Calli-ope music from the merry-go-round, playing "After the Ball Is Over," fills Cass's ears as she stumbles along the gravel path, hands bound behind her back.

"It's pepper oil, man," Rap says. "Take it to your lab and test it." If his hands were free, he'd be making an expansive gesture; since he's handcuffed, he can only lean toward the canister, now carried by an impassive deputy. "Worst thing that stuff'll do is give you a humongous case of heartburn."

Cass lets out a sigh of relief. How can they possibly be charged with a crime when they haven't done anything?

"Shut up," the blond cop says, giving Rap a shove.

Rap gives Cass a sidelong glance. "What exactly are we charged with?" he asks in a taunting tone. "Possession of Tabasco in the first degree?"

It is Tarky who finally silences Rap. "I'd advise you to stop talking," he says. "Wait till Harve gets here."

The blond cop wrinkles his brow. "You mean Harve So-bel?"

The partner speaks up now. "Wasn't he the lawyer on that Black Panther case? Geez, and now he's representing this bunch." He shakes his head. "Hell of a thing," he says. "Fucking Panther just walked up to the patrol car and blew a cop away," he went on. "How could anybody represent a piece of shit like that?"

"You're speaking of my future father-in-law," Rap says in mock indignation.

They reach the parking lot. One of the cops walks toward the station wagon and opens the door. Wes says, "Don't you think you ought to get a search warrant?"

To Cass's astonishment, the cop stops in his tracks.

"What are we going to do with this stuff?" the blond cop asks. "I don't like the idea of riding around with deadly poi-son in the back seat, if you get my drift."

"I keep telling you, it's not—" Rap begins.

"Will you shut the fuck up?" Tarky cuts in. In the distance, the merry-go-round stops, then starts up with a spirited rendition of "Happy Days Are Here Again."

"We got an expert on the way," the balding cop tells his partner. "Some guy from the Department of Agriculture."

A big black car rolls up, bouncing through the ruts in the dirt parking lot. The door opens and a man in a plaid sport shirt steps out. He walks toward the canister and nods at the cops. They nod back. He pulls on a pair of rubber gloves, the thick, heavy kind used in industry. He reaches up and turns the top of the canister, opening it. He takes a handkerchief out of his pants pocket and holds it against the opening.

Standing in the dusty parking lot, the music of childhood ringing in her ears, the smell of manure in her nose, Cass feels a bubble of laughter welling up in her throat. This solemn little man with his polyester shirt and his handkerchief is about to make a scientific declaration that the canister contains . . . hot sauce!

But before the bubble explodes in a giggle, the little man takes the handkerchief away and brings it, slowly, toward his face. He stops when the cloth is about eighteen inches from his nose. He sniffs the air, then says, "I don't dare bring it any closer, boys." He lowers the handkerchief.

"And get that plastic bag over here quick. I don't want to end up dead. It's parathion all right."

All eyes turn toward Kenny.

CHAPTER FOUR

August 26, 1969

Jail is a metal world of hard edges and clanging noises. Cass lies on the thin mattress, sweating in spite of her gauzy Indian dress, coasting in and out of sleep. Her dreams are nightmare visions involving cops and judges and a long, long prison sentence. What would she tell Mom and Dad? What was happening to Ron? How had the pigs known their plans?

And, above all else, how the hell had real parathion been in that container?

". . . still think it was Kenny's fault." The voice is Dana's and so is the cigarette smoke that brings Cass to full consciousness. In the distance, Elvis checks into the Heartbreak Hotel.

"I don't believe that," Jan counters, her soft voice stubborn. "Kenny wouldn't tell the cops anything. And he *did* empty the canister and fill it with pepper oil. I was there, remember?"

"Then how do you explain the fact that we're in this place?" Dana replies. Her cigarette smoke rises to the ceiling like a campfire in the forest. "And how do you explain that creepy guy who said the canister was full of parathion?"

Cass rubs the sleep out of her eyes and sits up on her cot. "How long have we been here?" She looks at her bare legs and pulls her skirt down. Her Keds are under the hard bunk.

She slides her feet toward the floor and slips them on.

Neither of the others even bothers to look at her. It is yet another reminder that whenever Kenny's not around, she's the kid, the one nobody pays attention to. The little sister, tolerated because she came with Ron.

Jan runs nervous fingers through her stringy hair. "Dana, will you please stop? Kenny didn't do this. The pigs just knew, that's all."

"Someone had to tell them," Dana insists. "Someone had to put a real parathion canister into the station wagon. Kenny's father's station wagon," she repeats with sinister emphasis.

"We're in deep shit," she goes on. "I mean, I've got faith in Harve to get us out of here, but if they can prove that stuff was really poison, they've got us for attempted assault at least."

"But we never even got to the bandstand," Cass protests. "We didn't really do anything."

"We printed up a thousand flyers telling everyone at the fair what we were going to do," Jan points out. She twirls a strand of hair in her fingers and looks at the concrete block wall with weary eyes.

A tide of cold, wet fear hits Cass like a sudden virus. Ron! He can't afford this. He can't afford the slightest hint of a criminal conviction. Not with his conscientious objector petition pending before his draft board back in Cleveland. And now that there are no graduate student deferments, the only way Ron can escape the draft is by obtaining CO status or fiddling his medical records—something he swears he won't do, since it means some poor kid will have to fight in his place.

It's not easy to get conscientious objector status, especially if you come from a standard white-gloves Presbyterian family. And once the draft board finds out Ron's been busted for attempted assault, any claim that he has moral objections to violence will fall on deaf ears.

Sweat beads her forehead; she reaches a shaking hand to her mouth. Ron could lose his petition, he could be denied CO status and get drafted—and all because of her. If she hadn't insisted they come to the fair . . .

Cass raises cold eyes to Jan and says, "If Kenny ratted us out, I'll fucking kill the little bastard."

Harve springs them by late morning. First the chicks, then Kenny, who's by himself in juvenile detention, and finally the guys. They have a court appearance in three days.

Back at the White House, Cass and Ron discover that they no longer have jobs. Cris Correra at Amigos Unidos can't afford to risk his federal funding by employing potential felons. Wes, Tarky, Jan, Dana, and Rap have also been cut loose. The summer migrant program is at an abrupt end.

Only Ted remains employed. Only Ted escaped arrest. He stood at the main tent, notebook in hand, waiting for the event to unfold. When nothing happened, he covered the fair the way the *Blade* expected him to, writing a nice human interest story about a boy with one hand raising a prize calf for the 4-H contest.

Rap explodes at the news. "Fucking shit. That Tio Taco we work for has all the balls of—"

"Don't blame Cris," Dana says with a weary sigh. "He has to dance to the government's tune if he wants his funding."

Rap's vulpine face breaks into an evil grin. "I've gotta blame somebody, babe," he points out. "Who do you suggest as a replacement for our fearful leader?"

"How about Kenny?" Cass says, her tone edged with venom. "He's the one who fucked this up. Either he didn't switch the canisters or he did all this on purpose."

"Why would he do that?" Jan challenges. "Give me one reason why Kenny would get all of us arrested. Including himself, I might point out." She's usually the quiet one, but her anger can explode messily, like a can of garbage thrown from a passing car.

"He's a juvie," Tark the Shark reminds her. "Whatever happens to the rest of us, Kenny will get out of this without a record. Think about that when you can't get a job because you've got a bust on your sheet."

"We'll talk about it later," Wes Tannock pronounces. He

stands on the staircase, halfway up to the room he shares with Tarky. "I suggest we all get some sleep and meet on the porch at six o'clock. Jan, call Kenny and tell him to be here, okay? And Cass," he adds, "why don't you make sure Ted's here, too?"

Cass nods. She's tired and hot and very, very worried about her brother. Ron says nothing, to her or anyone else. "Should we call the parents?" she asks him. He shakes his head. "What about your draft counselor?" Another head-shake. At last she says in a small, scared voice, "I'm really sorry, Ron." At this, he strides out the door, slamming the screen behind him. She hears the Chevy start up in the driveway; the sound of spewing gravel follows. From the house, the Beatles remind her that all she needs is love.

She calls Ted. "What the hell happened?" he asks, then cuts her off when she tries to answer.

"I know you all got arrested," he explains. "I found out when I got back to the *Blade*. But why? How did the cops know what was—"

"I don't know." Cass finds herself, to her utter humiliation, breaking into gusty sobs. "All I know is, Ron's going to lose his CO status, and everybody here thinks Kenny fucked up. We're meeting at six. Can you come?"

Ted agrees; he tries to say something comforting, but before the words leave his lips, Cass returns the phone to its cradle.

Six o'clock on a hot, humid August day in Ohio means gathering clouds, the promise of hard rain that will cleanse but not dry things out. There are rumbles of thunder and thick, humid winds and big fat drops that plop on the porch roof as the students gather to discuss the arrests. They sit in their accustomed places, even though those perched on the ledge are beginning to get wet.

Rap begins the assault. "Why'd you do it, Kenny?" he calls from his place on the porch glider. "Why'd you sell us out?"

Kenny's face is white. "I didn't. Why would I do a thing like that?" Sitting on the floor, knobby knees crossed, he looks even younger than his years. "I emptied the canister and cleaned it out and put in the capsicum oil, like I told you."

He swallows; his mouth is dry, the words sticking like peanut butter. "I put the canister in my dad's car. Jan drove me home. We left the car in the garage. When I went to bed, I swear, that canister had pepper oil in it." He crosses his heart with his nail-bitten hands, just like the kid he really is.

Cross my heart and hope to die.

Cass hopes he does die. She stares through the kid, her own eyes blazing righteous rage. She knows he screwed them up. She knows he sold them out, tipped off the cops that they were planning this demo. She knows it because she has to blame someone, has to hate someone besides herself for what she fears will happen to her brother.

"So you're telling us that somebody must have come by your house and switched canisters while you were asleep. Is that your testimony?" The cross-examiner is Tarky, whose tone of voice does nothing to conceal his disbelief.

"I guess," Kenny replies. Then he lifts his chin and stares directly at Ted. "But at least I was there. I got arrested with everybody else."

"Sorry, kid," Rap cuts in. "Not a strong defense. Getting busted along with the targets is part of the cover. The cops round us all up, but you're the one who gets a break when we get to court."

"What about the FBI guy at the museum?" Kenny turns his attention to Wes, who has always been his hero. "I saw him. I followed him inside. He met somebody in the Swiss room."

Wes asks the obvious question. "Who did he meet?"

"Assuming there really was an FBI agent," Rap murmurs.

"There was," Kenny repeats, sounding like a stubborn kid even in his own ears, "but I didn't see who he met. The guards chased me away. And I didn't recognize the voice."

Dana takes up where Rap left off. "Of course not," she says. "You didn't recognize the voice because there was nobody there. There was no FBI agent. Because if there had been, you'd have told us. You wouldn't have kept it to yourself and let us go ahead—unless you wanted us to get busted."

"I didn't tell you because I knew you wouldn't believe me," Kenny replies. His voice catches; tears are not far off.

The rain begins in earnest. A bright crack of lightning splits the sky across the street. Thunder follows a minute later.

"Well, you were right about that, kid," Rap says. "I don't believe you, and I don't think anyone else here does either."

"I do," Jan says into the heavy silence that follows. "I believe you, Kenny."

No one else agrees. One by one, heads are shaken, the equivalent of a Roman emperor's thumbs-down.

Kenny knows where Rap and Dana stand; their contemptuous refusal to believe him doesn't change the expression on his face. But when first Tarky, then Ted, then Cass, and finally Ron reluctantly join the consensus, his lower lip begins to tremble.

The last member of the group to be polled, Wes Tannock, looks down at the kid from his place on the swing and slowly, his features grave, shakes his head too.

Kenny can no longer contain his sobs. He jumps up and runs from the porch, slipping on the rain-soaked stairs, careening across the lawn as he makes for the station wagon.

Jan reaches for the porch swing and lifts herself up. "He can't drive by himself," she says and races after her cousin. Her bare feet slap the sidewalk and her hair flies behind her. She is a warrior goddess, a hippie Valkyrie.

The Stones rejoice in the fact that Mick's girlfriend is, at long last, under his thumb.

Kenny knows it all now. Has it written down, too. Times, dates, places, everything. In the steno book, just the way Ted showed him. Kenny doesn't think he wants to be a reporter like Ted, but his scientific mind approves of keeping records, of having documentary evidence.

Evidence that will prove he wasn't the one who got them all arrested. Evidence that will change everyone's mind about him. Evidence he intends to show as soon as the sun rises.

He waits at the tree behind the museum for the one person who can help him. The cool morning air is damp with dew and the world is bright and fresh after last night's torrential rain. He pictures the scene to come, when he faces down his accusers and shows them once and for all that he wasn't the one who sold them out.

But of course he isn't stupid enough to just write it down so that anyone could understand it. He's made his own code, something only he can interpret. That way if the notebook falls into the wrong hands, it won't mean a thing.

And he's hidden it, too. The notebook isn't in his pocket or his room at home. It's safe. Secret and safe.

Kenny only wishes he felt as safe as that notebook.

He pushes aside a branch and peers through the green curtain of leaves. No one coming—yet. That's the beauty of the weeping beech. You could sit inside, covered by foliage, and no one would know you were there. The tree's like a fuckin' tent. The trunk tough as iron, smooth and gray, a perfect climbing tree. You could climb up and sit, share a joint, and talk about life, and no one in the park would know.

It's 5:40 a.m. It's good that he's early. The person he's meeting will be coming to him, coming into his tree.

At first, he was pissed at Jan for telling the others about the tree. It was theirs, this weeping beech. It was where they'd played as kids while his dad waxed the car. It was where they'd first decided to explore the mysteries of their opposite genders—you show me yours and I'll show you mine. His was still a boy's, but Jan was already beginning to grow hair on hers, and her tiny breasts were rock-hard and rosy. Good thing his dad was a serious car-waxer; he'd trembled in fear as he'd touched his cousin's titties, knowing his dad would whale the tar out of him if he'd known what his son was doing beneath the green canopy.

But it was worth it, oh yes, and so was the first hand-rolled cigarette his cousin had offered him underneath these very leaves. He'd taken it the way he'd seen grownups handle tobacco cigarettes, and Jan had laughed at him. She'd shown him how to hold a joint, how to suck in the smoke and keep it in the lungs, taking in the heady perfume. He'd giggled and she'd giggled watching him giggle; they'd fallen on the ground like two fools and once again his boy-dirty hands had reached under her faded T-shirt to fumble with her green-apple tits.

The voice from below startles him; he's been so caught up in the past, he's forgotten to keep watch. He looks down. It still feels odd to see other faces inside the great green tree; after Jan shared their childhood hiding place with the others, it became a general meeting place—and, he suspects, a fucking place as well.

He scrambles down the branches and says, "Have I got something to tell you. Wait till you hear this."

His companion reaches into a jeans pocket and pulls out a crumpled joint. He clamps it into a hemostat and says, "Let's have a little hit first."

Turning down a hit is uncool. At only sixteen, Kenny Gebhardt lives in fear of the uncool response. He shrugs and slips his fingers into the handle. He lets his visitor light the tightly rolled end and sucks in a huge lungful of smoke. He chokes, his eyes widen, he grabs his throat—and then he falls, paralyzed, onto the ground beneath the tree. He gasps for air, his face turning blue, his fingers clutching at his neck as though to rip open an airway. His legs twitch and kick, hitting the ground like a drum tattoo. A dark spot appears on the front of his jeans.

The struggling stops. His body convulses and lies still.

His companion looks over the scene, nods once, and then walks out of the tree canopy into the rising sunlight.

"We have to talk," says Ron. It's six o'clock in the morning. Neither slept well, and both found themselves in the communal kitchen, where Cass made cups of instant coffee.

Cass nods; misery envelopes her, especially when she thinks about Ron. "Not here," she says, glancing around the porch of the White House as if the ghosts of the other students still sat in their accustomed places, ready to eavesdrop. "Let's go to the tree."

Ron nods. They walk toward the huge weeping beech in

the little park behind the art museum. "Listen, I—" Cass begins.

At the same time, Ron's deeper voice says, "It wasn't your fault, Cassie."

Cass turns hot, teary eyes on her brother and demands, "Wasn't it? Would you have gone along with it if I hadn't pushed? If I hadn't been so fucking militant?"

"Hey, who knows?" His smile is the tender one she recalls from years of little sisterhood. "I have an ideal or two of my own, you know."

Tears overwhelm her. A convulsive sob grabs her throat. She begins to run, jerkily at first, then gaining speed. The tree, she has to get to the tree. Wrapped in its protective leafy arms, she can sob out all her pain and guilt.

Tears whip her cheeks. Ron's sneakered feet echo behind her; he could easily catch up, but he lets her take the lead. At the tree, she will beg forgiveness for what may not be forgivable.

A sharp pain stabs her side as she reaches the park. It slows but doesn't stop her; she pumps her legs harder as the tree comes into view. The treehouse from *Green Mansions* comes to mind as she races toward the inviting canopy of leaves; she is Rima the bird girl, heading home at last.

She reaches the tree and grasps a strong gray branch in one hand as she catches her breath and waits for her brother. She pushes a fist into the place in her side where the stitch still hurts. Her breath comes in panting, heaving sobs. As Ron comes closer, she parts the branches and steps into the cool world beneath the canopy of leaves.

Kenny lies on the ground. Sleeping? But—

What was he doing in her tree, anyway? She steps forward, about to wake him, then steps back with a cry. Kenny's face is blue, his body still as a doll's. He can't possibly be alive.

She raises her hands to her mouth and stifles a scream. "He killed himself," she whispers. But then something strikes her. She looks at the area around the body—the only way she can look at it is to think of Kenny as "the body"—and sees no glass, no bottle of pills, no means of ingesting poison. No hemostat, although she has no way of knowing that one is missing.

Ron reaches her and grabs her by the shoulders. "Don't get any closer." He steps past her and blocks her view. "I think it was parathion. If we so much as touch him, we could be dead too."

CHAPTER FIVE

As always, it was the chair I noticed first. Not the smile on the bearded face or the warm welcome in the brown eyes, so like mine and yet so different. Not even the startling increase of gray in hair and beard caught my initial attention. Instead, my eyes traveled first to the wide rubber wheels, then up to the strap that secured the twisted torso in place, finally to the hand and breath controls on the armrests. Even to me, my brother *was* his chair.

It still gave me a jolt to see Ron's basketball player's body folded like a carpenter's rule into the ugly hunk of metal that made his life possible. I pasted on a smile and tried to act as if meeting my brother in federal court were an everyday occurrence.

I knelt next to the rubber wheels and said the first words that entered my head. ''You could've stayed in Cleveland and fought extradition. You didn't have to make it easy for them.''

''It's good to see you, too,'' Ron said with a wry smile. I put my arms around his shoulders and hugged hard, steeling myself against the realization that he wouldn't hug back.

He leaned down and brushed his lips against my cheek. His beard tickled my face.

''Cass, it was nice of you to come,'' Ron said, ''but Harve Sobel is my lawyer.''

''Not anymore he isn't,'' I retorted. ''Haven't you ever

heard of conflict of interest?'' Without waiting for an answer, I went on. "Maybe it was okay for you both to have the same lawyer back in '82, but with Jan facing new charges, Harve should keep Jan and I'll represent you.''

"The reason I waived extradition and had Zack drive me here from Cleveland,'' Ron said, replying to the question I'd all but forgotten I'd asked, "is that they'd have won eventually, so why drag it out? Besides,'' he added in a tone just a shade too firm, "I wanted to be here for Jan.''

"Jan!'' All the pent-up rage I'd been feeling since I first saw her on the news exploded. "I can't believe she talked you into this in the first place, let alone running away when things got heavy. I can't believe she used you. I—''

"Cass.'' Ron's tone was commanding. "If you don't stop talking about Jan like that, I'll get another lawyer. Maybe it won't be Harve, but it won't be you either unless you shut up. Got that?''

Ron's face was red, blood pounding to his head. He strained forward in his chair, chest pressing against the strap that held him in place. His hands made claw motions that didn't seem entirely planned.

There were a number of things I would have liked to say, starting with the fact that I for one had been hoping Jan had overdosed years ago and lay buried in an unmarked grave instead of popping up like a zombie in *Night of the Living Dead*, dragging Ron and me back to Toledo and all of us back into the sixties.

I didn't say it. I thought about Ron and Jan the way they were in the summer of '69 and I said nothing. If Jan still had the power to bring out a protective masculinity in my brother, so be it. So be it as long as it didn't get in the way of what I had to do in court, which was to put as much distance as possible between Ron and what Jan had done.

"Did they let you see her?''

"No,'' he replied. "Not yet. But Dana said Harve saw her and that she was ready to face whatever happens in court today.''

"She'd better be,'' I muttered. I had no doubt that the court was prepared to take a hard line against a woman who'd killed a federal law enforcement officer and then gone underground. My only concern was that whatever anger the prosecutor and judge had toward Jan wouldn't spill over onto Ron. It was my job to make sure that didn't happen.

A burly man in a Harley-Davidson T-shirt and black jeans stepped up to Ron's chair. He was carrying a cardboard tray of cellophane-wrapped pastries and three cups of steaming coffee.

I guessed he was the latest and best in a long line of home attendants. Stories about him had filled Ron's letters for almost a year, although we'd never met. I tended to blitz in to Cleveland every Christmas, bearing a Jon Vie chocolate cake and presents from the Museum of Modern Art. I knew only as much about my brother's life as I could learn in three or four days.

Fortunately, Ron's letters prepared me for the burly man who extended a beefy hand connected to a tattooed arm. "John Zachowicz," he said. "But call me Zack, okay?"

I let my hand be swallowed in the big man's grasp, trying not to stare at the tattoo on the hairy arm: a devil's face superimposed with the words "Born to Raise Hell." Wasn't that the sentiment Richard Speck had on his arm when he murdered eight nurses in Chicago? I consoled myself with the knowledge that the other arm read "Jesus Saves."

Like Ron, Zack was a Vietnam vet. Unlike Ron, he'd been a "lurp," a long-range reconnaissance patrol sniper who'd spent too much time in what Ron called "the bad boonies." He'd gone from the jungle to a biker gang, from a perpetual marijuana haze to a hard-core heroin habit, from drug rehab to born-again Christianity.

"Bought some sweet rolls," Zack said. He set the cardboard tray on a wooden bench next to Ron's chair. I was back in the Midwest; Danishes were sweet rolls, soda was pop, and I'd better not ask for an egg cream. I sat down on the bench and opened one of the coffees.

Zack opened a pastry and cut it with a plastic knife. When he had a pile of kid-sized pieces on the cellophane, he set them on Ron's lap. My brother moved his hand slowly toward the pieces, took one, dropped it, picked it up and finally succeeded in conveying it to his mouth. I could have eaten a whole Danish in the time it took him to take one bite.

Zack opened a straw and placed it into one of the coffees. He held the coffee under Ron's chin and Ron took a sip. "Hot," he said. "Let it sit a minute, okay?" Zack set the cup on the bench next to me.

"Look in the bag," Ron said, tilting his head to the right. I focused on the canvas book bag I'd given him five Christmases ago. I leaned down and pulled out a manila envelope. "You mean this?"

Ron nodded, a barely concealed grin of anticipation on his face.

Even before I opened it, I knew what it was. A photograph. I steeled myself to look into faces from the past.

But the picture wasn't a snapshot of old buddies. I held the eight-by-ten black-and-white glossy on my lap, taking care to keep my fingers at the edges so I wouldn't smudge the shiny surface.

It was a typical northwest Ohio landscape. Rows and rows of beet greens, as straight and narrow as a Presbyterian conscience, being hoed by hunched-over migrant workers wearing big straw hats. A short distance away, under an elm tree, stood a rickety baby carriage. Next to the carriage, her round face beaming, stood four-year-old Belita Navarro.

The picture was hand-printed and dried far too hastily on an ancient print-dryer. I knew because I'd printed it, back in the summer of '69. Printed it and given a copy to Ted Havlicek, who managed to get it published in the local section of the *Blade*.

"You kept it." My voice was a whisper, barely there at all.

"Hey, it was my sister's first published photograph."

"It was your sister's only published photograph."

"I didn't know that then, did I?" Ron's voice was lazy, teasing. "The way you carried that camera everywhere you went, I thought you were going to be the next—I don't know who. But famous."

"Imogen Cunningham," I murmured, "or Margaret Bourke-White. Every photo a masterpiece of social significance. The downtrodden as Art with a capital—"

"There's something else in the bag," Ron said.

I reached in, digging to the bottom before my fingers grasped an envelope. It was business-size, with no return address.

The handwriting was large, the letters round and childlike, yet written shakily, as though the writer were an elderly woman with the soul of a ten-year-old.

I glanced at my brother. His face wore an expectant look, but it wasn't the pleased anticipation he'd shown when I'd looked at the photograph. Instead, he seemed tense, ready for trouble.

Inside the envelope were four sheets of typing paper written in the same awkward script.

"Dear Ron," the letter began. "Thank you for writing to me. Your letters meant a lot. I feel like I'm starting my life all over again. I have a lot of things to make up for.

"In the Program, we have this thing called the Ninth Step. You have to make a list of people you've harmed and then try to make amends. When I did my Ninth Step, I closed my eyes and remembered all the faces of people I'd hurt when I was drinking. One of those faces was yours. And one was Kenny's."

I stopped reading. "God," I murmured. "That's a hell of a thing to do. Think of all the people you've harmed. And what does she mean"—I stared directly into my brother's eyes—"when she says she harmed you?"

Ron looked away, his cheeks reddening. "That's another story. Keep reading."

"I mean, I remember you and she were—"

"Keep reading, Cass." I opened my mouth, then shut it as I caught a glimpse of something in his eyes that told me to quit while I was ahead.

I kept reading. "I can't make amends to Kenny because he's dead. I can't tell him I was wrong, that I know he wasn't the one who sold us out to the cops back in '69. We all thought he was the traitor who got us busted, but the truth is that the FBI had an informer in our group.''

The letter fell from my hands. ''What is this woman smoking? Is she serious? Does she really believe this crap?''

Ron nodded. He leaned down and sipped the coffee Zack held under his chin. ''Keep—''

''I know, keep reading.'' I suited action to words.

''Kenny didn't sell us out, Ron. The cops knew everything before we got to the county fair, but it wasn't from him. One of us was working for the feds all along, and I'm going to tell everything when I turn myself in.''

A wave of nausea hit me. I felt hot and cold, sweaty and chilled. Sick to my soul.

The guilt flu. I had only been three years older than Kenny when I'd looked at him after the arrest with cold, rock-hard eyes and said, ''I don't talk to traitors.'' Then I'd walked away, my head held high with righteous fervor. I had no idea he'd take our rejection so hard, that he'd poison himself with the very pesticide we were protesting.

I was a child. A dangerous child.

''Cass?'' Ron's concerned voice broke in. ''Are you okay?''

''Yeah, sure,'' I said. My teeth were chattering. ''I got a little drunk on the plane is all.'' A little drunk, a little maudlin, a little guilty. Some people do the Ninth Step sober, some have to drink in order to remember.

The letter ended with a signature. No truly, no sincerely, and no love.

''God, Ron,'' I began, ''I already felt rotten about Kenny, and now—if he didn't even sell us out, then—''

''Then we're even more guilty than we were before,'' he finished. ''We jumped on that kid so fast.'' He shook his head. ''I mean, I never even thought of anyone else. As soon as the bust went down, I said to myself, 'Kenny, you little fuck. You're going to pay for this.' And then he did pay for it.''

I looked at the wheelchair. ''So did you, Ron. So did you.''

''Yeah, well, sort of.''

"Sort of, my ass. It was because of the arrests that you got sent to 'Nam."

"What do you think of the letter?"

I let Ron change the subject. "She sounds pretty flaky. And besides, she just got sober. Does that sound to you like somebody with her head on straight?"

"Does to me," Zack said. I looked across Ron at the wild black hair and shaggy beard, the tattooed arms and studded wristband, the leather vest with the motorcycle patches. His huge face glowed with joy. "Kicking juice and shit and coming home to Jesus was the best medicine I ever took, praise the Lord."

"Well, maybe for some people," I muttered, aware of Ron's suppressed laughter.

A hand tapped my shoulder. I jumped. A uniformed officer said, "Court's in session, Counselor. Better get inside. Judge Noble's a stickler for punctuality."

I nodded and rose from the bench. Zack took the handles of Ron's chair and wheeled him toward the courtroom, where I came face to face with a piece of my past. Dana Sobel Rapaport, Harve's daughter and Rap's ex-wife, stood waiting outside the big double doors. She wore a navy blue suit that cried out for brass buttons and epaulets, flat shoes, and an Oxford cloth shirt with a straight gold pin through the collar.

I knew it was her by the shiny, straight black hair. Indian hair, I'd always thought, particularly in the old days when it hung down to her butt. Now it was short-cropped and gray-streaked, but it was still the hair of a Native American princess.

"Cassie, is that you?" she asked. "I almost didn't recognize you."

Me? What's different about me? You're the one who got old, who cut her hair and put on forty pounds and started dressing out of a Land's End catalogue. I'm still the same—

"Dana," I said, forcing enthusiasm into my tone. Pretending this was a reunion, not a court appearance that might end with my brother in custody, awaiting trial as an accessory to murder.

"Where's Harve?" I asked. "I wanted to talk to him for a minute or two before the case was called."

"He'll be here," Dana replied. "He had a case in Common Pleas, but he'll be here by the time our case is called."

This was the Harve Sobel I remembered, always running late, always dashing into court at the last minute with a breezy apology, always having to cool out the judge before getting down to business. I'd hoped having the first two rows of the courtroom packed with media people would have been reason enough to adjourn his other cases by phone and show up on time.

"He's going to piss off the judge before we even open our mouths on bail."

Before Dana could reply, an ebony-black man with a shiny shaved head stepped up and said, "We have to talk."

"Do we?" I answered, raising an eyebrow. "And you are . . . ?"

"Luke Stoddard," he replied, "assistant United States attorney."

The enemy. The man trying to put my brother in jail. But if he was ready to talk, that meant what he really wanted was a deal. A deal that would cut Ron loose, in return for . . . what?

I nodded my willingness to discuss the matter and followed him down the corridor to a spot where the others couldn't hear.

I jumped the gun, letting my opponent know I intended to control the situation. "What do you want?"

A small smile crossed Stoddard's smooth face. "I want Jan Gebhardt."

Not a news flash. "In return for what?"

He shrugged. "A clean walk for your brother."

I refused to make the obvious remark. "All charges dismissed? He leaves town and forgets the whole thing?"

"Not exactly," the prosecutor replied. "There's the little matter of his testimony at trial." His smile grew broader. I was reminded of a poem from my childhood, about the fish with the deep-sea smile. The smile of the big fish who always eludes the hook, who swallows up the smaller fish.

"Ron can't add anything to your case," I said with more

confidence than I felt. "He was a passenger in the van." *A mere passenger* was the way I intended to phrase it when addressing the judge. "He didn't know the other passengers were illegals."

"It *was* his van, Counselor," Stoddard reminded me. "That makes him a little more than a passenger. Besides," he went on, "those original charges of smuggling illegals pale beside the murder of a federal officer."

"Ron was nowhere near the scene of the crime," I pointed out. "Jan was on her own during the whole thing."

"But he was waiting for her back at the church. It's my guess he knew exactly where she was and what she was doing."

My face reflected my complete astonishment. Stoddard smiled his deep-sea smile and said, "It seems your client hasn't told you everything." He put the slightest possible emphasis on the word "client," managing to needle me not only for walking into court unprepared but for being the kind of sister whose brother hadn't seen fit to tell her the whole story.

Before I could reply, the prosecutor said, "Think about it, Ms. Jameson. We'll talk again after the arraignment. You and your client may see things a little bit differently then."

He strode down the hall and into the courtroom. I followed, thinking as I walked. Would a deal be so bad? All Ron had to do was deny any knowledge of Jan's intent. Whatever went wrong was her fault, not his, so why should he suffer?

The first two rows of the courtroom were filled with reporters. I scanned them, hoping to recognize Ted Havlicek. It would be nice to have a friendly ear into which I could drop pro-defense tidbits.

Ron's chair sat at the defense table. I had barely reached my seat when the cell door opened and out came a phalanx of guards, all surrounding a prisoner in a faded print dress.

I stared frankly and openly at the woman whose untimely return from the dead had caused all this trouble.

Thin, tense, her mouth working and her fingers idly twisting a hank of stringy hair, she looked like a haggard prostitute emerging from the drunk tank. Her face was pale as oatmeal and there were old track marks on her skinny arms. A fine shiver ran through her body as I watched her; it was as if my eyes had somehow touched her in a sensitive place.

Her face lit up as she caught a glimpse of Ron; the smile took twenty years off her face.

Breaking from the guards, she rushed toward the chair. Before they could stop her, she threw her arms around his torso and kissed him. It was a long, deep kiss with plenty of tongue.

I had never thought to see a woman kiss my brother that way again.

Luke Stoddard wanted Ron to testify against Jan.

It was my job to sell betrayal as a viable option.

But how could I ask Ron to betray a woman who kissed him as though he were still a whole man?

CHAPTER SIX

It was like being on speed. Black beauties with a hit or two of grass to fuzz the hard edges. Jan gunned the motor as the van sped along the black-topped T-square road toward Lake Erie. The summer wind licked her face, swished her long fine hair into her eyes, her mouth. She leaned back and laughed. This was alive—the most alive she'd felt since the day she stopped drinking and doping seventy-nine days ago. Seventy-nine long days without a high, gray days in spite of golden summer sun, days as flat as the farmland on either side of the blacktop. The danger only heightened the high. Was this what Harriet Tubman felt leading slaves to freedom? Was this what Raoul Wallenberg felt smuggling Jews out of Hitler's Reich? Were all heroes danger junkies at heart?

"Eh-slow down, *por favor*," the man in the passenger seat said, his Spanish accent heavy. Jan, loving the feel of summer wind in her hair, bristled at the peremptory tone behind the polite words. Miguel wasn't asking, he was ordering her to reduce speed.

She glanced at the speedometer. Sixty-five and rising. But hell, there was nobody around, even if it was afternoon. What was wrong with a little speed? She gunned the motor, taking the van another five miles over the limit.

A quiet voice from the back of the van said, "He's right,

Jan. The last thing we need is to be stopped for speeding. Slow it down, okay?'' It was Ron Jameson, strapped into the back of his specially equipped van like precious cargo.

He was right; she lightened her foot and the van slowed. But damn it, she was right too! If Miguel used that tone in front of anyone else, he'd never pass as a migrant farm worker. Humility was as much a part of his disguise as the *guyabera* shirt and calloused hands.

Anyway, Ron owned the van. He called the shots. So do the double nickel all the way to the lake. *Fifty-five, stay alive.* Her mind repeated the words like a mantra as her sandaled foot touched lightly on the accelerator. *Fifty-five, stay alive. Fifty-five . . . five.*

Five. Five years. Five years if they got caught. That mantra, stronger than *fifty-five, stay alive*, took root in her brain. *Five years, five years*, she said to herself. Five years in a federal pen for transporting illegal aliens.

Could she do five years? No booze, no drugs—hell, as far as getting high was concerned, she was already in jail. Sobriety jail.

No men. Jan thought about that a moment, remembered Hal, her ex-husband, still actively alcoholic. Remembered the nameless, faceless men from the bars, men who'd reeked of booze, just like her Daddy. No men. She shrugged; no loss.

No loss for her, but what about Ron? Would they really give five years to a man already imprisoned by paralysis? No, of course they wouldn't.

Right. And maybe the tooth fairy would drop by and slip some coin under her pillow for the two teeth Hal had knocked out just before he left.

''How far?'' Miguel asked, not for the first time. He looked like a typical Mexican-American migrant worker: face dark as a buckeye, wearing a loose shirt and a straw hat. Shorts and dusty huaraches. He had the look of a man who'd spent his life squinting into the sun, squatting over strawberries, sweating over rows of sugar beet seedlings.

That was what Jan was counting on. That the weeks of working in the fields, sun beating down on their faces, had transformed Miguel and Pilar into people who could pass for Mexican-American migrant labor, not a Salvadoran university professor and his family running from the death squads. Running toward Canada, where the asylum laws were more lenient than in the United States.

The trouble was, they looked like *campesinos* but she couldn't count on them to act as deferential as real migrants. Pilar had a way of holding her head erect, of staring straight at people, that spoke of a Central American *doña* used to weekly leg-waxings, not a woman who started the day at five a.m. by putting a pot of beans on the stove. And Miguel—his situation galled him. He was an educated man forced to pretend ignorance, a man who had been respected forced to act deferential, a man who had earned a place in society forced to flee with only the clothes on his back. His hair-trigger temper had led to confrontations back at the Migrant Rest Center; could he pass as a migrant if they were stopped, challenged?

"It's about ten more miles," she said, keeping her eyes on the road, consciously not looking at Miguel's face. Not wanting to see the chip on his shoulder, reflected in a slight sneer around the mouth. Wanting to pretend that he was playing his role.

Ten miles to the lakeshore, ten miles to the boat, Rap's boat, that would ferry Miguel, Pilar, and little Manuelito to Canada. Ten miles more of heart-pounding fear, of adrenaline rush. Ten final miles on the underground railroad that had begun in El Salvador, traveled overland to Mexico, then forded the Rio Grande into Texas. Now safety was within reach, within tasting distance.

"We're almost there," Jan said, glancing at the face beside her. Underneath the bravado, she sensed worry. She knew that feeling; how many times had she done things in spite of the fear, drowning the fear in booze and pretending a cockiness she didn't really feel? She let her voice fill with confidence and reassurance. "Only ten more miles."

Ten more miles of high, then back to emotions as gray as Lake Erie, as flat as the beet fields.

God, a beer would taste good.

She clamped down hard on the thought, her first booze-thought of the day. Instead, she concentrated on driving, ostentatiously looking into the rearview mirror despite the emptiness of the rural road.

There was a car behind her. A silver-gray late model that glinted ominously in the noonday sun.

How long had it been there? She didn't know, thought of asking Ron if he'd noticed it, but decided not to cause panic. That was how it had started before; a car innocently following, then the police descending on them with siren screaming.

Oh, God, her first run by herself and she was going to be stopped. Just like last week, with Ramón and his family. She and Dana had been driving the church van—was it only three days ago?—when the Highway Patrol pulled them over. At first they thought it was a routine stop, although Jan swore they'd been doing fifty miles per hour max. But then a gray government car drove up and out stepped Walt Koeppler, head of the local Immigration and Naturalization Service, *La Migra* to the thousands of illegal immigrants who crossed the U.S. border every week.

First line of defense: phony ID showing that the Escobars were American citizens from south Texas, up in Ohio to pick crops like hundreds of other migrant workers. Dana's ex-husband Rap had copied passport photos onto real Texas driver's licenses obtained from the genuine Escobars of Brownsville.

Second line of defense: a strong offense. So while Jan sat quietly behind the wheel, Dana, in the passenger seat, went into a carefully rehearsed tantrum.

"Green cards?" she'd said, her tone dripping contempt. "They don't need green cards. As you perfectly well know, Mr. Koeppler." She'd raked him up and down, her eyes blazing. "They're American citizens." Which was true of the vast majority of migrant farmworkers who came into northwest Ohio for the season; they were Spanish-speaking Texans who lived only slightly better than their cousins across the Rio Grande.

Walt Koeppler didn't back down. "Can they prove it?" The voice was softer, but no less menacing.

Dana motioned to Ramón, who put his newly calloused hand into his work pants and laboriously withdrew the forged papers.

Jan had taken the papers from Ramón and passed them wordlessly to the immigration officer, hoping the shaking of her hands would be put down to anger instead of nerves. "This really sucks," she said as he perused the documents, lifting the sunglasses from his pink nose to peer more closely at the signatures. "These people were born in the U.S.A., same as you, and everywhere they go they get hassled just because they look Mexican." She hoped her tone was as sarcastic as Dana's.

It was four agonizing minutes before Walt Koeppler handed the papers back to Jan. Her fingers were so damp she was afraid she'd melt the ink, but all she did was leave a smudge. He let them go. He had no choice.

She couldn't believe she was driving illegals again after the scare Walt had put into her that day. But glancing back into the rearview mirror, watching the silver car come closer and then fall back, she understood why.

She'd thought it was because Miguel and Pilar and especially Manuelito needed her. Because she needed to be needed. She was doing good, doing important work.

But that wasn't what had put her behind the wheel of Ron's van. It was the high. She glanced back at the silver car in the rearview and felt the rush of danger and knew: she was doing it for the high.

"How many are left?" Dana asked. "After Miguel and Pilar, I mean." She pushed hair off her sweat-soaked forehead and puffed out her cheeks as she expelled hot, humid air from her lungs. Summer in the fields took a lot out of Dana; every year she swore she'd get to the mountains or the ocean—hell, even Michigan—and every year she stayed in the same sun-baked landscape, hating summer with every sodden pore.

"Twelve Indios from Guatemala," Rap replied. "And I

have one more Salvadoran family over at the Henderson farm.'' He pushed his Mets cap back and wiped sweat from his brow with a hand that left a streak of dirt. His eyes strayed from his ex-wife's face to the sailboat moored at the deserted pier.

"Don't lie to me, Rap.'' Dana cut him off, her voice hard. "I know there are others. Those guys in the trailers at the van Wormer farm make it more than twelve. I don't know what side deal you have going on, but I want the whole truth. How many *total*?''

Rap spread his bony hands in a placating gesture, smiling the open, friendly grin that had captivated Dana Sobel fourteen years earlier. The grin that said he had nothing to hide; the grin that she knew from long bitter experience meant he was lying through his crooked teeth.

It wasn't fair. He was even sexier than he'd been in those days, when she'd first fallen under his spell. She took in the lean face, the wiry torso, the long, tanned legs in cutoff jeans. At forty, Joel Alan Rapaport was a good-looking guy; at thirty-eight, she was a dumpy broad with thirty extra pounds, crow's-feet around the eyes, and gray streaks in her once-black hair.

"Look, I don't care who those guys are,'' she said, her voice edged with the mock patience of a mother dealing with a teenager. "I don't want to know. I sure as hell don't want to know if it's something illegal. Which, knowing you,'' she added, "it most likely is. Just get them the hell out of the factory as soon as possible. We're being watched, Rap. It's only a matter of time before—''

"Oh, Christ, not this old song and dance.'' Rap's lateral lisp sprayed saliva in her direction. "You're starting to talk like Jan, and you know what a flake she is.''

"Flake or not, she may be right. That police car last week had no business knowing we were there. It wasn't a coincidence, Rap. Somebody informed—''

"Yeah, yeah, yeah.'' Rap's agreement was no agreement at all; he waved away the words with a bony hand. "Truth is, babe, it's not the feds that worry me. It's Joaquín's buddies from back home.''

"Joaquín Baltasar? The guy in Ted's *Newsweek* article?" Dana squinted at Rap. "The guy who found the *contra* hideouts in the jungle?''

Rap nodded. "He's in south Texas right now, signing on with a sugar beet crew. He should be in Liberty Center by tomorrow or the next day, and then it's up to us to get him to Canada.''

The full implication of Rap's remarks finally sank in. "You think the *contras* would follow Joaquín all the way up here?" She looked around at the peaceful freshwater beach as if guerillas hid behind every dune. "Here, in Ohio?" Dana's voice rose in disbelief. Her own worry that the cops were on their trail paled in the light of her ex-husband's fears. Talk about paranoia—the idea that Nicaraguan *contras* could and would make their way north just to take out one refugee . . . it was crazy.

Wasn't it?

"Hey, look, I'm just telling you what I've heard," Rap went on. His lean body moved in rhythm to music only he heard as he paced the marshy sand. "You know I hear things, Dane. Those dudes are heavy. They don't like it that Joaquín told the world what they were doing, they don't like Ted making him a hero, and they sure as hell don't like it that he got out of the country before they could take him out. It's like when Stalin iced Trotsky. He didn't have to do it, but—''

"Oh, Jesus. Stalin and Trotsky. What the fuck year is this?" But she said the words under her breath.

Rap had a point. Joaquín had beaten the government forces in his own country and by escaping he'd made them look weak. Their balls were on the line, and when men had their balls on the line, there was nothing they wouldn't do to get even.

"So have you seen anything? Are the other families in danger? Should we move them?''

Rap shook his head. "Moving people too much calls attention. We'd better sit tight after we get Miguel and Pilar out of here. I'll check out my sources and find out what's shaking.''

You'll check your sources, Dana thought. *You'll check your wiretaps, run the tapes on your hidden microphones. Sources, my ass.* She took a moment to wonder just where Rap had hidden his little bugs, whose phones he'd tapped into, whose secrets he'd plundered to get his information.

Then she stopped herself. She didn't want to know. For her own safety and that of their twelve-year-old son, she really didn't want to know.

The silver car drew closer. Jan didn't dare raise her speed; she couldn't give the cops an excuse for pulling her over. The silver car honked, just like any driver on a two-lane road annoyed at a slower car in its path.

''Go ahead and pass, idiot,'' Jan muttered. ''This is the straightest road God ever made, there's no double line, so—''

Why wasn't he passing? Why was the damned car playing tag with her? Was this part of the game? Maybe Walt Koeppler was in this car, not his government-issue clunker. She peered into the mirror, trying to see a face behind the driver's seat. But all she could tell was that he was male.

''Is he following us?'' Miguel whispered, low enough that Pilar in the back seat couldn't hear.

''I don't know,'' she replied. ''I hope not.''

''How does he know we are here?'' The *h* sounds came out more like *j*'s; Miguel was losing his English in his anxiety.

It was a good question. Dana and Rap had talked long and hard about changing the route, varying the site of the boat. So this was not the same road she and Dana had taken last week, nor was it the same time of day. Even the van was different. They'd done everything they could to remain unobtrusive.

So what was this silver car doing here?

And what should she do about it?

The turnoff was coming up. She was supposed to make the turn right after the one for Crane Creek State Park, where fishermen or swimmers went for a day's recreation. The road she was to take was the one used by occasional boaters, much less traveled.

But would that lead the silver car and the police to where Dana and Rap waited with the boat? Should she keep going and double back to make the turn?

Blood pumped through her veins as if she'd done a serious dose of speed. She was learning that natural highs were even harder to manage than artificial ones. She knew what to do to ensure a soft landing after speed: a little grass, a snort of coke, a glass of wine. Not sleeping pills, that was for housewives. But what do you do to bring yourself down from a high you didn't make?

God, I need a drink. Or two. Or six.

Second booze-thought of the day.

And meanwhile the miles slipped away under the rolling black tires. The turnoff was coming up; what should she do?

Before she had to decide, the silver car abruptly peeled off to the left, following signs directing fishermen to the inlets off the lake. Was the driver really intent on lake perch or had he just telephoned her location to *La Migra*?

No way to know. But her turn was next, and she swerved the car to the left. No oncoming traffic, yet her turn was awkwardly done. Nerves.

It was a dune road, bumpy and sandy and gravelly and not much used. Serious boaters rented slips at marinas up and down the lake; this road had long since been supplanted by blacktopped routes to the water's edge.

She could see water for the first time, ditches and marshes and inlets sparkling in the sun. Manuelito, in the back seat, pointed and said something in Spanish. Pilar murmured a reply; Jan caught the word *agua*, but not much else.

They were going to make it. Relief, in the form of a waterfall of sweat, flooded her skin. Her first trip as conductor on the underground railroad, engineer of the Enchilada Express, and they were going to make it. She could picture the boat moored at an old pier at the end of the dune road.

A siren sliced the air like a razor cutting a throat.

CHAPTER SEVEN

Judge LaMont Noble strode onto the bench, his robes flying behind him like the wings of a bird. He was tall; I recalled someone saying something about a college basketball career before law school. His face was angular, his limbs fleshless. Ichabod Crane with African ancestry. His voice was harsh, ravenlike. Allergies? A cold? Or a reflection of an inner impatience with things human?

I watched and listened as the judge called the room to order, then asked where Lawyer Sobel was. Dana answered; I wondered if she'd become a lawyer since I'd seen her last, or if the judges simply permitted her to address the court out of familiarity with Harve and his ways. She was in the middle of an elaborate explanation when Harve himself swept through the doors, followed by an entourage of very young-looking law students.

Before he was halfway up the aisle, Harve started apologizing. I gave him full points for theater; it was like one of those Broadway shows that begin with an actor popping up out of the audience and commanding attention. Taking all eyes off the stage and focusing them somewhere in the middle of the house.

The judge wasn't pleased that the spotlight had been commandeered. ''I'll hear you when you reach counsel table, Lawyer Sobel,'' he said in his croaking voice, "and not a moment before.''

I noted the use of the title. Southern black people used that term, Lawyer So-and-So. Did that mean Noble had a memory of the old civil rights days? Could I get away with reminding the court that Jan and Ron had been working for the freedom of refugees in the same way that civil rights lawyers had worked for the freedom of Southern blacks?

Before I turned my attention back to the bench, the big wooden doors opened once more, this time admitting a tall priest with Marine-short gray hair and an ascetic face. It took me a minute, but when the penny finally dropped, so did my jaw.

It was Father Jerry Kujawa, pastor of Our Lady of Guadalupe. The Radical Preacher we'd all met in the summer of '69, the man who'd declared his church a sanctuary for the fleeing Central American refugees during the summer of '82.

What the hell was he doing here? Didn't he realize that his presence would only serve to remind everyone, the judge included, of those radical years when civil disobedience seemed as American as apple pie? Didn't he know he was doing more harm than good by striding up to the third row and squeezing himself into the seat next to one of the law students?

Luke Stoddard's voice rumbled like the Mississippi in flood as he summarized the charges. "On July 15, 1982, these two defendants were arrested for transporting illegal aliens," he began. "And a scant three days later, Ms. Gebhardt was once again engaging in illegal activities along the same lines, showing a complete and total disregard of the laws of the United States." I jotted a note to myself to remind the court that Ron, in contrast, had done nothing beyond the original charge.

"On July 18, 1982, Ms. Gebhardt was stopped while transporting yet another illegal immigrant, as a result of which she shot and killed Agent Dale Krepke."

"Agent Dale Krepke of the Drug Enforcement Administration," Harve interjected in a booming voice. The judge gave him a withering stare, but I was grateful for, yet puzzled by, this new information. In all the press accounts, Krepke had simply been identified as a federal agent. I'd assumed he was Border Patrol, like Walt Koeppler. What was a DEA agent doing making an arrest for immigration violations?

"He was an agent of federal law enforcement," Stoddard said in a firm tone, "and he was shot and killed while performing his duty. It makes no difference which agency he—"

"He was shot and killed," Harve repeated in a voice that overrode the prosecutor, "but not by Janice Gebhardt. The truth is, Your Honor, that Agent Krepke had no business being where he was at the time he was shot. He was in fact specifically ordered by his superiors not to follow or harass any member of the so-called sanctuary movement. He disregarded those orders and he died because he was in the wrong place at the wrong time. He interrupted something far more serious than the crime he thought he was pursuing."

"Mr. Sobel," the judge said, hammering the desk with his ebony gavel, "I insist that you hold your arguments until it is your turn to address the court on bail. Kindly permit the United States attorney to continue."

And continue Stoddard did. A sucker for deep male voices, I found myself lulled by the man's delivery. It was smoother and more sophisticated than the old-time preacher style, but it had some of the same cadences and all of the same passion. A passion that was being directed toward one end: holding Jan without bail.

To hear him, you never would have suspected that he'd just offered one of the defendants a deal. I gave him full marks for strategy; he was showing me just how bad things could get should Ron refuse his offer and insist upon going to trial.

Old Lefties have better faces, I thought as I watched the old warhorse, the Bill Kunstler of northwest Ohio, rise to his full height. Harve Sobel had to be seventy-five, but his eyes still burned and his voice still choked with a passion for justice that made me wonder where my youthful passion had gone. How had he managed to keep his rage and his love alive all these years?

"My client," he began, placing a huge hand on Jan's thin shoulder, "ran away when Agent Krepke was shot to death in front of her eyes. She ran away not because she shot him, but because she was afraid that those who killed Agent Krepke could and would kill her. The identity of the actual murderers of Agent Krepke will be revealed in due course, Your Honor, but it will have to be revealed very, very carefully, since I assure this court that the ramifications will reach far beyond this courtroom.''

Stoddard jumped to his feet, but before the words left his mouth, Jan spoke up. ''I want to say something, Your Honor,'' she announced. ''There were a lot of things going on that summer. Illegal things. The sanctuary stuff was the tip of the iceberg. I came back to tell the whole truth about all of it.''

Harve touched Jan's arm and she fell silent. ''What my client means,'' he said, ''is that a number of illegal activities were going on around her—none of which she was involved in herself. But her contention is that the government of the United States not only knew about these activities, but covered up for them and in some cases actively supported them. In fact,'' he went on, lowering his voice to a confidential tone that had the first row of reporters leaning forward in their seats, ''the defense intends to prove that the government of the United States violated my client's most basic civil rights by planting not only an informer but an agent provocateur in the sanctuary movement.''

''Your Honor, this is outrageous,'' the prosecutor interjected. His voice was steady, but a vein in his temple throbbed. The man was reining in a gigantic rage.

''Counselor,'' Judge Noble said, his tone heavy with disapproval, ''are you asking this court to believe that the government of the United States would engage in the kind of illegal conspiracy you're alleging here?''

Harve smiled his own deep-sea smile and reached into the open briefcase on the defense table. He took his time in pulling out a sheaf of photocopied cases, the names of which he proceeded to recite for the record. I recognized them after the fourth name: each case involved FBI illegalities, ranging from the planting of illegal wiretaps to the use of agents provocateurs, and each case involved left-wing organizations. Each case also ended in a dismissal of all charges against the defendants.

Harve made his point. Judge Noble cut him off with a wave of his long-fingered hand. "Lawyer Sobel, this court sees where you are going with this. And I must agree that the government of this country has at times overstepped its bounds in enforcing the law. But a mere recitation of case law does nothing to prove your assertion that the government did any such thing in this case."

Harve smiled, as if the judge had said exactly the words he wanted to hear. "Which is why, Your Honor, my client wishes to speak openly and frankly, under oath and on the record, about what she knows, at the earliest possible opportunity. She seeks a public forum because she fears, even now, that there are agents of the government who would silence her if they could."

Luke Stoddard had heard all he could stand. "Your Honor," he broke in, his voice cracking with outrage, "can't you see what's happening here? This defendant is the one charged with the murder of a federal agent, and she's trying to put the government of the United States on trial instead of herself. There is absolutely no foundation for her statements, and I move that they be stricken from the record."

"These allegations are too serious to be dismissed, Mr. Stoddard," Judge Noble said. "I will hear the defense out on this matter and make my decision accordingly."

I had the feeling I ought to stop this runaway train, at least long enough to find out what was going on and how it could affect Ron. But the look on Stoddard's face kept me in my seat; the fact that he was openly upset by this turn of events led me to believe it could only do us good in the long run.

The long run. The trouble with that thinking was that I hadn't intended to be here for the long run. Hadn't I promised Harry the Toop—and, far more importantly, old Pops—that I'd be back in Brooklyn in three days? A hearing like the one Harve was proposing could last weeks, with the government pulling out all the stops to keep the truth from coming out.

And when had I decided that what Jan was saying was the truth?

It was too paranoid not to be true.

"My client wishes to make a formal statement, Your Honor," Harve said.

Jan stood and read from a sheet of spiral notebook paper that shook ever so slightly in her hand.

"I've been running too long," she began, her whisky-and-cigarette voice ragged. "Living a life off the books, working for minimum wage, using someone else's name, and moving to another shit job after a year or two because I was afraid somebody would recognize me and turn me in." Her voice dwindled as she spoke; I craned my neck around Ron's chair for a glimpse of her wan face.

"That was a joke, wasn't it?" Her eyes rose from the paper and engaged the judge with a bitter honesty. "Because nobody would have recognized me, nobody cared anymore. When I first ran away, I thought I'd be living underground, like those Weathermen. Only there wasn't any underground, not really. Just a few people who got me phony ID, slipped me a little cash, told me to keep the faith, and then went home to their little sellout lives." The paper in her hand fluttered to the defense table, forgotten.

"That's what I thought then, Your Honor. Sellout lives. But after a few years, I realized they were the ones who had a life. I had nothing. So I started drinking again, and then I really had a shit life. Excuse me, Your Honor, but that was the truth. My life was shit, and I didn't see it until I started in the Program again, started to get sober for the second time. I was afraid," she confided, dropping her eyes and lowering her head. "I was honestly afraid to go to meetings, afraid the government would find me through the Program. But that was just another excuse to keep drinking." She stopped and drew a long, ragged breath, steadying herself against the table edge.

"That's when I realized I had to come back. I had to tell the truth. The whole truth. No matter who it hurts."

"I move," Harve said, "for full disclosure of any and all government documents related to the surveillance of the sanctuary movement in northwest Ohio for the years 1981 and 1982,'' Harve said. ''I request in particular the name of the undercover informant used by the government to obtain its search warrants and the names of any and all witnesses, informants, or undercover operatives, along with full, unredacted copies of any statements made by them.''

All Stoddard had to do was deny that any such statements existed. All he had to do was say that he couldn't turn over names of informants because there were no informants.

But that wasn't what he said.

''The prosecution will present all relevant discovery material at the proper time,'' the U.S. attorney replied.

I sucked in my breath. Unless I was missing something, Stoddard had just confirmed Jan's suspicion that someone had tipped off the cops. If there'd been absolutely nothing in the allegation that someone tipped off Walt Koeppler, Stoddard would have worded his denial very differently. Jan was right; someone in the sanctuary movement had been working for the feds.

Another triumph for good old sixties paranoia.

It was time to move on to the bail application. Stoddard cited all the reasons why Jan needed to be locked up. They were pretty convincing; if I'd been on the bench, I wasn't sure I'd have let Jan walk out of the courtroom.

But then Harve weighed in.

''Your Honor, my client was safe from the law. She was working in a Wal-Mart in Kansas under another name. No one there, or anywhere else for that matter, had the slightest clue who she was or that she was wanted by the police. She could have stayed there another twenty years. She could have died and been buried under that phony name. But''—he held up a finger made crooked by arthritis and fixed his burning eyes on the judge's impassive face—''but, Your Honor, my client felt guilt. My client felt a need to return to this court and set the record straight. My client walked into a federal office building and turned herself in. And she did it without making a deal in advance, the way some other fugitives have done. She took her chances. She announced her willingness to submit to the justice system. And that, Your Honor, makes her an outstanding bail risk.''

Stoddard snorted audibly, but said nothing. I held my breath; was it possible that Harve Sobel could actually secure the release on bail of a woman charged with the murder of a federal agent? A woman who'd eluded capture for fourteen years?

Then I found out why Father Jerry was in the courtroom. Harve called him to the defense table and asked the judge to release Jan into Father Jerry's custody. It seemed there were small cottages behind Our Lady of Guadalupe church, cottages used to house battered women and their children. Jan could stay in one of them pending the hearing. She would be under house arrest, Harve explained, permitted to leave the cottage only to attend Mass and AA meetings held in the church basement. For no other reason would she be allowed to leave her private prison.

The judge bought it. He set bail at one hundred thousand dollars, under the conditions Harve set forth. My co-counsel gave a satisfied nod; Jan could make bail. I wondered who was footing the bill. Surely Jan hadn't saved a hundred thou working at Wal-Mart.

I winced as the bailiff read the next case into the record. "United States of America against Ronald Douglas Jameson" sounded as if the whole country stood arrayed against one man in a wheelchair.

". . . permission to amend the indictment to include a violation of Title 18 United States Code section 3 in that the aforesaid Ronald Douglas Jameson did act as an accessory after the fact in that, knowing that Janice Gebhardt had committed a federal offense, he did offer comfort and assistance to her in order to hinder prosecution."

What was Stoddard talking about? What did he mean, Ron offered comfort and assistance? How in hell could a man confined to a wheelchair aid and abet a fugitive?

I found out soon enough.

It was the Internet. I raised my eyes to the ceiling. It was for this that Ron had studied computers at Kent State's program for the disabled? He and Jan had communicated by e-mail, with her using a phony identity.

And then there was the letter Ron had shown me, in which Jan told him she was going to turn herself in.

Ron had known where Jan was and he had known she was going to return from the dead. He had known, and he hadn't told me.

What other secrets had my brother chosen to keep from me?

I got Ron released. There had never really been any doubt in my mind that I'd do that. But I'd hoped the old charges would be so remote in time, so minor compared to Jan's, that the court would either dismiss outright or send strong signals that a dismissal was inevitable. Instead my brother was facing charges for crimes he'd committed within the past week.

We were mobbed as soon as the judge left the bench. Every reporter rushed toward Harve or me, begging for a statement. Harve promised to answer questions on the courthouse steps. I made no such promises, but I'd learned a thing or two about high-profile criminal trials, and I knew it would be in Ron's interest for me to say something as well.

When bail was posted and we were free to go, Harve strode toward the gaggle of reporters and news cameras at the courthouse entrance. He positioned himself directly in front of the columns, where the minicam operators shooting stock footage for the B reel couldn't miss him. He spoke into the fuzzy mikes that dangled from long booms like huge dusters. His white hair was a flowing mane; his voice already lifted in indignation even before he reached the waiting newspeople. "... an outrage," I heard him say, and then caught the words "physically challenged veteran."

The combination of blatant pathos and political correctness was pure Harve. He couldn't say "helpless cripple," yet if the disabled were fully equal with everyone else, why shouldn't the government prosecute Ron? And what was he doing talking about my client when he was Jan's lawyer?

I turned to Dana, ready to tell her that her father had better confine his remarks to his own case from now on. But instead of Dana, her ex-husband Rap stood at my shoulder.

I'd have known him anywhere. That lean body, the faded Antioch sweatshirt, a Toledo Mud Hens cap over his eyes. Rap always wore hats, always shaded his eyes from the sun, or from human scrutiny. As though to glimpse his eyes full-front would be too much for frail humanity.

"Can't you do anything to shut her up?" he asked. His gray eyes bored into mine. "I mean, I enjoy a good pig roast as much as the next guy, but doesn't anybody notice that Jan's a flake and a half? All that bullshit about an informer. Who knows what the hell she's going to tell the court?"

"She always was a nut case," Dana remarked. "Remember what a nervous wreck she was? Always chewing on her hair, her fingernails? Taking every drug that came her way? She's out to wreck our lives because she screwed up her own. We'd be a lot better off if she'd never come back. Why the hell didn't she choke on her own vomit and do us all a favor?"

Dana's words were extremely close to the thought I'd had when Jan first surfaced. Why didn't she die of an overdose and leave us all alone? Cold, brutal words that sounded a lot colder when someone else said them.

"Your old man's her lawyer," Rap pointed out. "If anyone can convince her to shut up, he can. You could talk to him."

"Harve doesn't listen to me," Dana said, her tone bitter. "He's on his high horse, he's riding the sixties again. Happy as a pig in you-know-what. He doesn't give a damn about what all this could do to me, to Dylan. His own grandson, but Harve doesn't care. All he can see is the Big Case, the head-lines, him saving the fucking world. That's all it's ever been about for him."

Rap looked at me, calculation lighting his cold gray eyes. "You're part of the defense team," he said. "You can shut her up. Cut a deal. Tell Harve to cut a deal."

"I am not part of a team, Rap," I said, making my voice as cold as his eyes. "You watched too much O.J. There is no team. There is Harve, representing Jan the way he sees fit, and there is me, trying to get Ron out of the whole mess. There is no team."

"There better be some teamwork, Mama Cass. If all the dirt

gets dug up, it's going to stick on all of us—including your precious brother. Got that?''

"Is that a threat?"

"If it has to be."

He strode through the crowd before I could reply. Always an exit line. I wondered how serious his threat was—and what exactly he was afraid of. Even a million-dollar drug deal from twelve years ago couldn't hurt him now. In fact there was only one crime he could still be worried about: murder.

CHAPTER
EIGHT

July 15, 1982

Rap held up his hand for silence. Behind him, Dana watched the lazy lake waves lap the shore. Trees grew along the edge of the beach, giving shade and cover. That was the blessing of fresh water; near ocean, they'd have been exposed on all sides.

"Do you hear something?"

Dana listened. At first, nothing. Just a wan, overheated breeze ruffling the leaves of the trees that sheltered the little inlet from the road. The persistent lapping of the waves, the pitch and toss of the boat. Then, underneath but growing louder, a whine like a mosquito circling your head on a hot summer night, zeroing in for the kill.

A siren. Close. Too close.

"I'd better get the *Layla* out of here," Rap said, moving toward the boat, lying lazily in the hazy sun. "Jan could be in trouble."

"Jan!" Dana's wrath, heated by the relentless sun, exploded. "We should have known better than to let her make a run by herself. I should be with her, not out here with my thumb up my ass. Who knows what she's gotten us into?"

"Which is why I should move the boat. We don't want her impounded if the cops roll up." He turned toward the rickety pier where the cabin cruiser was tied.

Something about Rap's haste rang a bell in Dana's mind.

Something about his eagerness to cast off, to take the *Layla* out of reach of the police—

"Rap," she said sharply. "What the hell have you got on that boat? And don't give me that innocent look. I remember the first run, when it turned out you had Roberto pay you in—"

She broke off, panic and anger struggling within her. "You didn't. You couldn't be that stupid. That greedy. Oh, Jesus, tell me you don't have dope on that boat."

Even as she said the words, even as Rap opened his mouth to protest his innocence, she knew the truth. Of course he had dope on the boat. He was ferrying people who were fleeing the drug wars of South America; what better currency for them to pay their passage with than white powder?

"Fucking shit!" She wheeled around in frustration. "This is supposed to be a rescue mission, you asshole. We're taking these people to Canada because their lives are in danger. And you're using the trip to make a buck. I can't believe—" Words failed her; she regarded her former husband with a loathing she did nothing to conceal.

A sinewy hand reached up and grabbed her T-shirt, pulling it into a hard knot. The other fist rested lightly against her damp cheek. Rap's gray eyes were granite chips and he spaced his words with a deliberate slow contempt she'd heard before.

"What the *fuck* do you think I am, babe? The fuckin' Red Cross? You think I take this boat out, risk going to jail, just to help suffering humanity? You and Father Jerry wouldn't have an underground railroad without me."

His hot breath licked her face; she glared into his eyes, praying the deep fear in her stomach didn't show on her face. She went rigid, just listened, let him blow it off. Like always.

"So don't ask stupid questions about what's on the boat, and we won't have any trouble. Okay?"

"Okay," she whispered. Then gathered courage and said, "Get the boat out of here before the cops come. I don't want to get busted on your drug rap."

The siren had stopped now, but that was no guarantee of safety. Cops could be on their way along the dune road even as they spoke. Rap let her go, let the T-shirt knot go limp, and sauntered toward the *Layla*.

As she watched her former lover, former husband, the father of her son amble, then trot toward his beloved boat, Dana knew that as long as white powder made its way north, Rap would make money from it. And as long as she was part of the sanctuary movement, needing Rap and his boat to ferry refugees to safe Canadian water, she would live in dread of the day he was caught and his boat thoroughly searched.

For today, she could live with it. But she swore to herself that next time she would take the hull apart with her bare hands before she loaded the refugees on board.

The siren zeroed in on them, homing like a missile seeking its target. Jan speeded up at first, then slowed as she bowed to the inevitable. Next to her, Miguel turned eyes huge with fright on her. *"Qué pasa?"*

Jan shook her head. What was happening? The worst, probably.

In the back seat, Pilar began to moan. *"La Migra,"* she repeated, over and over, her voice a lament. *"La Migra* will find us. *Madre de Dios."* She rocked back and forth, keening like an Irish widow. Panic turned Pilar from self-assured professor's wife to peasant. She had never played her role better.

Manuelito whimpered. Jan's high dissolved in a cold-sweat bath. The danger rush had congealed into the certainty that this trip wasn't going to end well, that capture was at hand. She had a sudden, sharp memory of wheeling Manuelito in a shopping cart while they bought him clothes for the journey. He'd pointed and giggled and kicked his little feet into her stomach.

For one wild moment, she considered speeding up, racing the cops to the water's edge in a mad hope that the family could get on the boat and make their escape before she was caught.

Jan pulled to the side of the road. There wasn't much shoulder; the road edged off into a ravine designed to catch rainwater.

The car was a blue and white Ohio Highway Patrol vehicle, but Jan wasn't surprised when the man who strode toward the van, sun glinting off his glasses, was Walt Koeppler of the Border Patrol.

As if he'd known they'd be on this road. And driving this van.

The van was the first line of defense this time. It wasn't the church van, with Our Lady of Guadalupe written on the side in Gothic script; this was Ron Jameson's specially designed vehicle, with a hydraulic lift for the wheelchair. He sat in the back, strapped in, wearing a bathing suit, an orange towel draped over his whale-white bony shoulders. Playing his part of cripple being taken on an outing by a friend.

The theory was that the police would be watching for the white, green-lettered church van, not a red van with no lettering on the side. The theory was that not many cars travelled the old dune road to get to the lakefront. The theory was that the stop three days earlier had been a fluke, a coincidence, not to be repeated.

The theory was full of shit.

Second line of defense: the forged papers, the indignation bit. Jan watched Walt Koeppler's determined glare as he approached the van, accompanied by a uniformed Highway Patrol cop. She decided abruptly to jettison the tantrum. He'd already seen Dana do that number. It wasn't going to work a second time. Just be cool, pass the papers to him, and act as if the whole thing were a giant hassle. Boring, annoying, but hardly threatening.

Koeppler's first words were less than reassuring. "You again. I thought I warned you about transporting illegals."

"Who said they were illegal?" She tried for the flip, bad-girl tone that came so easily when she'd had a few belts. It was a lot harder to pull off sober.

"You gonna run phony paper on me again?"

Stay cool. Not easy, with relentless farm-loving sun beating down on the roof of the van. Not easy, when a family's life hung in the balance, dependent on the nerve of a woman sober seventy-nine days.

Not easy, when your eyes were level with the single cyclops eye of a blue-barreled gun.

"I'm going to give you the identification this man gives me." Her voice shook slightly, as did her hand when she passed the documents from Miguel to Koeppler. Once again, they were phony birth certificates from Texas, a driver's license with Miguel's picture superimposed upon that of Eduardo Peña, a genuine Mexican-American migrant. A letter from the van Wormer farm certifying them as employed for the sugar beet season.

Koeppler took the documents and tossed them into the dirt. "These are crap, lady. We both know that. Now get out of the car—slowly—and tell Pancho there to do the same."

This time the indignation wasn't rehearsed. "His name isn't Pancho," she replied, her voice steady now. "And none of us is armed, so you don't have to be so—"

"—the fuck do I know you're not armed? Just get the hell out of the van. Now." The softer Koeppler's voice got, the more dangerous he seemed. Jan opened the van door and was relieved to see Miguel doing the same. No heroics, she prayed. Please, no heroics, no arrogance, no challenge to Koeppler's authority. Just be cool. Snow-cool, coke-cool.

Pilar whimpered as she hauled herself out of the back of the van. She'd been sitting on a jumpseat next to where the wheelchair locked in place. She pulled Manuelito close and looked at Koeppler with terror-filled eyes. In her world, *la policía* shot first, asked questions later. "No my baby," she pleaded. "Don' shoot *mi niño*." In some corner of her mind, Jan wondered how much of Pilar's incoherent pleading was real and how much role-playing. They'd worked long and hard to turn this well-to-do San Salvador couple into passable migrant workers; Pilar at least was believable.

For a moment Koeppler looked almost ashamed, almost human. Manuelito at three was a beautiful kid, all huge black eyes and infectious grin. Understanding nothing but his mother's fear, he looked up at the cop with a face full of incipient tears. He clung to Pilar's shapeless dress, carefully chosen to add to her migrant farmwoman appearance, like any kid gone suddenly shy in the presence of a stranger.

It was time for the third—or were they up to the fourth?—line of defense. Miguel, true to his instructions, let himself be searched. Let Walt Koeppler put his free hand into the pockets of the baggy shorts, gun held at stomach-level. Let *La Migra* find the Mexican identification papers that would at least guarantee deportation to a country that wasn't El Salvador, a country that wouldn't torture the little family.

Once back on Mexican soil, they could try again, perhaps going through Arizona instead of Texas. There were churches down there ready to help.

It all depended on how much Walt Koeppler knew. He'd known they'd be on this road, driving a vehicle other than the church van. How much else did he know—and how had he learned it? Jan studied the immigration officer's deceptively bland face, searching for a clue that wasn't there.

"This is more like it," he said. "At least these papers show a little finesse. A little style. I like that. Of course," he added, giving Miguel a shove with the gun, "they're just as phony as that batch." He waved the gun at the papers he'd thrown in the dirt. "Where are you really from?" he asked Miguel, his tone conversational. "El Salvador? Guatemala?"

Jan sighed softly, exchanging a glance with Ron, who sat rigid in his strapped-in chair. Walt Koeppler knew a lot more than he had three days earlier. Then he had been content to accept the Texas forgeries; now he questioned even the Mexican papers. Then he had let her and Dana go; now it was clear arrests were in the picture. She glanced uneasily at the Highway Patrol cop who stood guard behind Koeppler. He was a tall blond with a bright sunburn; his hand rested lightly on the handle of his gun.

A second officer stood next to Pilar; his gun was out and pointed directly at her. They'd come prepared to take prisoners.

Oh, God, prisoners. She and Ron were prisoners. Her first crazy thought: Would they handcuff Ron? Was there any point to handcuffing a man who needed braces to lift his arms as far as his shoulders?

For the first time she felt true kinship with Miguel and Pilar; for the first time she felt vulnerable. How, goddamn it, *how* had this happened? How had Koeppler found them? Short answer: Somebody told him.

Somebody who knew she'd be on this road, in this van, ferrying people who weren't Mexican-Americans, who weren't even Mexicans, had tipped off *La Migra*. She looked again at Ron, still locked into the back of the van. His chest and arm muscles strained against the strap; he looked as if he wanted to break his bonds and fly, Superman-like, to the rescue. He drew in a deep, ragged breath and visibly willed himself to a stillness she knew wasn't natural.

Who? The question burned in her brain even as she watched Koeppler reach for the handcuffs on the back of his belt. Who would do this to them? Who would send this family back to hell?

As the cuffs closed on Miguel, Manuelito squirmed free of his mother and ran toward Koeppler. "*Papi, Papi,*" he screamed, his three-year-old lungs bursting with anguish. Tiny fists beat on Koeppler's khaki-clad leg.

"Manuelito, no," Pilar cried, rushing toward her son.

"Don't come any closer, ma'am," Koeppler warned, pulling his gun from his waistband and pointing it at Pilar.

"You," he said to Jan, "get this kid off me."

Jan stood numbly at first, unable to will her body to move. Both Highway Patrol cops had drawn their guns. "Everybody stand still," the older, dark-haired cop said. Jan would have felt better if his voice hadn't been shaking.

She moved with a speed she couldn't believe. She snatched Manuelito around the waist, registering in a few accelerated seconds the child smell of his damp hair, the pudgy roundness of his tummy under her thin arms, the red of his new K-Mart sneakers. She pulled him away, breaking the hold his tiny hands had on Koeppler's pant leg. It was like pulling a kitten off a sweater.

At the same time, Pilar rushed forward, keening. Not even Spanish, just the wordless howl of an animal mother watching her young face a predator. Her body, lithe under the shapeless

housedress, moved with speed and power. Koeppler turned the
gun on her, his hand shaking.

"Stop right there," he shouted. Miguel, hands cuffed, lowered his head and drove into Koeppler's stomach like a bull,
butting him backward onto the dirt road. Both uniformed cops
ran toward him, dust flying under their hard shoes.

A shot rang out. Jan screamed; Pilar shrieked. Manuelito
began to howl. "Fuck," Koeppler shouted, then repeated the
shout as blood appeared on his khaki shirtfront.

The two Highway Patrolmen reached Miguel at the same
time. One reached for the handcuffs in his belt; the other shook
his head as Miguel fell forward into the dirt.

"God, no." The words were wrung from Ron; his face
gray, he gave up all pretense of stillness and pushed himself
against his bonds. The claw hands stiffened into what might
once have been fists. Pilar threw herself over the still body of
her husband, and Manuelito sobbed, "Papi, Papi."

Jan begged God to take back the last five minutes. She'd
stay sober, she'd give up smoking, she'd go back to Toledo
and have nothing to do with refugees ever again if that was
what He wanted. She had the message now; please don't make
Miguel pay for what she had to learn.

Please, God, take back the last five minutes, let them all be
sitting in the van, air conditioning on high, bumping over the
dirt road on their way to the lake. Let Manuelito point at the
agua like any little kid on his way to a beach.

The blood on Koeppler's shirt was Miguel's. The Immigration officer holstered his gun and then bent down and lifted
Pilar to a standing position. She shook her head and fought,
but the uniformed cops cuffed her hands behind her and
walked her toward the waiting car.

Koeppler knelt in the dust and turned Miguel over. He
opened one eye, then bent over and breathed into Miguel's
open mouth.

One of the Highway Patrolmen came back from the car, but
made no move toward the wounded man. His drawn gun
caught the bright sunlight and made reflections as hurtful to
the eye as the glinting lake water.

Back at the blue-and-white, with Pilar sobbing in the back seat, the other cop picked up a hand radio and called for an ambulance. But how far away was the nearest hospital?

Jan stood motionless except for the hand that stroked Manuelito's damp hair. The boy was still crying, but it was quieter now, as if even he understood that what was happening couldn't be changed by tears.

Miguel made an ugly noise somewhere between a gasp and a clogged drain. His hands grabbed at his shirt, sodden with blood where the bullet had struck. The shirt grew redder and redder.

"Grab a towel or something," Koeppler called out. "Somebody stanch the blood."

Jan moved toward the van, Manuelito hefted on her hip, her breath coming in short puffs. There were towels in the back, orange beach towels just like the one draped around Ron's shoulder. Camouflage in case they were stopped. She opened the hatch with one hand and pulled them out, her hands shaking.

Ron was shaking too, still rocking, working to break free of the straps that held him in place. She reached out a hand, wanting to touch his cold flesh, to reassure even though she knew he could feel nothing. Then she pulled back. It was Miguel who needed her now. Ron would have to wait.

This couldn't be happening. Not on her first run without Dana.

One of the patrolmen stepped up to Koeppler. "County says they can be here in fifteen minutes, give or take."

Koeppler's eyes told Jan Miguel didn't have fifteen minutes. She leaned on the van, suddenly light-headed, dropping the orange towels onto the road. Getting them dirty.

No. They shouldn't be dirty. Miguel needed them, needed them to stop the bleeding. They shouldn't be dirty. Jan leaned down and picked up the towels. First one, then the other, with careful precision. She had to do this right, had to get the towels over to Miguel. If she did it right, he would live until the ambulance came. If she dropped them again, if they got dirty, he would die.

It was that simple.

CHAPTER NINE

$\mathbf{M}$y beeper vibrated against my waist. I looked down at the number. Local. I nudged Ron and said, "Don't answer any questions. I've got to return a call." I pushed my way through the press crowd and walked back into the courthouse.

The phone was picked up on the second ring. "Governor Tannock's campaign headquarters," a woman's voice announced.

John Wesley Tannock. The man I'd lusted after in 1969, the man who'd gone on to an active career in Ohio politics. He'd been governor for only one term and was now running for the Senate.

"May I speak to the governor, please." I deliberately lowered my voice at the end, making it a statement and not a question.

"May I ask who's calling?"

I smiled, visualizing Wes hearing my name again after so many years. "Cassandra Jameson."

I was put on hold for a maximum of ten seconds. An efficient office operation.

"Cass?" The deep voice startled me. It took a moment to realize it wasn't Wes's rich baritone, but a heavy-sounding bass. The tuba to Wes's trombone. I should have known I couldn't call John Wesley Tannock without running into his perennial campaign manager, Paul Tarkanian. Tark the Shark.

I pictured him as he'd been in the summer of '69, leaning back in a swivel chair, his feet propped up on a desk, a wet cigar clamped in his teeth. The picture of a ward heeler. Of course, when I'd known him, the ward heeler had sported a mountain man beard and the longest hair in northwest Ohio. Black and curly, it hung down in waves.

"I suppose you cut your hair." I hadn't realized I'd said the words aloud until I heard Tarky's laugh.

"Bought a suit, too."

"If memory serves," I said, "I'm returning your call. Before the operator cuts me off, what's up?"

"We need to talk."

"About what? And who's 'we'? You and I and Wes and who else?"

"All of us. Including Jan, unfortunately. I want to set up a meeting, discuss the implications of her return."

"Implications for Wes's campaign, you mean." I'd only been in Toledo for a couple of hours and I'd seen at least one hundred "Tannock for Senator" posters.

"I'm only concerned with one implication," I said, highlighting the word, "and that's how this whole mess affects Ron. Everything else is decidedly secondary."

"I can understand that," Tarky said slowly, "but I still think you should hear us out. Wes is due at a fund-raiser at eight, but we could meet after six. The question is, where?"

The operator cut in; I fished in my purse for a nickel and fed the pay phone. Someday I'd give in all the way and get a cellular.

"If you want Jan there," I said, "then it has to be at Our Lady of Guadalupe in Oregon. Jan's been placed under house arrest until the hearing. She's staying in a cottage behind the church."

"That's a hell of a long way from the Heatherdowns Country Club," Tarky complained. "I don't want Wes showing up late at his own testimonial."

"Look at it this way," I pointed out. "The press won't make the trek either. If you don't roll up in a stretch limo,

you have half a chance of getting there without being followed.''

"We'll be there at six." Tark hung up without a goodbye.

At five, after checking in to the fanciest motel in downtown
Toledo, chosen because it had the best accommodations for
the disabled, Ron, Zack, and I headed east on Route 2 toward
Oregon, the little town where Father Jerry Kujawa had his
church.

I was in the front seat, next to Zack. I turned my head to
look at Ron, who was strapped in his chair in the rear of his
specially equipped van. "Somehow I pictured us all meeting
on the front porch of the White House, but that doesn't make
sense, does it?"

"I don't even think that house is there anymore," my
brother replied. "I think they tore it down when they put the
expressway through."

"Too bad," I said, keeping my voice light. "That house
had a lot of character. And a lot of memories."

"You think they should have put up a plaque?" Ron raised
one eyebrow; a talent I'd always envied.

"Absolutely." I filled my voice with a teasing quality I
didn't really feel. I wasn't at all certain I was up to this reunion. Seeing Dana and Rap had been hard enough. And I
didn't want to know Jan any better than I already did.

I quoted from my imaginary plaque: " 'In this historic Victorian house a small band of revolutionaries lived for one short
but significant summer. Thanks to their untiring efforts on behalf of the poor, absolutely nothing has changed. In fact,' " I
went on, warming to my theme, " 'in the twenty-odd years
since they lived here, more people are homeless, more children
are hungry, and more people are unemployed than ever before.' "

The teasing glint in his eyes was gone. "Are you that cynical about what we did?"

"Why not?" My tone sounded coldly flippant even in my
own ears, but I couldn't seem to soften it. "Look what we
wanted to achieve versus what actually happened. We had

high hopes, big plans, bigger mouths, and all we succeeded in doing was getting ourselves arrested.'' *And getting you sent to Vietnam* was the part I didn't say.

He'd intended to become a VISTA volunteer, joining the domestic Peace Corps instead of the Army. His service with Amigos Unidos was supposed to be a down payment on the conscientious objector status that would allow the draft board to okay VISTA as an alternative to combat. Instead—

It was hard to see the summer of '69 as anything but a gigantic failure. The sense of futility might have been lessened if every migrant farmworker received a living wage, medical care, education—all the things we'd fought for. But with the conservative Right in ascendency and LBJ's Great Society mocked on talk radio, none of that summer seemed worth the price.

As we drove along the T-square roads, checkerboarded by corn and wheat fields as far as the eye could see, it felt as if we were spanning years as well as miles.

The van sped past Pearson Park, where we'd spent one memorable night drinking Cokes laced with rum from a jelly jar and feeding the swans. One particularly aggressive bird, demanding more Oreos, chased Jan up a hill, while we all laughed. I tried to capture the moment on film, but all I got were blurred images of tree and sky and a ghostly white object that might have been the swan. Or it might have been Jan herself, who was in her Indian gauze period and often appeared swathed in thin cotton skirts, looking like a member of an Asian religious sect.

It was the night Ted Havlicek first kissed me.

I'd closed my eyes and pictured Wes Tannock's lips on mine.

Zack turned at the edge of the park and headed north toward Oregon. Our Lady of Guadalupe was outside the town, near the fields where its parishioners worked. I remembered Spanish bingo nights and used-clothing drives and a fiesta with children dancing in ruffled skirts and bolero jackets. And the day care center where I'd played Candy Land with Belita Navarro.

The building was the same: cinderblock painted adobe brown, with a crude image of Our Lady of Guadalupe surrounded by Diego Rivera–style peasants in huge straw hats painted on the side. Father Jerry's house was a tiny white cottage with a crucifix over the door.

Zack drove the van down a dirt driveway behind the church, where little tan houses squatted like chicks behind a mother hen. They were dilapidated, roofs sagging and screen doors unlatched. A plastic wading pool sat in front of one house, a broken swing set stood beside another.

Jan Gebhardt sat in a kitchen chair on the cement slab that served as the porch of the last house in the row.

She waved as we came up. Zack was driving, and Ron wasn't able to wave, so I lifted my hand in a half-hearted gesture. Two cars were parked on the sparse grass at the side of the house; I wondered who was already here.

Zack pulled up next to the red convertible. It looked like a vintage something-or-other, the kind of car good girls didn't accept rides in when I was in high school. I decided it had to belong to Rap.

I opened the door and jumped down from the van, not sure whether I should wait for Ron or go ahead. Zack pushed the buttons that opened the back door and lowered the lift that would put Ron and his chair on the ground.

"I'll see you inside," I said, and marched toward the little cabin.

Jan wore an oversized man's dress shirt with hand-painted irises on it. They were dusted with glitter and sparkled in the waning sunlight. Her black shorts revealed thin white legs with marks that might have been bruises or varicose veins. Her feet were in sandals, and her long toes looked like part of a skeleton.

She reached out a hand. I took it without thinking. It was so slender, the bones so pronounced, that I was afraid I'd break it, but the handshake was surprisingly firm.

"Thanks for coming to represent Ron," she said. "I was really glad to see he had someone in his corner."

I was not about to let this woman thank me for helping my

own brother. I took back my hand. "Who else is here?"

"Rap and Dana are out back."

"Thanks." I walked past her and opened the screen door.

I stepped into what might have been a nun's cell. One ancient iron bed, one pine dresser with no mirror, one bed table upon which was a book I took to be the Bible until I got closer. It was bound in dark blue leather and embossed with the words "Alcoholics Anonymous." A white plastic rosary hung over the bed, knotted around the iron bars so that the crucifix dangled over the single pillow. I wondered whether it belonged to Jan or if it had been put there to inspire whoever occupied the little room.

I also wondered whether Jan might not be more comfortable in jail.

There was a back door. I opened it and went out, realizing only then that I could just as easily have walked around the tiny cottage. Had I deliberately opened the front door instead so as to catch a glimpse of Jan's private life?

Rap met me at the door. This time the hat was a white Borsalino. "If it isn't the Little Sister," he greeted me, using the nickname he'd coined back in '69 when he discovered I was a fellow Raymond Chandler fan. I hadn't liked it; I desperately wanted my own identity, and the reminder that I was Ron Jameson's little sister rankled.

I gave my standard reply, the one it had taken me the whole summer to come up with: "The Little Sister wasn't as innocent as she looked, Rap."

"Too true," he said, his crooked grin infectious. "Innocent girls aren't what they used to be. But then, what is?"

He took my hand and helped me down the concrete steps. I considered reminding him that he'd threatened me earlier in the day, then decided to play along with the pretense that we were having a pleasant reunion of old friends.

Dana sat at the picnic table, cigarette smoke wafting from one hand. For a moment I thought it was a joint, but then I noted the brown filter tip. She waved and called out, just as we used to do on the front lawn of the White House, "Red Rover, Red Rover, let Cassie come over."

In spite of myself, I began to run. The childhood game, the fact that we were wearing jeans instead of court clothes, brought back some of the old feeling. Dana's faded lavender T-shirt said "Women's Writes."

"I didn't know this town had a women's bookstore," I said when I reached the picnic table. I was out of breath even from the short run across the grass.

"It doesn't," Dana said shortly. She dropped the cigarette butt to the ground and stepped on it with her hiking boot. "Not anymore. It closed about eight years ago. It was my store."

"I'm sorry," I said. "I bet it was a great place."

"Yeah," she agreed without enthusiasm. "Trouble was, I wanted it to be strictly political. Lesbian, sure, but no crystals, no wicca, none of that New Age bullshit that's setting the women's movement back to the goddamn fourteenth century. So some little twinkie opens up a store called Goddessworks and I'm history. She's got a full line of tarot cards and a complete set of Lynn Andrews and I'm up shit creek."

Ron's chair appeared around the corner of the house, but it wasn't Zack behind the handles. Jan pushed the chair, a smile of proprietary pleasure on her face. She propelled the chair toward the picnic table, settled Ron at one end, then bent down and kissed the top of his head. He looked up at her and smiled. It was a moment of almost unbearable intimacy.

Intimacy? Ron and Jan intimate? I remembered the kiss in the courtroom. But Ron couldn't feel anything below T-6; so how could they—

But was sex everything?

"Where's Zack?" I asked, looking around for the huge biker.

"There's a meeting at 6:30 in the church basement," Jan replied.

"What kind of—" I broke off in embarassed silence. "Oh."

Jan smiled and said, "If we finish early, I'll catch the end of it."

Ron lifted his hand, slowly, and touched a heart-shaped plastic medallion around his neck. "Don't worry," he said,

"I'm as safe as that old lady in the commercials."

I didn't get the reference until Rap clutched his heart, fell over on the picnic table bench, and squealed, "I've fallen and I can't get up."

"If I need Zack," Ron explained, "I just push this button and he'll hear it. He's got the receiver box with him."

"So, how was Vietnam?" Rap asked the question with the mock brightness of a TV game show host.

"Hey," he said, when we all glared at him, "it's what everyone else is thinking, right?"

"I don't believe you," Dana muttered. "That was just about the crudest thing I ever heard."

"Look, it's like the elephant in the living room," her ex-husband countered. "We can spend the whole night pretending Ron's not sitting here in a wheelchair, or we can talk about it up front and then get past it."

"Well, if you're expecting me to burst into tears and admit that I killed babies, you can forget it," my brother said. "I was only there five months, not even long enough to buy postcards. And I was a clerk-typist in Saigon. I had a boring war—up until the time I got hit."

"And how did that happen?"

"I went out on a field assignment. Notifying an ARVN family that their son was killed. A milk run to a nearby ville. Just a little jaunt into the countryside—but a sniper in the area shot at us and got lucky."

"I knew a guy went to 'Nam," Rap said. "'Course he was no hero. He was just another stoned-out fuckoff."

"You don't get it, do you?" Ron's tone was as contemptuous as I'd ever heard it. "In 'Nam, the stoned-out fuckoffs were the heroes."

Even Rap fell silent after that. Jan walked back toward the house. The silence grew as oppressive as the humidity. Mosquitoes buzzed around my legs and arms; I slapped at them, grateful for the diversion.

"How did she do it?" Dana asked nobody in particular. "How did she stay underground all those years?"

"Probably did the dead baby thing," Rap replied.

That was not a remark that could go unchallenged. "What dead baby thing?" we all asked at more or less the same time.

Rap smiled his crooked smile; his favorite thing in the world was to know what no one else knew. "You find a baby who was born at about the same time you were, but who died shortly after. Then you take the name and birth date of that baby, apply for a Social Security card, and, voilà, you have a new identity. People do it all the time. Once you have the Social Security card, you get a driver's license and any other ID you might need."

"You sound as if you speak from personal experience." I wasn't entirely sure whether I was teasing or cross-examining.

He shrugged bony shoulders. "I get around," he said. "I know a lot of things I don't actually act on."

"Thank God for that," Dana murmured. She squashed another cigarette butt under her heavy soles.

"Are we sure Wes is coming?" I asked, glancing at my watch. It was ten after six, and Tarky had said they'd have to cut the visit short. If they were going to be late arriving, it would be even shorter. But maybe that was the idea; maybe Wes didn't like this meeting any better than I did.

The screen door slammed. Jan stood on the porch, a big stoneware bowl in her hands. She stepped slowly and carefully as she walked across the grass. When she reached the table, she set the bowl in the middle. Potato salad. We were having a picnic, just like in the old days.

"Cass, could you help me bring a few more things?"

"Sure." I rose from the table and followed her back to the house.

There were stacks of paper plates, plastic forks and glasses, bottles of soda. I reached for the nearest items, but Jan touched my arm.

"I wanted to talk to you alone."

I pulled my arm away and stepped back. Her face was pale and intent. Her eyes bored into mine. "You have to listen, Cass, please."

"I can't. I represent Ron, and you have your own lawyer. There's a conflict of interest, and I—"

"I don't care about all that legal shit." The control she'd shown in court was gone; she looked ready to snap, to start pouring herself a drink, to do or say just about anything without regard to consequences.

But I had to consider the consequences. I was here for my brother, and however close this woman was to him, she wasn't my responsibility.

"I can't, Jan. I'm sorry but I can't." I made for the door before she could stop me. I was moving so fast I didn't notice the man walking toward the picnic table. We collided, and I looked up into the tanned, handsome face of John Wesley Tannock.

CHAPTER
TEN

July 16, 1982

The cell door opened. Jan, newly awake after a night of stormy sleep, looked up with wary, bloodshot eyes. God, she hadn't been in jail since . . . when? The time she was picked up for d & d in the parking lot of the Rampage Saloon out on Alexis Road? Or, no, the last time was the shoplifting beef at the Woodville Mall. She'd been drunk then, too, had thrown up on herself and was marched into court smelling of vomit and vowing never to pick up another drink. That was three years ago; a lot more drinks had gone down the hatch, but at least she'd managed to stay out of jail.

This was her first time behind bars sober. It didn't look or feel a whole lot better, but at least she hadn't tossed her cookies. The blessings of sobriety.

She'd been half asleep, her mind replaying the scene on the dusty dune road, a childish rhyme ringing in her ears. *All of us went out to play; Rap and Dana ran away.*

Rap and Dana ran away.

Rap and Dana

got

away.

Rap and Dana. How far away had they been? A half mile at most. So why did Walt stop her before she reached the shore? Every cell in her body told her Walt had been tipped off, that he'd known she'd be on the dune road. He could have had all of them; he could have had the boat. Could have had whatever Rap had hidden in the boat.

Jan was under no illusions about Joel Alan Rapaport. She remembered the grass runs to Ann Arbor when they were students, the fine coke he'd bring from trips home to Long Island, the 'ludes he handed out like cough drops. It was impossible for her to believe all his crossings to Canada were clean. So why had the feds let him get away?

Or did the question answer itself? They let him get away. They wanted him to get away. Rap had always believed in plowing profits back into the business; maybe he'd paid off Koeppler, or someone even higher, to leave him alone and grab the van instead of the *Layla*.

Jan barely noticed the squat, middle-aged matron who stepped into the cell with an air of hostile authority. She was slow to realize that the woman with her was a fellow prisoner, and that the matron was going to leave her here, in the cell.

I don't need company, damn it. I have to think.

"Hi," the newcomer said shyly, "my name's Marie."

"I'm Jan." Nothing more; no indication that conversation would be welcome. She turned her eyes toward the sand-colored cinderblock wall.

Rap and Dana got away. Why?

Bits and pieces of whispered conversation, hastily shushed when she came near, slipped into her consciousness. Dana had mentioned a "factory" hidden somewhere in the boonies. Something about illegals in trailers, people she wasn't supposed to know were there. What were Rap and Dana doing besides transporting political dissidents?

"Uh, do you mind if I smoke?" The voice was small, child-like. Jan barely looked at her cellmate as she nodded her okay. She took out one of her own, lit up. Smoking helped her think, helped keep her hands from nervously twisting her long hair.

"I've never been arrested before," the young woman on the opposite bunk said. "I guess I'm a little scared."

And you want me to be your Big Sister. Forget it. You got your troubles; I got mine.

Thanks to whoever had dropped a dime, she and Ron were under arrest, Miguel was dead, and Pilar and Manuelito faced deportation. Back to El Salvador, not just Mexico. Back to where General Duarte had sworn to execute them so the whole country would know what happened to academics who spoke out against the regime.

Who the hell could do such a thing?

Rap and Dana got away.

"It wasn't my fault. Really." Marie seemed intent on telling her little story. She leaned forward on the bunk, her pale skin tinted fluorescent-green, her platinum hair wispy.

Jan hated wispy little child-girls. Especially ones who figured nothing was their fault.

"I mean, it was my boyfriend's idea."

"Look, could you do me a favor and maybe shut up?" Jan dragged on her cigarette. God, she sounded like Ma Barker. The experienced con talking to the new kid, setting her straight about life in the joint.

"If that's the way you want it." Marie turned her head toward the door, her shoulder-length hair shimmering in the eerie light. Dark roots. No surprise; people really didn't have hair that color. But somehow the dark roots made Marie human. A real person, not a doll.

"You work in a beauty parlor?" Jan asked.

"Howdja know?" Marie turned back, her face animated. "I'm just a shampoo girl now, but my friend Patti says I've got a real flair for hair. She did my color."

"Looks great." Jan was sorry already that she'd opened communications.

"So what are you here for?"

Jan pulled out another cigarette from the pack in her pocket. "Long story."

"Yeah, well, I bet it wasn't your fault either," Marie said. "Like me believing my boyfriend when he said the old guy signed the check over to him. Instead of which Joey's ripping the guy off, stealing his Social Security check right out of his mailbox. Which is two kinds of federal crime right there. And just because I went with him to the grocery store to cash it, they think I was in it with him. Is that fair?''

Fair. She wants to talk about fair. Was it fair that Miguel was dead? Was it fair that somebody wanted her ass in jail— that somebody *used* her, set her up?

Heat flooded Jan's face; she shook so badly she leaned against the cool cinderblock wall. Her teeth chattered; her sweat turned to ice on her clammy skin.

''Hey, you okay?'' Marie asked. ''You detoxing or something?''

Jan shook her head. She'd never felt like this before.

Or had she? Yes, it came back now. The night she pulled a knife on Hal, the night she decided he'd hit her for the last time, she'd been filled with this fury.

Fury. Like one of the Furies. Avenging women who—who avenged. Who fought back, who didn't let themselves be used as pawns in anyone else's game, who destroyed out of sheer, purifying rage. That was Jan: a Fury stripped of all emotion except the healing fire of rage.

It didn't matter anymore who had tipped off Koeppler. It didn't matter why Rap and Dana got away. What mattered was that she was through, finished with being used. *Whoever dropped that dime better look out.*

Fire filled her soul. *Because when I find out who did it, I'll—*

''Would it help to talk about it?'' Marie leaned forward, an eager light in her pale blue eyes. A light Jan recognized in her newly transformed state as a Fury. It was the light of avarice, of consuming curiosity, of betrayal.

''Why?'' Jan rapped out the word, hard as a boxing glove. ''So you can run to Walt Koeppler with whatever I say?''

She stood up and began to roam the cell. Looking up at the ceiling, peering into corners. ''Or has he got this place bugged? Huh? Which is it?''

Jan strode to where Marie still sat on the edge of her cot, swinging one leg. ''I ought to slap it out of you,'' she said, her voice harsh, ''but that would only give them more ammunition.''

She sat back on her own bunk, motionless, wordless, arms crossed over her thin chest. Inside she seethed like a pressure cooker, her thoughts hissing, steaming, raging. They'd done it again. Just like last time. Just like when Kenny died.

They wouldn't get away with it this time.

It was no surprise that within five minutes the matron came back and removed Marie.

Where there's a will, there's a way. Words to live by. Words Walt Koeppler lived by. Okay, so Marie had failed. Marie, who'd conned confessions out of some pretty tough broads, had been made in thirty seconds by this leftover hippie. But there had to be someone she'd open up to. He'd considered letting her see the boyfriend, the guy in the wheelchair, but decided that was too obvious. It was then that routine paid off, the way he'd always told rookies it would.

She had a visitor. Not her lawyer; Sobel hadn't been around yet. And there were problems, legal problems even Koeppler wasn't ready to face just yet, with monitoring conversations between lawyer and client. But where was it written in the goddamn Constitution that a prison visit with a civilian was sacred?

He nodded at the guard who'd brought in the request. "Put them in room six," he said. "And turn up the volume on the mike, okay? I don't want to miss a whisper."

Jan walked into room six on rubber legs. Harve Sobel. It had to be Harve, her lawyer. Her lawyer and Dana's father. *Rap and Dana got away.* Could she trust Dana's father to represent her? She'd wrestled with that problem for the better part of last night, but still hadn't resolved it. Harve was a good lawyer, the best, and he believed in the cause, but if Dana had dropped that dime, she couldn't afford to trust him.

On the other hand, if Dana had turned informer, Harve would disown her.

Her breath whooshed out with relief when she saw her sponsor, her AA lifeline, sitting on the other side of the Plexiglas partition.

"Ritamae," she breathed. "Thank God it's you." She looked long and hard at her sponsor's black-coffee skin, her thick shiny hair, her bright magenta lipstick. The one person in the world she could truly trust.

"God, if there'd been a bar on the women's side of this prison," Jan laughed, "you'd be looking at one fallen drunk."

"Honey, I been in jail myself. It's a damn good thing they got no bars behind bars." Another reason she was grateful to have Ritamae as a sponsor. She wasn't some yuppie drunk who'd come down to the jail afraid to get dirt on her white gloves. She'd walked the same walk.

Ritamae had known fame; she'd been a Vandella for about five months, until booze and dope ended her dreams of Motown glory. She'd done time in a Michigan prison before coming home to Toledo. "If only I'd known—" Jan began. *If only I'd known someone was selling us out*, she wanted to say. But what if Ritamae thought she was paranoid? What if the one person she trusted didn't believe her?

"Uh-uh," Ritamae interrupted, shaking her head violently, "don't be talking that trash, girl. None of that 'if only' crap. Jan, girl, you cannot change that man's death. He is gone, honey, the cops done shot him right in fronta your face."

Jan dropped her eyes to hide the fury—no, the Fury—who lived inside her now. Last night, alone in the cell, she'd punched her pillow, screamed without noise into its meager softness, like a dried-up breast. She'd pounded her fists till the knuckles were raw into the hard-spring mattress and pictured Walt Koeppler dead, bloody dead with hundreds of stab wounds from the kitchen knife she'd used on Hal.

"Look," Ritamae said, her tone brisk, her voice devoid of accent. Over the phone she could have passed for white. "You got a lawyer, or what? I can get on the phone and find someone from the Program if you—"

"Harve Sobel is my lawyer," Jan said. Like saying the rosary, she'd repeated the words over and over after her arrest, to any cop who came near her. "Harve Sobel is my lawyer." Words like charms to keep the vampires away.

But could she trust Harve? Could she trust Dana's father? Could she trust Dana?

She already knew she couldn't trust Rap.

"I've heard them talking," Jan said, staring into her sponsor's deep brown eyes. "Just bits and pieces, but I know there's some kind of factory somewhere. And there are more refugees, but I don't know where they are either. Rap—he's the guy with the boat—I think he deals drugs. But I don't know where he gets it or what he does with it. All I know for sure is there's a whole lot more going on than I knew about. They used me. They fucking used me." Jan's voice rose and her throat ached with tears she wouldn't shed.

She paused and took a deep, ragged breath. "Not only that," she went on, more calmly, "somebody tipped off Koeppler. Somebody told him we'd be out there. Just like before."

Ritamae's brow creased in a frown. "What you mean, like before?"

Jan felt light-headed; she'd said forbidden words, told secrets, named her suspicions, and she was still alive. "Like when my cousin Kenny—" She broke off and swallowed hard. "Somebody called the cops then too, and we were all arrested and Kenny died."

Ritamae pursed her lips. "This Kenny," she said, "how long ago the boy die?"

"Thirteen years ago," Jan said, almost dreamily.

"Then what the fuck you messing with it now for?"

Jan looked up, fear flooding her. All sense of safety had fled with her sponsor's accusing tone. "But—but Koeppler stopping the van, knowing just where we were—it's the same thing all over again. Somebody tipped him off. Don't you see, it's the same informer, still working, still selling us out." *Please, God, please*, she prayed, *let Ritamae see this. Don't let her laugh at me.*

Ritamae stared ahead, a black Buddha. A seer staring into an African fire for visions.

"Way I see it," she said at last, "this shit is not where you need to be at right now. You need to worry about it later."

Jan melted with relief. "Later like the Ninth Step?"

Ritamae laughed. "Girl, eighty days ago you thought the Big Book was a telephone directory, now you quotin' it at me like a Bible-thumpin' Baptist. I'll tell you when you ready for the Ninth Step and don't you even be thinking about it until then. Got that?"

Jan nodded, but some of last night's fury welled up and came out her eyes and burned into Ritamae.

"Honey, you ain't thinkin' about no Ninth Step," her sponsor pronounced, her tone a warning. "You thinkin' about paybacks and that is in no way the same thing. Hear?"

Jan heard. She didn't like it, but she heard. Her sponsor sat on the other side of the visitors' table, talking too loudly into holes that didn't let the sound through. Jan felt caged. Caged by the cramped, ugly quarters and trapped by Ritamae's clarity. Caged by the truth.

"The Ninth Step," Ritamae shouted into the holes, "is about asking forgiveness for what you done to others. Not about carrying grudges for what you think they done to you."

Jan nodded. She felt her face go stiff. Wood-stiff, like a little puppet. The same face she used to wear when Sister Mary Whoever would call her into the office and ask how things were at home. She'd wear the wooden mask and nod and say quietly that things were fine and she didn't know what Sister meant. All the time knowing, her inner face burning with shame, that somebody'd seen her daddy drunk again.

It had served her well, her wooden outer face, her mask that could smile or look just plain puzzled while the inner face raged and cried and blushed and nobody could see it.

Except Ritamae. Sometimes. Like now.

"Jan, talk to me," Ritamae called, her voice reaching through the holes, grabbing out to her. Trying to pull her to her side of the barrier. "Tell me what you thinkin', babe."

Paybacks. She was thinking paybacks. A nice word, one she hadn't used before, not even to herself. Ritamae had given it to her, like a precious gift. Even if she hadn't meant to. Even if she was trying for a warning instead.

But the word struck a deep chord in Jan's heart. The inside

face, the one that wasn't made of wood, smiled at the word. Paybacks.

She rolled it around on her tongue like single-malt.

Walt Koeppler ran the tape back as soon as Ritamae Johnson was ushered out of Jan's presence. He smiled as he listened to the talk of Rapaport running drugs. As an agent of the Immigration and Naturalization Service, he didn't have jurisdiction over narcotics trafficking. But he knew someone who did. He picked up the phone and dialed a number from memory.

The phone was answered on the first ring. "Drug Enforcement Administration, Krepke."

"Dale, it's Walt. I've got a line on that guy you were after a while back. Joel Rapaport. Yeah. Let's have some lunch and I'll fill you in."

There was more than one way to skin a cat, Koeppler decided as he and Dale agreed to meet at Tony Packo's on the east side, far, far away from downtown ears.

A factory, Jan Gebhardt had said. To Walt, that meant only one thing: Joel Rapaport and his ex-wife were using illegal aliens to make methamphetamines. The five years max Gebhardt and Jameson might get for yesterday's arrest would pale in comparison with the nice long sentences the whole group would receive for conspiracy to manufacture and sell hard drugs.

And what was even better was that he could use Jan Gebhardt as a stalking-horse to lead him into the inner workings of the sanctuary movement.

CHAPTER ELEVEN

All the times I'd dreamed of seeing Wes Tannock again I'd visualized myself as: (a) glamorous, in a silver lamé sheath gown, hair tossed back like a tawny mane; (b) sophisticated, in a designer silk suit and jade green pumps; (c) professional, swaying a recalcitrant judge with my eloquence while he looked on, admiration in his eyes; (d) sexy, in a red leather miniskirt and skintight sweater, boots up to God knows where; (e) all of the above, an unlikely combination of Sandra Day O'Connor and Frederick's of Hollywood.

The upshot of these fantasies was that Wes saw me for the first time, saw Cass, not Ron's little sister, not tagalong Cassie who worshiped from afar.

Instead, I'd crashed into him like a clumsy idiot.

I stepped back and made my apology, trying to regain some veneer of dignity.

"Cassie," he said in a pleased tone. I shook his hand numbly.

It was strange seeing Wes grown up. Jowlier, heavier in the face. Hairline receding, but in a sexy way. Manicured hands veiny, fingers knobby with early arthritis.

Still sexy as hell. Just looking at the dark curly hairs on his wrist sent my pulse racing. What would it feel like to have those manicured hands roving my soft naked skin? How would it feel to run my fingers through the thinning hair, gaze into his eyes and watch the sun glint off the little green flecks in the iris?

Not that I was going to find out. I'd just recovered from one charismatic, driven, stimulating man and I had no intention of starting anything with another. The attraction I felt was powerful—but that very power warned me off.

An olive-skinned man I'd never seen before stepped briskly toward the picnic table. Wes turned toward the new arrival. "Everything went okay at the focus group?" The man nodded, then smiled broadly.

"Cassie," he said, his deep voice warm. He reached out a hand on which a class ring shone like a ruby firefly. His other hand held a stub of cigar.

My God, Tarky! Gone was the Dutch Master haircut, the thick beard, the faded sweatshirt. In place of the Armenian hippie I'd known that summer stood a stocky lawyer in a blue three-piece suit, a gold watch chain spanning his broad belly, cordovan wingtips on once-sandaled feet.

Shock must have shown in my face. Tarky gave a single harsh bark—what passed for laughter with him—and said, "Hey, we all grow up."

"Yeah, sure, Tark," I muttered. And reminded myself that I'd traded in her own stick-straight hair for a salon perm ten years earlier. And started buying clothes at department stores instead of the Rajarani Indian Boutique. Times change.

One thing that hadn't changed: As soon as Tarky came, Wes grew larger. Even though Wes was the one working the room, meeting each of our eyes in turn with his compelling gaze, Tarky's presence was, in some mystical way, the source of his energy. As though Tarkanian had always been his campaign manager, even when both were radical law students with nothing but contempt for conventional politics.

While Wes strolled over to the picnic table to press the flesh, Tarky sidled up to me and said in a low voice, "Why now?"

Even when I'd been young and in love with Wes, it had been Tarky whose opinion really mattered. He was the one who when you made a joke or said something really radical, you kind of peeked over to see how he reacted. If he laughed, you'd been funny; if he said "right on," you'd been politically out there. I'd wanted Wes's body, but when it came to approval, Tark the Shark was the arbiter of all I'd said and done.

So I wanted to answer his question with something so clever, so intelligent, that he would know once and for all that I was now a grownup, not to be patronized.

But what the hell did he mean, *Why now?*

At least the cigar he held wasn't lit. It reeked anyway, but it would have been far worse with smoke emanating from it.

An impatient frown knotted the bushy black eyebrows. "Why now?" he repeated. "Why did Jan come back three weeks before Election Day?"

"You think this whole thing is about you and Wes? My brother's facing jail time and all you care about is the election?"

"Cassie, I get paid to worry about the election." He shifted the cigar to the other side of his mouth.

I turned and walked toward the others without a word.

Wes leaned on the edge of the picnic table. "We can't stay long," he said. "We can't eat anything either. When on the campaign trail, the candidate eats nothing that isn't provided by a constituent. One of the basic rules of American politics."

"It is not enough to eat," Tarky intoned, "one must be seen to eat."

He settled himself on one of the benches, his ample rear end sagging like a beanbag. I sat next to him, as far away as possible from the mixture of cigar, aftershave, and male sweat.

He fixed his penetrating eyes on Jan and said, "I'll repeat the question I just asked Mama Cass: Why now?"

Jan stood next to Ron's chair, as if gathering strength from his nearness. Her fingers twisted together as though to remove an invisible pair of gloves.

"It started out as a feeling," she explained. I sat forward, elbows on the picnic table, listening to a voice from the past.

"I mean, the arrests came out of the blue. There was no reason for anybody to be following us on that road."

"Which arrests?" Tarky cut in. "What year are you in?"

She dropped her eyes, her hair falling over her forehead. "Eighty-two," she murmured. "And I guess I'm talking about both times. The time Miguel died and the night the whole thing fell apart. We were set up. Somebody who knew about the sanctuary movement tipped off Walt Koeppler and that's how Ron and I got busted. There was an informer in the group, just like in '69."

"Of course there was an informant in '69," Rap said, "and his name was Kenny Gebhardt. If you weren't obsessed, you'd see that as clearly as any of us. That stupid little fuckup ratted on us and that's why we got arrested. No mystery, Jan."

"And I suppose Kenny dropped a dime from the grave and tipped Walt Koeppler that we'd be on the dune road in '82?" Ron retorted.

I stared at my brother. Could he really believe all this nonsense about informers and Kenny being murdered?

"Of course it's completely impossible that *two* people fourteen years apart are capable of betrayal," Tarky replied. He stared at the tree behind the sagging wire fence, as if his remark were totally academic, addressed to no one in particular.

Wes raised his hands in a peacemaking gesture; his wedding band caught the light and glared into my eyes.

"Look, this may sound monumentally selfish, but all I want," he said, "is for all of you to keep me out of this. This sixties bullshit isn't going to help the campaign one bit. I had nothing to do with the sanctuary thing anyway," he pointed out in a persuasive tone that edged a little too close to a self-serving whine for my taste. "Which is something my opponent isn't going to give a damn about, by the way. If my name pops up in this mess, I'm going down with the voters of this state, even if I get a clean bill at the end of it." He looked at me. "I'm counting on you for this, Cassie."

Why did everyone suddenly seem to think I had the power to make all this go away? Anyone who thought I could talk Ron into keeping Jan quiet didn't know either of them very well.

At least Wes and Tarky weren't making honest-to-God

threats, I told myself, remembering Rap's words in front of the courthouse.

"I'm on it, Wes," Tarky said. "You know as well as I do that the public has the attention span of a flea. The day after the hearing, there'll be a new scandal. This thing's a three-day story at best."

"That's three more days than I want to spend wandering down memory lane, Tark," Wes replied evenly.

"I think Kenny found out who the real informer was and that's why he was killed." Jan's soft voice was stubborn.

"Jan, he wasn't killed." I spoke slowly, as if to a child or a foreigner. "He killed himself."

"Just listen, Cass," my brother said.

"I kept having this dream after Kenny died," she began, her voice thin and childlike. "His body was all full of worms. They were white, but kind of greenish, like they'd glow in the dark, you know? They were going in and out of these holes in his body, but the real bad part was, he wasn't dead. He was alive, in that horrible narrow box, and the worms were going in and out and he was begging me to come get him out before they ate him up. I used to wake up shaking and sobbing from that dream—and then I'd have to take a drink to warm me up, I was so cold."

She rubbed her arms with her nervous hands, as if chilled by too-strong air conditioning.

There was a terrible honesty about her. I didn't believe a word she was saying, yet I couldn't take my eyes off her. She fumbled in her jeans pocket for a cigarette. Dana handed her a lit one from which to get a light. She handed Dana back the butt and held her own cigarette between two fingers, as if it were a joint.

"He was trying to tell me he didn't kill himself," Jan said.

She looked older than her years. Her teeth were yellow and chipped; the translucency of her skin spoke of the damage done to her body by the years of abuse.

It was then that I had my epiphany: If Kenny was murdered, then I was innocent. If he hadn't killed himself, then my harsh rejection of him hadn't caused his death. I could lay down at least one of the guilt burdens I'd been carrying since that summer.

If I believed Jan.

It was like asking me to believe in healing crystals or tarot cards. A pretty fantasy, even an elegant system of thought. But not reality.

Reality was Kenny's white face as he begged me to believe him. "It wasn't me," he'd said. "I didn't call the cops. Honest."

"I don't talk to traitors," I'd replied, my face a stone. Nineteen years old and hard as nails. No forgiveness for betrayal.

Reality was Kenny's twisted, still body under the weeping beech.

If I accepted Jan's assertion that Kenny was murdered, would it be for his sake, or for my own?

My voice was more vehement than I intended. "Bullshit. Sheer, unadulterated bullshit."

"You don't think Jan could be right?" Ron's voice was carefully neutral.

"Oh, well, dreams are good solid evidence, everyone knows that. Anyone appears in a dream and says he didn't kill himself, you can take that to the bank." I was hitting my stride now, sarcasm protecting me as always. "The worms are a wonderful touch."

A hand touched my shoulder. "Easy, Cass," a man's voice said. But all the men at the table were within my line of sight, so who—

I turned my head and looked up at the face of Ted Havlicek, the man I'd searched for in vain among the press people in the courtroom.

He was the same old Ted, Midwestern-bland in looks and manner. Glasses instead of contact lenses, a haircut at least ten years out of date, slacks and a sport shirt instead of shorts and T-shirt.

"So the circle is unbroken," Rap said. "We're all together again, one big happy family. Except of course for Kenny. Maybe Jan can hold a séance and bring him back."

"Shut up, Rap," Dana said through a mouthful of smoke.

She gave Ted a look that held no friendliness. "What the hell are you doing here, anyway?"

"I asked him," Wes replied. "Since this mess is bound to end up in the newspapers, I thought it made sense to give Ted an exclusive in return for the opportunity to, shall we say, shape the story?"

"There's another reason he's here," Jan added. She gave Ted an intense stare and said, "Tell them, Ted."

"Wait a minute." I held up a warning hand. "I have a client to protect here. Maybe Jan doesn't mind talking to the press without her attorney present, but I'm not letting Ron make statements without a clear understanding about how they're going to be used."

I looked up at Ted, willing away memories of his hand grasping mine as we walked through the little park behind the art museum. "First of all, will you please sit down before I get a crick in my neck. And second, who are you working for?"

Ted smiled and walked around the picnic table, settling himself next to Dana. "I'm with the Cleveland *Plain Dealer*. I've been covering the campaign, and this looks like it might have some repercussions. But I'm here on deep background. No quotes, no attributions. Nothing said here will find its way into the paper, believe me."

"Now that we have all that settled," Rap said, "let's get back to 'Tell them, Ted.'" He waved a hand in Ted's direction and said, "Go ahead, tell us, Ted."

Ted cleared his throat. "I made some inquiries." He looked at me. "Under the Freedom of Information Act," he explained. I nodded. I could deal with this. We were talking law now, not dead teenagers.

"And the feds admitted there was an informer?" Dana's voice was sharp with skepticism.

"No, of course not," Ted replied. "But a lot of the documents were blacked out."

"Redacted," I murmured, using the legal term.

"Which means," Ted went on, "that they have something to hide. And some of the entries don't make any sense unless they were getting information from somewhere.''

"Yeah," Tarky cut in, moving his unlit cigar from one side of his mouth to the other, "they were getting it from Kenny. He was a sad little twerp who killed himself because we didn't like him anymore. And we didn't like him because he called the cops on us. It's that simple. It's a fucking shame the kid's dead, but it's no mystery."

"Do you really think the feds would rely on a sixteen-year-old to play undercover cop?" Ron asked.

"But we were working for the government," I protested. "Why would they spy on us?"

Rap's answering grin was one of pure malicious pleasure. "Maybe we weren't all working for the same government."

Tarky lifted his bulk from the table and began to pace. "Why," he asked the maple tree, "do all paranoids think they're the center of the goddamn universe? Every nut who believes in reincarnation thinks she was Cleopatra, and everybody who was remotely on the Left in the sixties thinks the FBI has a file on them."

Suddenly he wheeled around and thrust his cigar at Jan. "Do you really think we were that important? That a bunch of half-assed kids playing revolutionary posed such a threat to national security that the feds would bother paying somebody to keep an eye on us? Get real, Jan."

The Jan of twenty-five years ago would have ducked her head, hidden behind a curtain of hair, grabbed a joint and a drink, and dropped the subject. The Jan of today faced Tarky with a small smile, looked him in the eye, and said, "That's exactly the kind of logic I'd expect the informer to use. Because whoever sold us out back then is still part of the group now. So it could be you—or Wes."

"Do you hear yourself?" Dana muttered. She glared at Jan, who glared back.

"There's one more thing," Ted said.

"I'm not sure I can take one more thing," I said under my breath.

"Kenny was keeping a notebook," Ted said. "He got a steno pad from me and said he was going to write down everything that happened. He was going to show us that he wasn't responsible for all the fuckups that summer.''

"So where's this notebook now?'' Rap challenged.

Ted shrugged. "I have no idea. But I think if we found it, we'd be well on the way to knowing whether Jan's right or not.''

"So what if she is?'' Tarky asked. "Who the fuck cares if someone informed on us?'' He faced Jan squarely, his bulk overshadowing her frailness. "It won't do you a damn bit of good in court, and it'll focus press attention on the sixties and hurt Wes.''

"What about 1982?'' Ron replied. "What if the whole reason it all went bad is that the government infiltrated the sanctuary movement?''

"I repeat,'' Wes said, his hands spread in a gesture of pleading, "Tarky and I had nothing to do with the sanctuary movement.''

"Look,'' Jan said, raising her voice, "there's something about 1982 that you don't know.'' Then she looked at each of us, one by one, her gray eyes seeming to stare through us, as if she could x-ray our souls. "Or should I say, there's something all but one of you doesn't know. Something that changes everything. Something I have to tell the judge.''

I looked at Ron. He shook his head, which I interpreted as his telling me that he had no idea what Jan meant. I didn't like the prospect of my client's codefendant exploding a bombshell in court, but there wasn't much I could do about it. I'd just have to wait for the hearing to find out what Jan was talking about. At least the hearing would be closed to public and press; I wasn't going to have to pick up the pieces in the full glare of publicity.

"Why tell us?'' Tarky demanded. "Why not just go into court and do whatever it is you think you have to do?''

Jan bit her lip, then drew a deep breath and said, "Because I'm trying to be fair. I'm trying to work the Ninth Step, to make amends. There was a lot of shit going down in '82, but the only thing I care about is what the informer did. I won't talk about the rest unless I have to.''

"Oh, right," Rap cut in, his restless hands punctuating his words, "all you have to do is ask nicely and somebody will step up to the plate and admit they sold us out and killed Kenny and did whatever the hell you think got done in '82. Get real, Jan. In the first place, all of this is crazy shit. In the second place—"

We never got to second place. "We've got to run," Tarky said after a quick consultation with his Rolex. "Let's move it, John Wesley. We don't want to miss the fruit cup."

The candidate stood up from the picnic table, gave us all a wide, meaningless campaign smile, and strode across the lawn in the wake of his campaign manager.

The group broke up shortly after that. There was nothing more to say, no small talk that could follow accusations of betrayal and murder. Zack and Ron and I drove back downtown in the van, the setting sun a huge orange ball that filled the windshield.

At the hotel, I said I was tired and went to my room alone. I flipped on the TV and switched it to CNN, then took off my clothes and lay on the bed. I'd planned to read through the court papers, but instead I fell asleep with a story about the Middle East ringing in my ears.

The phone woke me. I reached for it, still groggy and displaced. I knew I wasn't in Brooklyn, but I couldn't have said for sure where I was.

"Hello?" I said, my voice rusty with sleep.

"Is this Cassandra Jameson?" a male voice asked.

I nodded, then realized that wouldn't help. "Yes," I said. I glanced at the clock on the bed table: 3:14.

"Do you know a Janice Gebhardt?" the voice asked.

"Yes. What is this about?"

"She was just airlifted to Toledo Hospital. We'd like you and Mr. Ronald Jameson to meet us there."

"Who is this?"

"Trooper Houghton of the Ohio State Police, ma'am," the man replied. "Ms. Gebhardt was the victim of an assault."

CHAPTER TWELVE

"They didn't hurt you?" Jan asked, for what Ron decided was the fourth time.

He shook his head. "It wasn't fun, but they didn't hurt me." He recalled, also for the fourth time, his urine bag overflowing on the floor of the cell. Nothing he could do about it, so he'd thought he was way past feeling shame. But he'd blushed when the guards went for the mop, blushed like a kid wetting himself in first grade. No, Jan didn't need to know that part.

"I was okay," he repeated, careful to keep the edge out of his voice. At least his attendant had cleaned him up before Jan was released. His bowel evacuation was also overdue, so Andrew had a few choice things to say when he did the rubber glove thing, but Jan didn't have to know about that either.

Jan leaned over and touched his cheek. "You shaved," she said softly. Ron inclined his head, accepting her euphemistic use of the active voice. When her bony fingers reached his lips, he pursed them into a light butterfly kiss that brought a smile to Jan's wan face.

They sat at a window table in Posner's Deli, a courthouse hangout in downtown Toledo, conveniently located across the street from Harve Sobel's law office. Ron had a half-eaten bagel in front of him, and a cup of coffee with a straw stuck into it.

"God, it's so good to see you again," Jan said. "I'm glad

you're here." Then her face darkened. "What a stupid thing to say. We've been fucking arrested, and here I am—"

"Stop it, Jan," Ron said. In the old days, he'd have lifted his hand to her mouth, stopped her words with a light touch. Now his tone of voice had to do all the work. "Don't blame yourself. I offered my van. I went along. I'm as sorry as you are that Miguel died, but it wasn't our fault."

"It was somebody's fault," Jan said. "Somebody tipped off Walt Koeppler. Somebody told him exactly where we'd be and when." Jan's face, devoid of makeup, radiated an intense conviction that struck Ron as just this side of madness.

"What makes you say that?" He kept his tone neutral.

"Think about it!" Jan's bony fist struck the table. "The feds let Rap get away with the boat. You'd think Walt Koeppler would have done anything to get the *Layla*. Without the boat, we're dead in the water, but instead of grabbing Rap and Dana, he screws around with us and gets Miguel killed. And Rap sails the hell out of there. It doesn't make sense, unless—"

"Maybe he was going to grab the boat, but when the shooting went down—"

Jan's voice overrode his, its stridency causing heads to turn three tables away. "Unless Rap or Dana made a deal with the feds."

"Why would they do that?" It wasn't the right question, but all Ron really wanted was to lower Jan's decibel level.

"I think Rap packs cocaine into the hull," she whispered, leaning over the table. "Runs it to Canada along with the refugees."

"How do you know?" Again, Ron had the feeling this wasn't the best question. But he'd spent his time behind bars worrying about her, not dreaming up conspiracy theories.

Jan's lips twisted into a cynical parody of a smile. "You forget, I was the Julia Child of drugs. I knew exactly what to take for the perfect high, knew just what you needed for a soft landing. Where do you think I got the stuff I used to hand out to my friends like chewing gum?"

Rap. Of course. Why deal with a stranger when you can

find an old friend who'll help you commit suicide the slow way?

Ron bit down on the remark he wanted to make. He'd smoked his share of dope before 'Nam, then gotten really wasted over there, where joints as fat as Havana cigars were made in Saigon factories and sold under brand names. Where cigarettes laced with heroin cost less than a carton of regular smokes. Back in the world, sitting in the chair, he'd graduated to harder stuff—though it wasn't easy being an addict who depended on a hospital orderly to get the stuff into his veins. He'd kicked the hard way, not wanting to admit to anyone who didn't have to know that he'd become the sorriest of statistics, the burned-out vet with a hole in his arm. So who was he to judge Jan? Who was he to wish she'd been able to say no when Rap waved his goodies under her nose?

"So you think Rap sold us out in return for the feds leaving him alone on the drug stuff? Would they do that?"

"Would they let a world-class drug dealer go free so they could nab a political refugee who never hurt anyone in his life?" Jan twisted a hank of hair around her finger. "Yeah, Ron, they would. After all," she went on, her eyes filled with the passion he remembered from the summer of '69, "it's U.S. policy in Central America that creates refugees. The government doesn't want a lot of people from El Salvador and Guatemala up here talking about what's really going on."

"I'm not a fan of the Reagan Administration either," Ron began, "but isn't this just a little too—"

"That's not all," Jan cut in. Her intense whisper was hoarse; the veins in her neck bulged. "I overheard Rap and Dana arguing at the church last week. They were talking about a factory."

"A drug factory? Packaging heroin? Making amphetamines?" Ron frowned as he considered the implications. Smuggling drugs across the border was bad enough, but if Rap was actually making the stuff, then he and Jan had to put a great deal of distance between themselves and their old comrade.

"I don't know," Jan replied, "but I'm going to find out."

"What do you mean, you're going to find out?" Ron worked at keeping his voice calm. It wasn't as if he had the right to tell Jan what to do—but he didn't like the idea of her going up against Rap.

Jan gave a slight, unconvincing shrug. "I'll just ask Dana a few questions, maybe see where she and Rap disappear to when they think I'm not around."

"Could be dangerous" was all Ron said, but his face must have said more. Jan hastened to qualify her remarks. "I won't do anything stupid."

Twelve years in the chair had taught Ron not to envy others for what they could do and he could not. Twelve years had taught him a brutal lesson in patience. But he hated the idea that he could only sit and wait while Jan risked her life. He wanted to beg her not to go out there, to leave everything to Harve, to—

He gave her his broadest smile. "Be careful, Jan," he said. "Don't do anything I wouldn't do."

Her bad-girl grin answered him. "How the hell should I know what you wouldn't do?"

In a temporary campaign headquarters in the same Spitzer Building that housed Harve Sobel's law office, the Democratic candidate and his campaign manager took a rare moment of rest to assess the situation. Posters of the highly photogenic incumbent congressman adorned the walls, while a dartboard in the corner featured a photograph of the smiling actor-president with several darts protruding from his forehead. Piles of flyers photocopied on pastel paper littered the desks. Boxes of political buttons were stacked against the wall; on the campaign manager's desk lay a glossy, full-color catalog from a company named Votes Unlimited, from which more political paraphernalia would be ordered.

"It was a nice hot crowd," the candidate said. He lifted his open soda can to his forehead and rolled its coolness across his skin. "I thought I had good connect, especially with that guy whose mother had her Medicare cut." He inclined his head in the direction of the dartboard. "Reagan keeps up this shit, he'll be a one-termer. You heard it here first, Tark. We win in '84 if we—''

"The Jan thing's gonna fucking kill us," Paul Tarkanian cut in. He sat in a swivel chair, his feet propped on a desk top. The Jan thing was not in fact the most important problem on his mind, but it had to be dealt with before he could address the really pressing issue of his life: where to get the money he desperately needed to pay a gambling debt.

He leaned forward in the battered swivel chair that came from his great-uncle Elia's secondhand furniture store on Cherry Street. "I was born in this town; I grew up working the precincts, getting out the vote. I know how these people think. And they don't want a dope-smoking ex-hippie representing them in Congress."

John Wesley Tannock sat on the leather couch, his tie loosened and his top shirt button undone. For a moment Tarky considered going for a camera and shooting a picture of his candidate at rest. Sitting there on the couch, at ease, drinking soda from a can, Wes resembled the young John Lindsay, the young John Kennedy. It could be a winning photo, blown up and pasted on every lamppost in town. But not if the Jan thing exploded in their faces.

"Depends on how we spin it, Tark. We let the other side define me that way, then, yeah, we're dead. But we aren't just going to sit here and take it. We've got to go proactive on this."

"Yeah?" Tarky replied. He shifted the unlit cigar from one side of his mouth to the other. "And just how do you plan to do that? How do you plan to explain to the voters that once upon a time, when we were young and dumb, we got busted for trying to poison the entire Lucas County Fair with a canister of deadly poison?"

Wes gave his old friend a smile the voters would never see. It was a smile of pure mischief, of joke-playing glee. "Easy," he replied, "we tell them we didn't know the canister was loaded."

Tarky snorted. "It's only a matter of time, John Wesley," he pointed out. "Some enterprising journalist, inspired by *All the President's Men*, is going to run a complete check on Jan Gebhardt and is going to find out that you and she were arrested together in 1969. The fact that the charges were dropped will have absolutely no meaning as far as the voters are concerned. You will be tried and convicted in the court of public opinion of being a bomb-throwing radical who can't be trusted no matter how short you wear your hair now.'' It was almost working; the demand made by Al Czik, Detroit loan shark, that his debt be repaid by midnight was almost receding from Tarky's mind as he addressed himself to the problem of Jan.

"You forget, old buddy, a lot of people had long hair and love beads. We're baby-boomers and we outnumber everyone else on the planet." Wes smiled his baby-kissing smile, the one that had young female voters lining up to volunteer at his headquarters. "Besides, campaigns in this state don't really start until after Labor Day, and by that time, this story'll be as dead as yesterday's mackerel.''

Tark shook his head and took the unlit cigar out of his mouth. "Ex-hippies are schizoid when it comes to voting," he said with a sigh. "They don't support their own. It's like they're all ashamed of what they did back then, don't want to be—''

"Ashamed?" Wes's voice rose; his face reddened. "What the fuck is there to be ashamed of? Should we be ashamed of trying to end a stupid war, of working to end poverty? Should we be ashamed of helping migrant farmworkers? Should we be ashamed of going a little crazy when a child was seriously injured in the fields?''

"It's a nice speech, Wes," Tark said, "but I think we're better off playing down the whole thing. All it's going to do is get us off-message. Our line is: Nobody got hurt, nothing really happened, it was a long time ago, you've had nothing whatsoever to do with Jan Gebhardt since then. No reason in the world for you to be connected with her now just because you worked together one summer a long time ago.''

"I've been thinking." The candidate's photogenic gray eyes fixed Tarkanian with Jerry Brown intensity. Tarky sat up in his chair; Wes thinking was always something he had to watch out for.

"Jan's not the only one who got arrested," Wes said. A glimmer in his gray eyes told Tarky the riddle was his to solve.

Tark the Shark gave a quick nod as the penny dropped. He'd have thought of it himself if he hadn't been rattled by the call from Czik.

"You want to put Ron Jameson out in front instead of Jan," he said. "Play the cripple card for all it's worth. He's a disabled vet to boot. Patriotic citizens who may have gone a little over the line, but are good people at heart. Throw in the priest for good measure. Lotta Catholics in this town."

Tarky stroked his chin with the same gesture he'd once used to caress his beard. God, he'd loved that beard. It made him look like a cross between an Armenian high priest and a wild mountain man.

But, like the beard, Wes's analysis was of the past, not the present. "I don't care how many priests declare their churches a sanctuary, Wes, the voters in this district are conservative Democrats." He pointed the dead cigar at the smiling face on the dartboard. "And I wouldn't underestimate Reagan, either. You were damned lucky to get this seat two years ago with him beating Carter; I wouldn't count on lightning striking twice."

The cigar made its way back into his mouth; he chewed on the end, shifted it to the other side of his lips, and went on, "So liberation theology as preached by Father Jerry Kujawa isn't going to fly in Toledo. You need to get as far away from Jan and Ron as possible. You need to—"

The phone rang. Tarky picked it up on the first ring and barked his name into the reciever.

It was Czik. The last man on earth he wanted to talk to with his candidate in the room. "I'll call you back later," he said, and slammed the phone down. He'd pay for that rudeness, but right now it was more important to conceal the identity of the caller from Wes Tannock.

Too late. Wes caught the implication; who else would his campaign manager dare to hang up on?

"How much?" Wes's voice was harsh, a lawyer cross-examining a hostile witness.

"What do you mean, how much?"

"Which word didn't you understand, Tark? How"—Wes spaced the words with insulting slowness—"much? How much do you owe Czik this time?"

"Wes, it wasn't—"

"Oh, yes it was. You need money to pay off the sharks and you owe the sharks because you put a bundle on one more losing horse, losing team, losing whatever." The florid face was bright red and the slender finger pointed straight into Tarky's face. "I told you last time, one more phone call from a loanshark and I find myself a new campaign manager. One who doesn't know where all the racecourses and poker games are."

"Wes, I'll clear this up. It's no big deal. I'll—"

"No big deal. My closest aide is paying off illegal gambling debts and it's no big deal." He lifted his hand to his forehead and wiped away sweat. "Okay. You get the fuck out of this mess, and then we'll talk. I don't want to dump you, Tark. You're the best campaign manager I've ever seen. But I can't afford you anymore."

After Wes left for his luncheon at the Toledo Club, Tarky sat at his desk, chewing his unlit cigar and seething with rage. How dare Wes Tannock, the pretty boy, the Face, talk to him like that?

He'd grown up political, stuffing envelopes at Democratic party headquarters with his father and three uncles while other boys were hitting home runs. To little Paulie Tarkanian, Election Day *was* the home run. He loved the cigar smell of party HQ—lavishly contributed to by all four adult Tarkanians—and the razzle-dazzle of rallies. He loved canvassing voters, that most boring of political tasks. Behind every door he knocked on lay a secret, and it was his dearest wish to unlock those secrets and use them to get his candidate elected.

When the sixties hit northwest Ohio, Tarky was a first-year law student. He'd turned his finely calibrated sense of the possible from traditional precinct politics to the War on Poverty, working for the local migrant farmworkers' union, the Farm Labor Action Coalition. He'd started with rallies, at which maybe twenty migrants would show up. By the end of the summer, he had organized a full-blown strike that paralyzed the tomato season and brought growers to the bargaining table. He'd helped create a real union where there had been only hopes and dreams before.

And he'd met John Wesley Tannock, fellow law student and Perfect Candidate.

God, Wes had been perfect then. So eager to learn. So ready to listen to Tarky's superior wisdom.

It wasn't that Wes couldn't think; he'd graduated sixth in his law school class (to Tarky's third). It was that he didn't have to think all the time. He was able to let someone else think for him, able to trust.

Which was fine with Tarky so long as the person Wes trusted was him. But now there was someone else influencing Tannock. Tarky knew it with the same intuitive certainty that tells a wife her husband is cheating.

Who the hell had Wes gotten in bed with?

Tarky sighed and closed his eyes. In a strongbox at the First Federal Savings and Loan on Summit Street, just three blocks away, there was a plastic bag. A bag containing one hemostat-turned-roach-clip, with a blackened end that spoke of hundreds of marijuana cigarettes burned to the nub. A hemostat Paul Tarkanian had plucked from Kenny Gebhardt's dead hand.

Divorce insurance. In case Wes had no intention of paying alimony.

CHAPTER THIRTEEN

There's nothing like attempted murder to wake you up. I scrambled out of bed and ran next door without putting on shoes. I knocked loudly, hoping I wouldn't wake the other motel guests. When Zack answered, I told him as much as I knew, becoming aware as I spoke just how little that was.

It took Zack fifteen minutes to get Ron out of bed and strapped into the chair. He handed me the keys to the van. I drove while he pulled off Ron's pajama top and put a shirt on him.

We sped down the freeway; I got off at the exit for the hospital and drove at top speed down the side street that led to the emergency room entrance. I raced inside while Zack extricated Ron from the van.

I walked up to a man in a tan uniform with the star-badge of a state trooper. "I'm here about Jan Gebhardt," I said. "How is she? What happened?"

"I can't tell you that, ma'am. You'll have to wait for the doctor."

"The guy on the phone said she'd been attacked. How? When?"

Zack pushed the chair through the sliding glass doors. The trooper stared; apparently he hadn't been prepared for Ron to be a quadriplegic.

A nurse stepped out from a set of double doors. "Can we see her?" Ron asked. He leaned forward in the chair, seeming to strain at his bonds. But that was impossible; he had no muscle control below his midchest.

"Miss Gebhardt is in intensive care," the nurse replied, her tone sympathetic but professionally cool. "Immediate family only, I'm afraid."

"I am her immediate family," Ron insisted. "I'm her husband."

I stared at my brother open-mouthed. Being at a loss for words is unusual for me, but there was so much I wanted to say that I found myself unable to say anthing at all. *When?* was one of the questions I'd have liked to ask. *Why didn't you tell me?* also came to mind. And finally: *Do Mom and Dad know?*

Why was the last question suddenly the most important? *Did you distrust everybody in your life, or just me?* Am I the only one in the family you kept in the dark?

But events were moving too fast. The nurse said, "In that case, I'll have Dr. Singh come in and give you the prognosis." She turned and walked away on soundless white shoes.

Dr. Singh was a small, bearded man with walnut-colored skin, a white turban, and a slight singsong accent. He said Jan was in a coma and that he had no idea when or even if she might regain consciousness.

"It is not looking good at this moment," the doctor said. "She is only at number four on the Glasgow coma scale, which means she is in a severe coma. She may not awaken, and if she does, she may suffer serious brain damage."

"Does she need surgery?" Ron asked.

"We are taking a CAT scan to determine that," Dr. Singh replied. "The great danger at this stage is internal pressure from bleeding and cerebral fluid. We will monitor her constantly and operate if we must."

"Can I see her?"

"As soon as she is finished with the scan and we have her stabilized, you may enter the room for a maximum of ten minutes. Then you must let her rest."

Dr. Singh murmured something about time being the great healer. I wanted to tell him to drop the Deepak Chopra act, but Ron and Zack nodded as if he'd said something profound.

I tried in vain to take it all in. Three days ago, I had no idea whether Jan Gebhardt was alive or dead. Then she reappeared, turned herself in, and claimed she'd been betrayed and set up in 1982. Now she was near death and married to my brother.

"When?" I asked, turning to him. "When did you marry her?"

"Summer of '82. Father Jerry."

The doctor left and the state trooper approached, notebook and pen in hand. "You two were with the victim earlier this evening, is that right?"

I nodded. "We came to see her at Our Lady of Guadalupe."

"And who else was present on this occasion?"

My lawyer antennae went up. Jan might be a victim, but she was also a defendant, and so was Ron. I didn't want to risk saying anything that could jeopardize his position.

"What happened to Jan?" I asked. I wanted the information and I also wanted time to think.

"You sat in that courtroom this morning," Ron cut in. "You heard what she said at the cottage. She was going to find out who sold us out and killed Kenny. Somebody obviously didn't like that idea, so they tried to kill her."

So much for keeping secrets from the cops. "Maybe someone broke in to steal—" I stopped myself when I remembered. There was nothing, literally nothing, in the cabin worth stealing.

"Who are these people you're talking about, sir?" the cop asked. I considered reading my brother his rights, then decided telling the police who was in the backyard with Jan wouldn't hurt him. It might hurt one of them—Wes came to mind—but they were neither my clients nor my brother. So I sat silent while Ron spelled all the names for the cop. I gave him points for not blinking when he heard that former governor and present senatorial candidate John Wesley Tannock was among those in attendance.

"How did it happen?" I asked when Ron's recitation was complete.

"She was hit on the head six or seven times with a heavy, blunt object. A baseball bat would fit the bill."

"God. My God." A baseball bat, hitting a human skull with full force six or seven times. Suddenly the attack became real. Suddenly I could picture Jan's frail body bending under the blows. I could hear the sickening thud as hard wood hit bone. My stomach rebelled; I swallowed sour bile and prayed that I wouldn't vomit on the state trooper's shoes.

"There must have been blood all over that room."

"There was, ma'am. There was." He snapped his notebook shut and gave me a card. "Call me if you need anything."

As the trooper walked toward the double doors, which whooshed open as he approached, it hit me that Ron would probably have been at the top of his suspect list if he hadn't been in a wheelchair.

Ted Havlicek, hair disarranged and shirt mussed as if he'd fallen asleep on the couch, raced through the automatic doors.

"How is she?" he asked.

"How did you know she was here?"

He answered without looking at me. "Scanner."

Ron started to fill him in. I interrupted. "What are you doing here?" I demanded. "Are you after a story or are you here as a friend?"

"Both. Jan's news, whether you like it or not."

"You said once that being a reporter was like having a free ticket to life," I reminded him. "Well, this isn't a show. Take your free ticket and get out of here."

"Actually, I see myself as a designated observer," he said in a tone that contained no resentment. "When people go out on a boat, there's one person who's supposed to keep an eye on anybody who goes overboard. Whatever else happens, that person has to focus attention on the guy in the water, no matter what else is going on. And that's what reporters do—we keep our eyes on the stuff everyone else gets distracted from."

"What does that have to do with Jan?" My anger was far out of proportion to Ted's presence. I was more upset than I wanted to admit about the attack on Jan. Especially since I'd refused to talk to her privately. I might never know what it was she'd wanted to tell me.

"This attack is already on the wires, so any minute now a couple more reporters are going to walk through those doors and start asking questions. You can refuse to answer them, you can refuse to talk to me, but they're going to get answers from somebody. Who do you want telling your story, Ron," he asked, transferring his gaze to my brother, "you or the cops?"

Ron gave a decisive nod. "Okay. They're saying Jan was attacked with a baseball bat."

"You think one of us did it, don't you?" Ted demanded.

Another nod. "Yeah. I don't like it, but I don't see who else had a motive."

I recalled standing on the sidewalk outside the courthouse waiting for Zack to bring Ron's van. First Dana and then Rap had made remarks that might be considered threats.

But would either of them actually bludgeon a woman to death to keep a secret that was almost thirty years old?

Yes, if that secret involved murder. And Jan claimed that someone in our little group murdered Kenny.

Time to play devil's advocate. "What about the family of that dead DEA agent? What about the FBI? If Jan was really going to reveal someone as an *agent provocateur*, maybe they tried to kill her to keep that secret. There are any number of people who might have wanted her dead."

As the words left my mouth, I realized that Jan was vulnerable to attack precisely because she'd been released on bail into Father Jerry's custody instead of spending the night in jail. Had someone inside the government engineered that release? Had former governor Wes pulled political strings attached to Judge LaMont Noble? And how paranoid was I getting?

Ted ignored me, addressing his remarks to Ron. He was crouched on the floor, eye to eye with my brother, talking as if they were the only two people present. I resented his ignoring me, but I respected it too. Ron was the one who mattered here. He was the one who really cared about Jan.

"I'll start finding out where everyone was when Jan was attacked," Ted said. "From what I heard on the scanner, someone interrupted the attacker. Came to the cabin and heard noises, then knocked and heard moans. Opened the door and there was Jan, bleeding from the head. The cops think the assailant fled out the back door."

"So if the attack hadn't been interrupted, Jan would probably be dead," Ron said slowly.

I refrained from pointing out that she might be dead even as we spoke, or that she might not make it through the night.

Ted stood up and stretched his arms and legs, yawning so broadly that I could see the silver in his back teeth. "I'm going to see if one of the troopers will talk to me."

A nurse in a blue smock stepped up. She handed me a plastic bag and said, "This is the jewelry she was wearing. I thought I should give it to her family; it might not be safe in the locker."

A nurse should know better. I looked her in the eye and said, "My brother is her husband. You can give it to him."

The woman looked around at our little group, then handed the bag to Zack. She fled before I had a chance to correct her mistake. Apparently the man in the wheelchair was her last choice as the patient's husband.

Zack grimaced and laid the bag on Ron's lap. "Sorry," he muttered.

Ron shook his head. "No problem," he said. "Happens all the time." He raised his hands slowly and reached for the bag. It was an oversized plastic job with a ziplock top. Zack reached over and opened the bag without a word, then stepped back to let Ron fish the pendant out of the bottom.

It was a silver butterfly, wings unfurled, hanging from an intricately knotted chain.

"I gave her that," Ron said. "On her first anniversary."

"Your wedding anniversary?" I asked, trying not to let the words stick in my throat. The idea of my brother having a wedding without me there hurt so much.

"No, her first anniversary of getting sober," Ron explained.

"The butterfly symbolizes her new life, her emergence from the cocoon."

He held the delicate thing in his twisted fingers and bowed his head. A single tear hit the silver butterfly; he wiped it on his shirt with a slow, clumsy movement, then dropped the pendant back into the plastic bag.

The next arrival through the automatic doors was Father Jerry. He wore his full priestly regalia and he carried a small black leather case. He stepped up to Ron, placed a hand on his shoulder, and gave it a squeeze. Then he walked over to the nurse's desk and spoke to her in a low voice.

Zack interpreted these events for Ron and me. "He's here to give the last rites," he whispered. "He's trying to find out whether he can see Jan."

The nurse shook her head. Father Jerry strode back toward us, the black skirt of his cossack swirling around his long legs. "She's still having the CAT scan," he told us. "They said I could go in as soon as she's finished."

Ron nodded. Although last rites was not part of our Presbyterian upbringing, he seemed to accept the fact that Jan would want a priest in what might well be her last moments of life.

"Ted said something about the attacker's being interrupted," I said. "Do you know anything about that, Father?"

The priest nodded. "I knocked at her door at three o'clock," he replied. "I heard noises. I didn't like what I heard, so I used my key to open the door. I found Jan bleeding and moaning."

It occurred to me that this story might raise an eyebrow or two. A priest who had the key to a single woman's bedroom, who was knocking at her door in the middle of the night.

"Pardon me, Father, but what were you doing at Jan's door at three a.m.?"

A small smile crossed Father Jerry's ascetic face. "You're not Catholic, are you?"

I shook my head.

"She was saying the hours," the priest explained. "In the Middle Ages, the monks used to pray every three hours.

They'd wake from sleep and say prayers at certain times. Compline, lauds, matins. Three o'clock in the morning is known as terce. I was going to pray with her.''

This was beginning to sound familiar. ''Like Brother Cadfael,'' I said, referring to the medieval monk-detective created by the late Ellis Peters. ''I love those books. But,'' I went on, ''Jan wasn't a monk. Or a nun. Why would she be saying prayers at three a.m.?''

''It's a kind of discipline. It was also done by squires in the Middle Ages on the night before they were to be knighted. It was part of the vigil they kept before their ordeal.''

Like the knights of old, Jan was facing an ordeal. It made sense that she'd prepare herself in some way.

I had a sudden vision of her in that spare, spartan room with the rosary over the bed. Kneeling on the bare floor with her prayerbook, waiting for her priest. Praying for strength to go through with what she'd promised to do.

Jan had come so far, she had so much life ahead of her, and now—

Now she might be dying. Dying before she could work her Ninth Step, before she could tell her truth.

It wasn't fair.

When we'd first come into the waiting room, I'd entertained the unworthy thought that if Jan died, the case would die too and I could go home to Brooklyn and forget the past. It was only a fleeting thought, and one that I'd suppressed at once. But the desire to let the dead past bury its dead was so strong that I'd let it overpower me for a brief moment.

Now that moment haunted me. The nurse came and said Jan was in the ICU and we could see her. Zack pushed the chair and Father Jerry and I walked alongside it, following her down the silent corridors.

The Intensive Care Unit was in a sealed-off section of the hospital. Those allowed to enter the room were required to don surgical masks and paper hats and gowns. The nurse gave a set to Father Jerry, who put them on with the ease of long practice. Zack helped dress Ron. They were the only two who would be allowed behind the thick glass partition.

I stepped over to the glass, shaded my eyes from the glaring fluorescent light of the corridor, and peered in.

It was hard to find Jan. The room was a maze of wires and cables, of tubes and IVs, of machines whose green numbers gave off an eerie glow. I had a momentary impulse to laugh. It was so sci-fi, so Robin Cook. Maybe they'd already harvested her kidneys and sold them to a rich maharajah on the tenth floor. Maybe she was dead and the machines were there to give the illusion that she lived. Maybe—

Father Jerry stepped into the room, looking like a space creature in his blue garb. He pushed the chair toward the bed from which the tubes and wires emanated. He opened the black leather case and took out little vials. He slipped his hand into his pocket and pulled out a long purple scarf. He raised it to his lips, kissed it, then placed it around his neck.

I shifted my attention to Ron. He raised his limp hand and moved it with excruciating slowness, toward one of Jan's motionless hands. Finally he managed to touch her. It seemed to me he tried to lift her hand, but with the electrodes weighing her down, he couldn't manage it. So he stroked her pale fingers with his.

I dropped my eyes. These rituals were not for me to spy upon. But one thing was certain: I wouldn't be going home to Brooklyn until Jan's attacker was brought to justice. I owed my brother that much.

The words of a Tom Paxton song floated into my brain. "Are you going away with no word of farewell? Will there be not a trace left behind? I could have loved you better, didn't mean to be unkind. You know that was the last thing on my mind."

I made a silent apology to the woman in the green-glowing room. *Sorry, Jan. It was the last thing on my mind.*

CHAPTER FOURTEEN

July 16, 1982

There was no one else in the elevator. No stares, no self-conscious, wooden attempts to ignore the man in the chair. Jan pushed the button for the Spitzer Building's mezzanine; if she'd been alone, she'd have dashed up the stairs. Maybe even taken them two at a time. Amazing how people took the ability to walk up a flight of stairs for granted.

Harve Sobel's office was behind a frosted-glass door straight out of a forties private eye movie. Jan strode ahead and rapped on the window, then opened the door wide and propped it with her rear end. Before she could pull the wheelchair inside, Father Jerry Kujawa appeared at her side and took over.

Father Jerry wore a navy golf shirt instead of his Roman collar. He greeted Jan with a platonic hug, and grasped Ron's shoulder as he settled the chair next to Harve's desk. Jan sat in one of the deep-seated leather client chairs.

"I thought we should all meet together," Harve explained. He stayed seated, a big man wearing a rumpled white shirt and a badly knotted, too-wide seventies tie with a hand-painted hibiscus on a bright blue background. "Saves me saying the same thing twice."

"What about Dana and Rap?" Jan asked. "Shouldn't they be here too?" Even the mention of their names gave her voice an edge she couldn't suppress. If they were here, would she be able to keep herself from accusing them, loudly and messily, of selling them out?

"Walt Koeppler would love that," Harve retorted. "The way it stands now, he has no proof that they were anywhere near the scene of your arrest. But if they're observed attending meetings with you and your lawyer, Koeppler will conclude they had something to do with what went down at Crane Creek."

"Observed," Jan repeated. "You mean you think he's watching us."

"I think," Harve replied, leaning so far back in his swivel chair that Jan was certain he was about to land on his butt, "that the feds would probably draw the line at bugging a lawyer's office. But anything short of that, we can and should expect. They probably got some nice photos of you two walking across Madison Street just now."

Jan shivered. When she'd been a frightened little Catholic schoolgirl, she'd believed quite literally that God was everywhere, that the nuns could see her every move. And that every little sin was marked down in a book from which God would punish her come Judgment Day.

Now Walt Koeppler was God: omniscient, ever-present, all-knowing. Had he seen her touch Ron's hair? Did he know how much Ron meant to her? Did he know what they did together after dark in the motel room, with Andrew the attendant having a discreet drink at the motel bar?

"What are we going to do, Harve?" Ron asked. "How serious are the charges, and what's our defense?"

Harve gestured at an open lawbook on his desk. "You'll probably be indicted under Title 8, section 1324 of the United States Code. I'm not sure whether they'll go for the felony or settle for a misdemeanor. They didn't look good out there, shooting an unarmed man. On the other hand," he went on, his bloodhound face solemn, "whenever the cops screw something up royally, they tend to take it out on everyone else. So they might throw the proverbial book at you. I have a call in to Cathy Sawicki at the U.S. attorney's office, but she hasn't returned it. My guess is that she wants to talk it over with her boss before committing herself.''

"Those are the charges," Ron said. "Now what about the defenses?''

Harve inclined his huge buffalo head. "I talked to a few people in Tucson," he said. "They've got a very active sanctuary movement down there. This lawyer named Travis something is sending me briefs. We ought to be able to use some of their arguments up here.''

"Successful arguments, I hope," Ron murmured.

"Nobody knows," Harve replied. "That's what makes this an exciting case. The clergy in Tucson is high on the sanctuary defense, on the theory that if you declare a church a sanctuary, the civil authorities can't touch you. Personally, I think that's a nice press angle, but it won't fly in court.''

"So what will?" Ron's hand gripped the arm of his chair. "I mean," he went on, "we knew we were running a risk, but I thought we had some hope of winning at trial if we got arrested.''

"You do," the lawyer answered. "At least I think you do. The problem is that none of this has been tested in court. My plan is to raise every possible argument relating to the right of the Salvadorans to political asylum. They're fleeing political persecution and they should be entitled to protection as refugees. That's our strongest argument, and it allows us to put the United States policy on trial.''

"You mean we'll be able to show what Miguel and Pilar were running away from?" Jan asked. Her fingers played with a strand of hair, curling it round and round.

"Once a jury hears the whole story, they might not convict at all," Harve replied. "If they do, I foresee a light sentence. First offense, for one thing," he said. "And of course, there's the other thing." He looked at Ron, then shifted his glance.

"The other thing being the fact that one of the defendants is a quadriplegic," Ron said dryly. "I can't say I like the idea of using—''

Harve turned and stared straight into Ron's eyes. "You want the truth?" He tapped a finger on his desk. "Walt Koeppler could have had your van. He could have filed forfeiture papers on it, claimed it was used in the commission of a federal crime. The only reason he didn't is that he knows damned well I'd have every newspaper in the country screaming its head off about stealing a van from a disabled veteran. So if we have to use sympathy, we'll use sympathy.''

"How about some sympathy for Miguel?" Jan cut in. "And Pilar and Manuelito. Where are they, Harve? Did Walt have them shipped back to El Salvador already?''

Harve gave a quick, sharp nod of his leonine head. "I filed every motion I could think of," he said. "I begged the judge to give us at least a couple of days, let me comb the cases for just one that might help us out. I put Father Jerry here on the stand to tell the judge what would happen to them if they were sent back. Know what the judge said?''

Jan shook her head. "He said that isolated incidents of torture against left-wing academics and their families didn't mean that Pilar was in any real danger from the authorities. He said we had to prove actual use of torture against her and Miguel in order to qualify her for political asylum.''

"Of course," Ron finished, his tone bitter, "if they were Cuban, they'd be given asylum automatically. That's what's so unfair.''

"So she's—" Jan couldn't finish the sentence. She groped in her purse for a tissue. "Where is she now?''

"El Salvador, we think," Father Jerry replied. "She's in our prayers.''

"Prayers! What the hell good are prayers, Father?" She turned on the priest. "If prayers did any good at all, Miguel would be alive and he and Pilar would be in Canada, where they'd be granted asylum. Where they'd be safe. So where was God, Father, when Walt Koeppler shot Miguel like a dog in the road?''

Father Jerry's ascetic face twisted with pain, but all he said was, "We have others to consider now. We'll pray for those who are beyond our help, but we have to act on behalf of those we can still help.''

Jan wadded up the tissue and shoved it in her pocket. That

little Catholic schoolgirl was dead, buried under layers of sixties rebellion and drowned in an ocean of booze. She'd grown
a hard shell, and she pulled it around her now.

"Boats aren't the only way," the priest went on. "We've
sent a group up to Sarnia in a truck and another is on its way
to Windsor by way of Detroit. But there are still quite a few
families left. And then there's Joaquín Baltasar."

"Do we know where Joaquín is?" Ron asked. "And should
we be talking like this in front of our lawyer?"

Harve raised a hand. "I'm not one of those who saves his
own skin at the expense of the client," he said. "I'm in this
because I believe in the cause, and I'm not running to the
authorities with anything I learn from my clients."

"He's due to arrive in Liberty Center sometime late tonight," Father Jerry said. "We've got to get him out of the
way as soon as possible. Given the publicity surrounding him,
Koeppler's got to want him pretty badly."

Jan pulled in a deep breath and let it out slowly. Now was
the time to say what had to be said. "Walt Koeppler knew
we'd be out there. So why didn't he arrest Dana and Rap too?
Why did he let them get away?" She looked closely at Harve's
face, trying to read what was going on behind the basset-
hound jowls.

Ron finished the thought. "We wondered whether there
might be a reason the feds let them get away. We wondered
whether one of them might have made a deal."

Harve sat still as a stone, then lifted a powerful fist and
slammed the table. Once. "I warned her," he said, shaking
his head. "I told her not to trust that bastard. Told her he was
a two-bit hustler." He fixed Jan with an accusing look.
"Know what she said to me?"

Jan shook her head, although she was sure she could give
a good guess. "She said, 'Takes one to know one, Pop,'—
and then she strapped on her backpack and followed the shit
to Nepal."

Harve sighed. "Came back six months later broke and sick
and pregnant."

"With Dylan," Jan murmured.

It was Ron who said quietly, "We don't know it's Rap. Truth is, the informant could have been Dana."

Harve shifted his attention to Ron. His booming voice was a hoarse whisper as he said, "You want me off this case, just say so."

Jan held her breath. If Ron said yes, who would defend them? Who could they trust? Hell, who could they afford? Harve was a pro bono lawyer, representing them for the cause.

"No," Ron said after an unsettling pause. "But I hope the attorney-client privilege means you don't tell Dana what goes on between us in this office."

"Of course it does," Harve replied. "And I haven't said two words to Rap since he came back here. He may be the father of my grandson, but he's nothing to me. Not after what he did to my little girl."

Jan wasn't convinced. Oh, it was clear Harve was sincere in his defense of Dana and his hatred of Rap. But a doting father was the easiest person in the world to deceive. She was still going to find Dana and ask her point-blank what she and Rap were doing with their so-called factory.

As she stood in the dimly lit hallway, waiting for the elevator, she had a quick vision of snow, piled high, sparkling in the sun. Cool and white and pure—a perfect refuge on a hot, humid summer day. She pictured herself diving into it like a child, picking up snowballs, making snow angels. Bringing a handful of sweet powder to her nose and—

To her nose?

It wasn't snow, she realized with a shock. She'd been playing, dancing, laughing in mounds upon mounds of pure cocaine.

"You were supposed to arrest them, Walt," the crisp female voice said, "not start a bloodbath."

Walt Koeppler stayed silent, although his mind formed pictures, lovely pictures of Assistant United States Attorney Catherine Sawicki roasting on a spit, turning ever so slowly over glowing embers. He was damned if he would defend himself. The state troopers had done what they had to do; any real law enforcement professional, male or female, understood that, and if this overeducated bitch didn't, then she had no business working the prosecution side of the courtroom.

"So what now?" Sawicki fingered the manila folders on her desk. Her desk, her territory. Her perfume hanging in the air like stale cigarette smoke. Koeppler had an animal defensiveness about meeting anyone on alien turf; he would have preferred this meeting at his own office in the federal building, not the U.S. attorney's lair in the courthouse.

Sawicki leaned back in her forest-green leather chair, clearly aware of the home court advantage. "You've busted probably the two lowest people on this totem pole. Because of that stupid shootout you let the boat owner and his wife get away."

It wasn't because of the shooting. The words stayed on the tip of his tongue, where they belonged. It wasn't this woman's business why Rapaport and Sobel hadn't been arrested. It was orders, orders he wasn't supposed to talk about, not even to the prosecutor.

"And then there's the little matter of probable cause," Sawicki went on. Her unpainted but neatly manicured fingernail tapped the top of her rosewood desk. "I assume you acted on a tip from a reliable informant." She emphasized ever so slightly the legal term. Just in case he was too stupid to pick up the implication.

"Yes," he replied. One-word answers. That was the best strategy. Let her pull it out of him like biting off a piece of Turkish taffy.

"You wouldn't care to name this informant, Mr. Koeppler?" It wasn't the cool sarcasm, the raised eyebrow, that infuriated him. It was the fact that he was a mere "mister" in a world where titles counted.

He shook his head. "Can't."

"Orders, I suppose."

A nod. Just one nod.

"You may have to disobey those orders," the prosecutor said, fixing him with her deep brown eyes. Just a touch of mascara, a hint of blusher, was all the makeup she wore. And yet he was acutely aware that she was a woman, he a large, bumbling male.

"I fully expect the judge to order disclosure of the informant's identity to the defense if they ask for it. And with Harve Sobel on the case, we can be sure they will ask for it."

They can ask all they want; they won't get it. But Koeppler took no pleasure in the thought. The reason galled him almost as much as the U.S. attorney's superior attitude. The defense wouldn't get the name because he didn't have it. The tip had come from the FBI, but the fibbies would drop the cases before they'd give up their sources.

"I repeat my earlier question," Sawicki said. "What now?"

Walt knew what he'd do now, but he wanted to see if this lawyer, with her smooth-as-a-polished-stone facade, had the brains to figure it out and the balls to do it.

She stood up and took a few steps. He noted with interest that she had slipped off her high heels; she paced her carpeted den in stockinged feet, her thin hips swaying ever so slightly. "Your office," she began, "is interested in stopping the sanctuary movement before they get any more publicity. And you want Joaquín Baltasar."

Walt stared. How had she known about Baltasar? It was supposed to be a top secret even within the INS that the Nicaraguan journalist marked for death by the *contras* had crossed the Mexican border into Texas and was on his way north.

She turned and faced Walt. He noted for the first time that she wore no jewelry except tiny gold earrings in the form of hearts. No rings, wedding or otherwise. No pin on her suit lapel, no gold chain at her throat. "My office doesn't give a good goddamn about refugees. We'll prosecute anybody you arrest, but we're more interested in a little matter of counterfeit airplane parts."

Walt nodded. "So that's what Rapaport and Sobel are doing with those trailers of theirs. We heard about them, but every time we went hunting, they moved the damn things. I thought it had something to do with drugs, myself."

"No," the attorney replied, giving Walt a superior smile.

"They're a little more imaginative than that. They're using their illegal aliens to rebuild small plane components—and then selling them as new."

"I talked to Dale Krepke at the DEA," Walt said. "He'd like to nail Rapaport's butt for smuggling coke. That's probably our easiest bust, and once we get Rapaport, we can scoop up the others."

"Not necessarily." Sawicki stopped pacing. She gazed out the window of her office for a moment, then turned the full force of her blue eyes on him. "Drugs are everyday. Drugs are nothing. But these airplane parts can and will cause deaths if we don't stop them."

Walt nodded, but a sour taste filled his mouth. "And an ambitious prosecutor doesn't make a name on routine narcotics cases. But she just might if she can grab the headlines on using illegal aliens to make bogus airplane parts."

"We can all win here, Walt." Sawicki's smile reminded Walt of the way his wife looked when he gave her a particularly romantic anniversary gift. "You, me, the DEA. All we have to do is exercise a little patience."

Koeppler nodded. Patience he understood. Patience and giving Jan Gebhardt a long, long leash—and then yanking her chain.

CHAPTER
FIFTEEN

There was nothing to be gained by staying at the hospital.

Ron wanted to be there for Jan when she woke up. If she woke up. It was with difficulty that I convinced him to go back to the hotel and get some sleep, then come back to keep vigil.

We drove in silence. I fell into bed and dropped into a dreamless sleep that left me groggy. I got up and checked the clock: 11:32 a.m. I splashed water on my face and went next door.

Ron was up and dressed, sitting in his wheelchair and gazing at his laptop computer. I leaned over and saw he was reading input from a newsgroup engaged in a passionate discussion of whether Jan should go to jail for the death of the DEA agent.

I lay down on his bed and groaned. "I feel like death warmed over."

Then I realized there was something missing. "Where's Zack?"

"Out jogging."

"You're not wearing the medallion."

"We're in touch," Ron explained. He inclined his head toward the desk. I followed his gaze and saw a white plastic speaker box. "It's an intercom," my brother said. "Zack has a receiver; he can hear everything. If I need him, all I have to do is call and he'll come back.''

"Which means I'd better watch my mouth," I said lightly. But the thought of Ron's always being monitored, having no sense of privacy, sent a chill through me. Even if it was absolutely necessary for his safety.

"So what did you think of Ted after all these years?" Ron asked. "Any old sparks rekindled?"

"Sparks. Ha. Ted Havlicek used to be the boy next door, and now he's the guy next door. The guy who not only lends you his power mower but shows you how to use it and ends up mowing half your lawn." It was an odd conversation, given that my brother's wife lay near death, but he seemed to welcome light banter instead of heavy confidences.

"Boy, what an indictment," he replied with a smile. "I can see why you wouldn't want a guy like that."

"I'm just not that fond of white bread."

"So that's why you and he never really got off the ground."

"It was the accordion picture that did it," I said. I gazed at the ceiling with the rapt attention usually reserved for star-spangled nights and cloud-picture afternoons.

"Try that again," my brother suggested.

"I'm serious," I said, but I ruined the effect by snorting a laugh in midword. "If it had been a guitar, it would have been cool," I went on. "If it had been a piano, it would have been okay. A trombone, even. But an accordion . . .''

"You dumped that poor guy because he once played the accordion?"

"He didn't just play it," I retorted. "His mother had a picture of him on top of her television set. A big, glossy eight-by-ten. He stood there with a big smile on his face, holding the most expensive accordion since Lawrence Welk. It was obvious he loved the thing. I simply could not go out with a man who—''

"And how old was he when that picture was taken?"

"What is this, cross-examination?" I sat up on the bed. "Okay, he was about twelve. Had one of those butch haircuts all boys wore in the fifties."

"So because he once had a bad haircut and played an unfashionable musical instrument, you, Cassandra Jameson, decided you were way too cool to go out with Ted Havlicek. Is this a fair statement, Counselor?"

"Yes, Your Honor," I shot back. "I plead guilty and throw myself on the mercy of the court. I was young. Young women make mistakes. Unlike young men, who never try to impress the prom queen instead of asking out the perfectly nice girl who sits next to them in Advanced Algebra."

"You never took Advanced Algebra."

"Incompetent, irrelevant, and immaterial," I countered, borrowing Perry Mason's most famous objection. "Besides," I went on, "it wasn't just the accordion. He was kind of a mama's boy, always sticking around home instead of doing things with us. He stood on the sidelines, taking it all down in that damned notebook of his instead of really getting involved."

"Ted looks pretty good," Ron remarked, with a casual air that didn't fool me one bit.

"If you're suggesting that we pick up where we left off in 1969, let me—"

Ron's voice overrode mine. "That would be an improvement on picking up where you left off with Wes Tannock."

"There's nothing to pick up on," I said. "Wes and I never had a relationship. It was just wishful thinking on my part."

"You might try looking me in the eyes if you want me to believe that."

I turned my eyes toward his. "It's true," I repeated. "I was a kid with a crush. That's all." And that was all. The fact that my crush had led me to one hot night of passion under the leaves of the weeping beech was not something I felt compelled to share with my brother. Especially since he hadn't seen fit to share with me the fact that he'd been married for fourteen years.

When Zack came back from his run, he showered and called the hospital. Jan had been operated on during the night for a blood clot. She'd jumped two whole points on the coma scale, but still hadn't regained consciousness. Ron and Zack prepared to visit her. I decided to begin my inquiries into Jan's attack by questioning Dana Sobel, on the theory that I could talk to her feminist-to-feminist. I rented a little red car at the hotel desk and asked directions to the garden apartment complex where Dana lived.

Dana's T-shirt proclaimed: "Life's a bitch, and so am I." She proceeded to prove it.

"If you want me to feel sorry for that stupid woman, you've come to the wrong place," she said. Her substantial body sat in a rattan peacock chair. If she'd worn a muumuu, she could have passed for a Polynesian queen about to throw someone into a volcano.

"Why stupid?" I sat on a Navajo-print-patterned futon in Dana's tiny living room. It was crowded with mismatched furniture, much of it the cheap, leave-behind stuff college kids use for their first apartment away from the parental eye. But Dana was fifty; how did she feel about still living like a student?

"Because she didn't tell Harve what she knew," Dana replied. She reached for a soft pack on the brass table and pulled out a cigarette. I wanted to beg her not to light it, but I knew she wouldn't listen. I steeled myself against an onslaught of smoke and hoped to hell Dana's information would be worth it.

"You think if she had, she'd be—" I broke off, realizing I'd almost said *alive*. And yet she was alive. Whatever alive meant to that still, frail body.

"I think whoever attacked her would have thought twice if he'd known it wouldn't do any good. And if she'd taken her own lawyer into her confidence, the person who tried to kill Jan would have had to kill Harve too. As it is, whatever Jan knew will die with her."

"You sound awfully sure she's going to die."

Dana's black eyes narrowed. "Don't try to trap me, Cassie. I was raised by one of the best cross-examiners in the business. For one thing, I wasn't finished. What I was going to say was, whatever Jan knew will die with her—unless she told someone else before she was attacked." She blew a cloud of smoke and let her lips form a near smile. "Like maybe her husband."

"How did you know?"

Now the smile became real. "Is that really the most important question?"

"I suppose not," I replied. I was growing more and more impatient, with Dana or with myself I wasn't quite sure. All I knew was that I was on the defensive, when I'd intended to take the lead. I was supposed to be asking tough questions that would have Dana squirming on her peacock throne. Instead I was the one scrambling for an answer, taking in new ideas and rolling them around in my brain, trying to assimilate them before the next onslaught.

"Okay," I said. "I get the point. If Jan told Ron what she knew, then Ron's in danger. But she didn't. Ron doesn't know any more than I do, and as you can see, that's not much."

"Nice try, Cassie. But if Jan did tell your brother what she suspected, then you'd definitely deny it in order to protect him. So I'm not so sure I buy this act of yours. Going around and asking everyone what they know, pretending you don't already have all the information you need." She stared at me with no friendliness in her dark eyes.

"And of course," she went on, "you'll take everything you know back to Luke Stoddard and cut a deal to get Ron out of all this. No matter who else it hurts in the process."

Dana ground her cigarette into a ceramic ashtray that looked as if it had been made by a kid at camp. And perhaps it had been. On the cigarette-scarred end table was a picture of a little boy, maybe five years old, with long curls and a tie-dyed T-shirt over his shorts. Dana and Rap's hippie kid.

I let my eyes roam around the cramped living room. There were bits and pieces of Dana's life scattered around—Indian-made pillows with silver-threaded puffy elephants embroidered on them, feminist books with torn jackets tumbling from bookshelves, a framed photo of a bride and groom on the mantel.

The groom had Rap's prominent nose and Dana's piercing black eyes. I pointed and asked, "Dylan?"

Dana's eyes followed my finger. "Yeah. And that's his

wife, Brittany. Can you believe it?'' A stream of smoke punctuated her words. ''My kid, named after Bob Dylan, with hair
like a Marine, marrying a Stepford Wife. They shop at Pen-
ney's and own a minivan.''

My smile was wry, remembering Ron's teasing me about
Ted. ''What a condemnation. They're actually normal people.
How humiliating for you.''

''Their oldest kid, Brianna, is getting to where she's
ashamed of Grandma Dana. Thinks I ought to wear skirts and
panty hose like her other grandma.'' Her belligerence was
mixed with sadness; some part of her would have liked to be
a grandmother to her son's children. But the price was too
high.

''The turning point of my life,'' Dana said, looking at one
of the elephant pillows, ''was when I was raped in Turkey.''

''You were what?'' Was she about to tell me that her son's
father might have been a Turkish rapist instead of Joel Rapaport?

She shook her head and looked into my eyes. ''No,'' she
amended. ''The turning point of my life was when Rap told
me it wasn't important, that it was just another symptom of
Third World anger against American imperialism.'' I began to
feel as if I were attending a seventies consciousness-raising
session. I considered reminding Dana that my consciousness
was plenty high already, but she continued musing aloud.

''As if I'd deserved to be raped because I was carrying an
American passport.'' She took another drag of her cigarette
and ground it out in the ashtray, which was near to overflowing with butts. ''And then on top of that, I found out that
he was using our so-called honeymoon in Nepal to buy and
sell heroin. When I learned I was pregnant, I ran home to
Daddy—only to find out he'd dumped Mom and married a
second-year law student named Mindy. They met me at the
airport, and Mindy was even bigger than I was. Her daughter
was born two months before Dylan.''

''What has all this got to do with Jan?''

''I'm coming to that.'' She waved her cigarette at me.
''Rap, as you might guess, wasn't big on paying regular child

support. Oh, he threw me a few bucks when he had money, and he bought Dylan all kinds of weird presents, like a gigantic African drum or an Indonesian shadow puppet. But steady money wasn't his thing, so when he offered to cut me in on one of his businesses, I said yes.''

"I hope to God both of you had the sense to make it something besides drugs.''

She nodded, sucking in a lungful of smoke and letting it out through her nostrils like a petulant dragon.

"He got a contract to rebuild used parts for small planes and helicopters. He hired migrant farmworkers to do the actual rebuilding. And when we started working with the sanctuary movement, we used refugees to do the work.''

I took a stab in the dark. "And Jan found out.''

To my secret relief, Dana nodded. "She stumbled on the trailers right after she and Ron were arrested.''

Trailers? What did trailers have to do with all this?

"She went into a long rap about ethics, accused Rap and me of running a sweatshop.''

Sweatshop. Trailers. Illegal immigrants rebuilding airplane parts in trailers. This was beginning to make sense.

"But it wasn't a sweatshop,'' I said in a flat voice.

"No. Not really. They were making motherboards. At least that's what Rap said. For airplane control panels.''

Again I kept my voice uninflected. "You were making counterfeit parts. The kind of parts the FAA says is causing plane crashes in Third World countries.'' Thanks to CNN, I was reasonably up-to-date on the bogus parts investigation going on in Washington.

"They can't prove those parts came from our factory,'' Dana said, but her voice sounded sulky, like a teenager hoping to hell her parents will buy her excuse for breaking curfew.

Dana sat with bowed head, the cigarette in her hand burning close enough to her fingers to cause pain. She came to with a start, and dropped the butt into her ashtray, where it lay smoldering.

"He told me they were legal,'' she said at last. Her tone had lost its belligerence; she sounded beaten.

"Right. People make legitimate airplane parts in trailers all the time. I'm sure Boeing has a few old Airstreams lying around in—"

"Cut the crap, Cassie." Dana raised her head and glared at me. "I didn't want to know, so I didn't ask, all right? I thought what I didn't know wouldn't hurt me."

My head hurt. I would have liked to ask for a glass of water to take an aspirin, but I didn't want to break the flow of our discussion. I let the pain charge my voice with impatience. "Why wasn't there a trial? Why weren't you and Rap even indicted?"

She spread her stubby hands in a gesture signifying that she'd come to the end of her knowledge. "I have absolutely no idea. One minute we were going to get Joaquín Baltasar out of the country and the next thing I know that DEA agent is dead and no one knows or cares about the factory."

"There's something else I've got to ask," I said. I stared into the inscrutable black eyes. "How could you go from sixties idealism to exploiting workers to make bogus parts? What were you thinking?"

"The sixties." The scorn in her voice was scalding. "Don't tell me you're one of those who get all misty when you see a hash pipe. The good old days of flower power and don't trust anyone over thirty. What a crock."

"I didn't say that." I hated being on the defensive, but I hated even more being called a sixties sentimentalist. "We were trying to do something good, trying to help some of the poorest and hardest-working people in this country. How do you go from doing that to putting those same people in trailers so they can make bogus parts that kill other poor people?"

She fumbled for another cigarette. The veins in my head were thumping in protest, but the one way to end this conversation was to take away Dana's smokes.

"And where did we get with our children's crusade, Cassie?" The words floated out on a stream of blue smoke. "Are migrant farmworkers better off? A little, maybe, but the truth is that if they are, we had nothing to do with it. We were playing at being radicals, but the minute we got busted, we turned to Harve to get us out of it. The one thing I learned from the sixties—and the seventies; don't forget, I'm also a casualty of the women's movement—is that for every gain made by progressives, there are two steps back. There's always a conservative backlash; we pay for every gain twice over.''

I remembered my cynical conversation with Ron on the way to Our Lady of Guadalupe. Dana's attitude was perhaps a shade darker, but the similarity in tone made me uncomfortable. But then I'm a born devil's advocate, driven by some inner force I can't control to take the opposite position in every argument. So where Ron's cheerful acceptance of our radical past pushed me into cynicism, Dana's contempt brought out a desire to defend at least our good intentions. I pushed away the realization that good intentions were also known as paving stones to hell.

Dana's passion culminated in a fit of choking. She put her hand to her chest and hawked out a gob of phlegm, which she spat into a tissue. ''God,'' she said, ''I sound like my grandfather used to in the mornings. Before he died of lung cancer.'' She stuffed the used tissue into a pocket and said, ''There was something else going on back then. Something I never got to the bottom of. One more thing I didn't really want to know. But my guess is it was a lot more important, and a lot more dangerous, than our piddling little factory.''

''Like what? Drugs?''

''Besides the drugs.'' She reached for her pack of cigarettes. I hoped I wasn't going to die of asphyxiation before this conversation was over.

''He used to take the boat out at night. And there were extra refugees, people Father Jerry didn't know about. People I wasn't supposed to know about. And some of them were armed to the teeth.''

Strange refugees with guns sounded like drugs to me. Unless—the thought crowded into my throbbing head as I drove away from Dana's nondescript apartment complex—unless Rap was also running guns.

Jan had accused one of us of working for the government as an undercover agent. Could she have been right—and could Rap have been supplying weapons to the *contras* under cover of the sanctuary movement?

CHAPTER
SIXTEEN

J an stepped out of the AA
meeting into hot, bright sunlight. After leaving Harve's office,
she'd passed up a downtown meeting to come to the 1:30 at
Our Lady of Guadalupe so she'd be on the spot to start her
inquiries. She decided there was no point in asking Father
Jerry if he knew anything about a factory; if Dana and Rap
were doing something illegal, they wouldn't have confided in
the priest. Instead she asked Belita Navarro, who was now
seventeen and worked part-time for the Migrant Ministry,
where Dana was supposed to be this morning.

"Ms. Sobel is out by the van Wormers', I think," Belita
replied, looking up from the typewriter on her desk. "You
know, where they got that trailer camp behind the big house."
She wore a peach-colored shirtwaist dress, and her long,
glossy black hair was held back by a matching peach headband. Her family had settled out after the parathion accident,
her father going to work at the ketchup factory, and her mother
cooking for Rosita's Luncheonette on Superior.

Jan nodded. She could find migrant camps with ease now,
even if they couldn't be seen from the highway. You took the
dirt roads, followed the line of poplar trees, aimed for what
looked like broken-down, abandoned shacks.

But she'd been to the van Wormer place before. She'd seen

the migrant camp. And there was nothing there that could remotely be called a factory.

Still, it was a lead. She thanked Belita and stepped out of the makeshift office. Shading her eyes with her hand, she gazed across the fields toward the van Wormer farm. Too far away; she could barely see the huge, newly painted red barn, with its Pennsylvania Dutch hex symbol on the front.

She opened the door to her ancient VW beetle and climbed inside. Driving along the back road toward the van Wormers' outer fields, the ones farthest away from the farmhouse, she caught a glimpse of something silver glinting in the sun.

Trailers.

Some farmers used old trailers as migrant housing.

But the van Wormers didn't; they had cinderblock cabins.

So what was causing that silver gleam?

Jan drove along the dirt road, willing herself to go slowly so as not to kick up dust. She wanted to approach as unobtrusively as possible.

The trailers were old-fashioned aluminum cylinders that gleamed in the sun like shards of glass. When you first saw them from the road, you thought maybe they were a mirage, but then you decided it was the sun glinting off a hidden pond behind the cornfield. Only after you'd bounced along the rutted dirt road did you realize that what you were seeing was man-made. And then you hoped they were unoccupied. Hot as hell in there, you thought. I just hope nobody—

You hoped wrong. Jan hoped wrong. When she'd first overheard Rap and Dana talking about "the factory" she'd figured that she was new to the underground railroad and didn't have to know everything. But Miguel's death and the growing suspicion that someone had tipped Walt Koeppler changed all that. Now there were no secrets she was prepared to tolerate.

She pulled her car into the tall weeds beside the road and stepped out. She was about a quarter mile from the trailers.

There were three of them. She walked up to the first and peered in the window. It was open about six inches, no screen. She heard Spanish spoken in the slow Mexican way, soft and lilting. Men and women sat hunched over card tables, hands moving with incredible swiftness in the moisture-heavy air. Playing cards? Dominoes? No, nobody could sit in that trailer, sun beating down, no ventilation to speak of, just to play games.

But the hands, she could see the hands. They were darting in and out, working with small boardlike things. Jan recalled a toy she'd had as a child, where you poked a blunt needle with yarn through a card with punched-out holes to make a picture. That was what it looked like they were doing.

Jan stood back from the window. This wasn't what she pictured when she thought of a factory, but then again, weren't there card-sized boards that went into computers? Could that be what the people in the trailer were doing—making computer boards?

Whatever they were doing had to be worth money. Rap didn't do things that weren't profitable. Three trailers, maybe eight people to a trailer. Twenty-four people making little board things. And maybe this wasn't the only shift. Maybe another group came in when these people left for the day. And maybe this wasn't the only site; you could stash any number of little trailer complexes like this behind the barns and silos of family farms and nobody would see them from the road.

She began to picture a network of trailers, a hidden factory complex that employed refugees. Miguel and Pilar had surfaced seemingly out of nowhere, yet now she suspected they'd once sat, for how long she didn't know, at these card tables, doing something with the little boards.

Did Rap and Dana bother to pay these people, or was hiding them from *La Migra* all the salary they received?

Bile rose in Jan's throat. They'd used her, Rap and Dana, they'd sent her out on a back road to watch Miguel bleed to death, when all the time they were bleeding their workers. Doing it for money, not because they cared about—

"Señora, por favor." A voice cut into her thoughts. Jan jumped and turned, clutching her heart.

"Oh, my God. You scared me. I was just—" She was just what? Passing by? Looking for someone? Fear clutched her bowels; she suddenly realized how dangerous it was to know things you weren't supposed to know.

Her fear deepened as she looked at the man's weathered face. His brown eyes were hard and bored straight into hers. This was no humble *campesino* used to taking orders from rich men, used to keeping his eyes respectfully on the ground as he listened to what others had to say. This was no migrant worker, American or Mexican. Nor did he seem like the educated, polite Salvadorans she had helped cross into Canada.

If anything, this man was what the refugees were fleeing from. A thug, a man used to holding guns on people. A cruel man whose cruelty had received official sanction back home. Wherever home was.

"You will come with me, señora," the man said. Jan took her eyes from the impassive brown face and looked down at his hands. He held a blunt-nosed blue revolver in one hand. It looked as though it belonged there, as though his hand and the gun were old friends.

Although she stood on the sun-drenched soil of Ohio, Jan felt the kind of bowel-melting fear she'd heard about from the refugees. She'd heard stories of the *desaparecidos* and wondered how it was possible in a civilized country to be subject to instant disappearance, to fear every knock on the door, every stranger.

Was it possible, could this cruel brown man disappear her, here and now, in the sunlit afternoon in Lucas County, State of Ohio, United States of America?

Damned right he could.

Paul Tarkanian was nothing if not a realist. Which was why he agreed to meet Joel Rapaport at Tony Packo's on the east side. Better, he decided, a highly public place where he would certainly be noticed than a hole in the corner where the meet would look furtive. With luck, he could pass it off as a campaign talk, shaking hands with the lunch crowd before sitting down at a table. And if Rap had any brains at all, he'd show dressed like a Toledo businessman and not a drug dealer.

When the handshakes were finished and the backs slapped,

Tarky, as if he'd completed the only thing he'd come for, sauntered over to the corner table where Rap waited. He slid the chair out and settled himself in it, giving the hovering waiter the kind of big campaign smile he usually left to his candidate.

"I'll take two Hungarians, extra onions," he said, patting his ample stomach as if it could hardly wait for the treat.

When the kid was gone, Tarky leaned over and said, "I hope to hell you've got Maalox. These dogs kill me every time I come here."

Rap's crooked smile answered him. "Then why don't you order the cottage cheese plate?" He held up a bony hand. "No, don't tell me. The Congressman's campaign manager can't be seen eating cottage cheese in a place famous for its heartburn. You have to show the voters you're a real man. You have to—"

"Cut the crap and tell me what I'm doing here." Tark the Shark said the words in a low voice; his face still wore the campaign-mode smile. No one observing the two would realize there was anything but casual small talk going on.

"There's a ballbusting U.S. attorney on my back." Rap lifted a beer to his lips and drank, then wiped away a foam mustache. "I need her off my back."

Tarky leaned over the table and whispered, "If you think I'm going to quash a drug charge for you—"

"I think you're going to do anything I need you to do," Rap replied. The lazy, insolent smile on his lips infuriated Tark.

"If, that is, you have any desire to get free of Al Czik. I hear he's holding your paper and wants the full amount by midnight. I could see to it that a substantial contribution is made to the Tannock campaign by a political action committee."

A substantial contribution. One that Tarky could siphon off to pay the loan shark and then repay from the winnings on his next decent bet. And with PAC money flowing like honey into political campaigns all over the country, the election commissioners were unlikely to investigate one little congressional race.

Tarky's mind was made up of watertight compartments, like the *Titanic*. Even those few people who thought they knew Paul Tarkanian failed to see the sealed-off compartments under the waterline.

In one compartment was his life with Wes, playing political wife, working behind the scenes to create the illusion that was John Wesley Tannock. In another was his secret passion. He gambled the way other men breathed; needed it the way other men needed sex. He'd never met, or even fantasized about, the woman who could give him the ecstasy a good long-shot win provided.

His partnership with Wes Tannock was the same kind of gamble. He'd spent ten years grooming and building John Wesley Tannock, and now he was gambling those ten years of his life on another man.

If Wes found out that he was taking money from Rap, Wes would fire him. If the election commission found out he was using campaign contributions for his own use, he could go to jail. He put these inconvenient facts into one of the watertight compartments and filed them away.

Then he proceeded to do what he did best: convince himself he was betting on a winner.

Who knew, maybe the money might never be missed. Maybe Wes would never find out that there had ever been a contribution by this phony PAC of Rap's.

But what did Rap want him to do for it?

He opened his mouth to ask, but Rap anticipated him. "No, this isn't about drugs. It's just a little side business Dana and I have."

"How illegal is this side business?"

"We rebuild electronic components for airplanes. Strictly on the up-and-up, according to FAA specifications. But some of our workers aren't exactly in this country legally, and we don't comply with every Mickey Mouse government regulation. Penny-ante shit, Wes, you have my word. But we don't need the hassle with this sanctuary thing going on. If you could just buy us a little time on it, I'd be in your debt.''

''Doesn't sound like anything a U.S. attorney would waste her time on,'' Tarky remarked. He steepled his fingers and gazed at Rap.

''But then,'' he went on, his voice silky, ''you've given me your word that this isn't going to blow up in my face. And your word, of course, has always been—''

He broke off as the waiter brought lunch. ''Those look fantastic.'' He picked up a hot dog dripping with onion sauce and lifted it to his mouth. He bit off a morsel and made loud noises of appreciation. Two guys at the next table turned their heads. One gave him a thumbs-up sign and the other said, ''Great food, huh, Tark?''

Tarky could only nod, his mouth full. He returned the thumbs-up and turned his attention back to Rap. His old friend had a cheese fry in his left hand and a derisive smile on his face.

''We're both going to be in the emergency room together from this *traef*,'' Rap said. ''Between my ulcer and your irritable bowel, we'll be in serious pain.''

''Which United States attorney are we talking about?'' Tarky mopped sauce from his chin. He was careful to hold the hot dog at a distance from his custom-made shirt and linen jacket. His tie was tossed over his shoulder to keep it out of the way of flying grease.

''Her name is Sawicki. Can't think of her first name. But she's on a crusade. Seems to think Dana and I are the Bonnie and Clyde of Lucas County.''

''Just tell me again that this has nothing to do with drugs. I can help with anything but that.''

''As God is my witness,'' Rapaport replied, his hand raised as if to take an oath in court, ''drugs are not involved.''

''It's a business, Jan. That's all. A perfectly ordinary business.'' Dana spaced the words as if talking to a child.

It was Rap's fault for enlisting Jan in the first place. Rap had assured her they had nothing to fear from Jan. She was a basket case, Rap said, a neurotic with a drinking problem and a coke habit. So what the hell was she doing snooping around the factory?

"It's a sweatshop," Jan retorted. "A portable sweatshop." She pointed to the three trailers, grouped behind the cornfield. "I can believe Rap would do this, but you? How can you—"

"How can I what?" Dana's color rose as anger infused her. Who the hell did Jan think she was? "How can I pay these workers three times what they'd get in Mexico? Almost twice what they'd get hoeing pickles? How can I take them out of the fields, give them a job where they get to sit down?"

"I suppose you pay minimum wage, too," Jan replied. "And take out for Social Security and FICA. And give them a pension. And what about day care? An old radical like you, I'm sure you have a day care center for the children some-where around here. Maybe in a chicken coop." She screwed up her thin face. "God, this is so disgusting. You and Rap exploiting the—"

"Exploiting! Don't talk to me about exploiting. Thanks to Rap and me these people aren't doing backbreaking physical labor. Thanks to us they learn a skill other than weeding and picking. Thanks to us they earn American money instead of worthless pesos back in Mexico."

"Thanks to you they live a life off the books. They work for peanuts, because even peanuts are better than pesos. Okay, I grant you that. They make more from you than they would in Mexico. But it's still under minimum wage. It's still against the law. Which is why it's hidden back here where the au-thorities can't find it. Because you and Rap both know what you're doing is wrong."

"It's illegal. That doesn't make it wrong." Dana's tone was flat; she'd thought this out long ago and her rationale was fully formed. No room for doubt. "You remember our old slogan, 'Fuck the System.' Well, that's all Rap and I are doing. No-body gets hurt, we all get paid, and Uncle Sam gets screwed. What's not to like?"

"I repeat, are these people—"

"Let's take a little walk down memory lane, shall we?"

Dana put her hands on her hips, legs apart, squared off and facing her opponent like a judo master.

"While you were boozing it up, doping your way through adulthood, I had a kid to support. After I left Rap in Nepal and came back home, I had no job, no skills, and a hell of a lot of anger. And if you think Rap pays child support—"

"Gee, that's tough," Jan cut in. "I hear worse than that every day at AA meetings, Dana." She gestured toward the trailers. "These people don't have any of your advantages. They take the shit you and Rap feed them because they've got no choice. Don't you see? When people have no choice and you do, and you take advantage of the fact that they have no choice, that's exploitation. And it sucks."

Dana looked at Jan, raking her eyes up and down the familiar lines of her. Thin, passionate, strung out, hyper Jan with her emotions on the surface. No protective layers of booze or dope to soften the hard edges of reality. There was a terrible honesty about Jan; she talked as though the whole world were an AA meeting where she could share her deepest truth and be heard without consequences.

But that wasn't true. She was in the real world now, and there would be consequences.

"What are you going to do about it?" Dana asked.

"What I have to do. See that it stops. See that these people aren't used anymore."

"You do that and you'll get them all deported." Dana's voice held a hint of gloat. "Is that your idea of helping the poor and downtrodden—have them shipped back to countries where they'll starve at best and be tortured at worst? You turn us in, Jan, and you condemn the people you say you care about." She paused and then moved in for the kill. "At least let us get Joaquín Baltasar out of here. He's at the Migrant Rest Center and we've got to move him quickly. After that, we'll get the others out and it will all be over anyway."

After a minute Jan said, "Okay. I see your point. But if it continues, I'll have no choice but to go to the authorities."

Unlike Jan, Dana was an able liar. She nodded her agreement. "Fair enough," she agreed. "Come back in three days and these trailers won't be here." She didn't say where they would be—Rap undoubtedly had several fallback locations. The factory wasn't in trailers for nothing. Mobility was a major asset to their operation.

But Jan wasn't stupid. "And I don't mean setting up again behind someone else's cornfield. I mean the whole show shut down. Nobody sweating it out in these sardine cans. Or else. I mean it, Dana. I'll do whatever it takes."

So will I, sister, Dana thought. *So will I.*

And if I don't, Rap will.

CHAPTER SEVENTEEN

The old Rivoli Bar was gone, a victim of urban renewal—or, as we used to call it in those days, Negro removal. So when Rap and I decided to meet for an after-dinner drink, we settled for a fern bar in the Portside shopping complex. There were no painted wooden airplanes hanging from the ceiling, no old-fashioned bowling game with a real wooden ball and miniature pins, no hookers lounging on barstools waiting for the guys from the third shift.

But one thing hadn't changed. "Still the same old Rapper," I said, my words coming out a tad slurred. Three rum-and-Cokes in thirty minutes will do that to you. "You always used to say there were two kinds of people: those who seduce and those who are seduced. And you're still a seducer, aren't you? You're still Coyote the Trickster."

Rap raised his glass in a mock-salute; he was still on his first gin-and-tonic. Always in control, the Rapper. Always watching and waiting for the other person to show weakness.

"At least I know where I stand with you," I continued. "Or should I say I take comfort in the fact that I never have known and never will know where I stand with you. That, at least, is predictable and therefore safe." I was under the illusion that my ability to construct complex sentences constituted proof positive of sobriety.

He spread his skinny arms wide in a gesture of openness

that didn't fool me for a minute. "Hey, Little Sister," he said, slurring the sibilants, "what you see is what you get."

"How many businesses do you have?" I considered this a very penetrating question.

"I own a store," he answered, his gray eyes widening to show sincerity. "Sounds of Silence. Stereos, radios, a little recording equipment—"

"Stop right there." I held up a hand. "Recording equipment as in little tiny gadgets you can put in a cigarette lighter? Telephone bugs? How much of the stuff you sell in there is legal according to the FCC?"

"I know you like murder mysteries, Cassie, but you're talking James Bond, not real life."

"Cut the shit, Rap. I've known you too long to believe—"

"Correction." The sharp voice sliced through my words. "You knew me for one summer a long, long time ago. Don't pretend you know thing one about me, okay? And don't believe everything you hear from my darling ex-wife, either. She'd like nothing better than to find out I'm up to my ears in illegal shit. It would confirm her good judgment in walking out on me. Never mind that it was nearly thirty years ago and that both of us were very different people back then."

"Were you?"

"Weren't you?"

He had me there. If I'd changed, why couldn't I believe he might have done the same?

Because he looked like the same old Rap, for one thing. Oh, thinner hair, a touch of gray, more lines in the lean face. But the same gimlet gray eyes, the same restless hands, the same whippet body. The same gleam of rapacious intelligence in those unforgettable eyes. The same hint of danger, the same go-to-hell attitude.

It was Wes I'd wanted. It was Ted I got. It was Rap, I realized with sudden drunken understanding, who'd made me shiver all the way down to my toes. What I'd thought was a mixture of fear and loathing turned out to be plain old sexual chemistry.

I shivered now. "Goddamn air conditioning," I muttered.

I picked up my glass and downed the watery dregs of my drink.

Rap signaled the waiter for another round. I promised myself I'd nurse this one. I glanced out the window, to where the High Level Bridge spanned the Maumee River. It was getting dark, and lights from the bridge twinkled against the violet sky.

"I just can't believe," I said, trying to get the conversation back on a logical instead of an emotional plane, "that you were involved in the sanctuary movement out of pure idealism. You had to have something else going on, and I can only come up with one alternative."

"How unimaginative of you," my companion murmured. I made a mental note to return to this point, but plowed on with my original remark.

"Drugs. Cocaine, to be exact."

My bombshell fizzled. "You've been talking to Dana," Rap said. He stretched his arm over the back of the leatherette booth. "She always had a one-track mind. I'd hoped you, on the other hand, would be able to—"

"But the problem is," I went on, raising my voice, "that even if you'd shipped half the coke in Colombia to half the noses in Canada, the statute of limitations has run. So why would you have tried to kill Jan? No matter how much she might have known about your activities, the truth couldn't really hurt you anymore. It's not as if you were running for Congress or anything."

"I have never sought the bubble reputation," he replied with a half smile that reminded me of the big bad wolf. "Unlike your old flame Wes Tannock."

"Not you, too," I said. "I've had about enough of that shit from Ron. Wes was not my old flame."

Rap was the master of deception, but he wasn't going to deceive me so easily. All of this banter was a way to keep my mind off the important fact: that he had things to hide, things he didn't want Jan talking about.

I went doggedly back to my point. "The statute of limitations has run on every crime in the book except one."

"And you don't need a law degree to know what that one is, do you, Sister Cassie?" The vulpine teeth showed.

"So who did you kill?"

"When?" Rap's smile reminded me of Luke Stoddard's deep-sea smile. "Are we talking 1982 or 1969?"

Any illusion I might have had that I was in control of this conversation fled at this point. "You don't mean you believe Jan's craziness about Kenny being murdered?"

"Your sainted brother does."

"My sainted brother has been married to that crazy bitch for fourteen years and never told me." To my horror, tears clogged my voice. "Fourteen fucking years and he never said a word."

Rap was out of his seat and in mine in less than ten seconds. His long sinewy arm stretched around me and his big bony hand squeezed my shoulder. He gently guided my head toward his chest and stroked my hair.

I fell apart. Four drinks hit me all at once and I let the full impact of Ron's betrayal sink in. Rap handed me a cocktail napkin and I pressed it against my eyes and nose. Within seconds it was a soggy mess of tears and mucus.

He handed me another one, and then another and another until I'd sobbed out all my pain.

"Oh, my God," I said. I straightened up and pulled back from Rap. "I can't believe I did that."

Rap lifted his hand and a college-boy waiter appeared. "Coffee," he ordered. "Make it two."

He made no move to go back to his side of the booth. He was so close I could smell aftershave and gin, sweat and another, musky smell that I couldn't identify but which sent an electric buzz through my skin.

Joel Alan Rapaport was not a good-looking man. His nose was too big and too broken-looking, his thinning hair was a mess of uncombed kinks, and his body was too lanky to be a comfortable resting place. His voice, while insinuating, lacked the deep sexiness of Luke Stoddard's. But he was alive—every cell of his body seemed deeply involved in the business of enjoying life.

It occurred to me that I'd never known a man about whom that could be said. From Ted Havlicek to Nathan Wasserstein to Matt Riordan, I'd been drawn to driven workaholics, to men who sacrificed for their ideals. If Rap had any ideals, which I doubted, they took a back seat to his own pleasures.

I wondered what it would be like to spend a night as one of his pleasures. No strings, no commitments, no long talks about Life—just good honest sex, given and received.

What was I thinking? Rap and honest in the same sentence?

The coffee arrived. I stirred in creamer and sweetener, making a small production out of the task, as if it demanded all my concentration. I didn't look at Rap, just lifted the cup and drank a healthy swallow. As if drinking it fast could restore me to sobriety and sanity, could wipe my mind free of thoughts involving Rap and a motel waterbed.

He touched my hand. I jumped; a tarantula couldn't have gotten more of a rise out of me.

"Hey, take it easy, Little Sister," he said, rearing back in the seat. "I promise, I don't have designs on your virtue."

"Why the hell not?" The coffee mixed with the drinks in a very strange way that allowed me to feel far more in control than I was. "In the first place, I'm not a kid anymore, and in the second place, I doubt that would have stopped you if you'd wanted me. So," I said, brushing hair off my sweating forehead, "why didn't you?"

"Why didn't I what, Cassie? Lay you down and fuck you under the weeping beech?"

I was not so far gone that this reference escaped me. "What the hell do you mean by that?"

His ugly-sexy face broke into a smile of pure mischief. "What do you think I mean by that?"

He couldn't know about that night with Wes.

Or could he?

And if he did—how had he found out?

That thought was eclipsed by another, more important, one. More than sex had happened under the weeping beech that summer.

"What do you know about Kenny's death?" I slid over to the edge of the booth and turned to face him.

"You've decided I didn't poison the little twerp after all?"

"Do you think he was poisoned?"

"You're the one asking the questions, Counselor. I don't know if he inhaled the stuff on his own or if somebody murdered him. I didn't care much then, and I care even less now. Poor kid's been dead longer than he was alive."

"Do you think he ratted us out back in '69?"

His long sigh sounded like a sincere reaction to looking back at our younger selves. "I did at the time. Hell, we all did at the time. And then when that DEA guy was killed in 1982, I thought Jan might have been right about someone tipping off Koeppler. But when she split, I decided maybe she'd been the one who sold us out."

"That doesn't make any sense. Why would the feds indict her if they—" I broke off. My own experience in criminal law told me how naive I sounded. "You think they set up the whole indictment thing as a cover? That they made it look as if they were after Jan, when she was really on their side? But then, when she ran away—"

He interrupted me. "At the time, I didn't believe she ran away. For one thing, she didn't have the kind of connections that could have kept her hidden for so long if they'd really wanted her found. I figured the feds had her in the witness protection program."

"But if they'd done that," I pointed out, "why wouldn't they have gone to trial? The witness protection program is for witnesses, and Jan never testified against anybody."

"One of the many flaws in my reasoning," Rap agreed cheerfully.

Too cheerfully. A complacent Rap was a Rap I wasn't getting to. I ran another idea up the flagpole. "Maybe they just wanted to shut down the operation. To strike fear into everybody's heart so that the sanctuary runs would stop even if nobody went to jail."

No salute. "Could be."

"Or maybe they wanted a deal. Use the threat of prosecution to get somebody else to roll over, and then drop the case once they had what they want. But who,'' I asked, my voice deliberately wondering, ''would they possibly want more than they wanted the sanctuary movement? Could it be that the feds' real target was the biggest drug trafficker in northwest Ohio?''

Still no reaction. No hint that I was hitting a nerve. ''If you mean me, then you're wrong on two counts. One, I was never more than a low-level middleman. And two, I was never arrested.''

''Maybe there was a good reason for that,'' I suggested. I let the idea roll around my mind. Rap as the informer. Rap as the agent provocateur—the guy who instigates crimes instead of just reporting crimes to the authorities. Hadn't it been Rap who'd come up with the parathion idea in the first place? Hadn't he always wanted to do the most radical, most out-there political action possible?

If I'd been a recruiter for the FBI, I couldn't have done better than Joel Alan Rapaport.

CHAPTER EIGHTEEN

Pumped high, pumped for action. Ready to rock and roll, brothers and sisters. *After midnight, we gonna let it all hang out.* The sounds of Clapton's guitar sang in Rap's head. After midnight was his time, Coyote's time.

He sprayed sand with the tires of his Jeep as he pulled into the tiny parking area behind the makeshift dock. He jumped out almost before he stopped the car, his own engine racing. After midnight, and he was ready for action. Ready for the real thing, not the do-gooder shit he did with Dana.

Night hung over the dune, yet the scene looked much as it had when he and Dana had waited for Jan to arrive with Miguel. The deserted lakefront, the hidden launching area. Moonlight instead of high summer sun glinting off the waves. Two broad-shouldered Spanish-speaking men in the back of the car instead of a refugee family. But the rest was the same; the *Layla* rocked in her homemade slip, eager to feel his hands along her smooth lines, ready to buck under his throttle like a fifty-dollar whore.

God, he loved the midnight runs. This was the real action, the dance with danger he loved better than anything.

The man Rap knew as *La Culebra*, the Snake, opened the passenger door. The second man he didn't know by name or nickname; the Snake did all the talking for both. All the talking and all the paying.

They all had nicknames. The sunlight refugees had families, had been dissenters, rebels, political activists back home. The midnight men had nicknames that told of their cruelty, their ruthlessness. *La Culebra, Señor Muerto, El Capitán.* The sunlight families fled terror; the moonlight men caused it. They were the *oficiales*, the torturers, the men with uniforms who came in the night and disappeared people.

Now they were disappearing. Rap loved the irony of it. They who had disappeared so many others would themselves disappear over the horizon of Lake Erie, never to be seen again.

La Culebra handed over the payoff, *la mordida*, the bite. A nice fat bundle that squished in his hand as he squeezed it. Rap opened the bag and stuck in a finger. It came out powdered with white crystals. He lifted the finger to his mouth and let the cold sting his tongue. Ice. Freeze. Like the stuff the dentist uses to numb your gums. This stuff would numb out a lot of noses up North. Primo. He nodded to the Snake and pointed at the boat. Passage paid in full. Now they could board.

At first one or two of the moonlight brigade had tried to hand him a genuine diamond ring or a bar of gold instead of coke. But word got around, and now there was no bargaining, no attempt to substitute goods that might be traceable for the one commodity South America produced better than any other place on earth. One thing about the moonlight men, they were very good at following orders.

In the bushes, behind a tree, Jan watched, binoculars held steady. If Rap had Coyote's shape-changing trickster ways, she possessed the unrelenting gaze of the owl.

She'd known Rap was up to something, something probably even Dana didn't know about. So she'd followed him along Route 2 heading east until she was certain he was heading for Crane Creek, for the boat. Then she'd hung back and entered the deserted dune road after giving him a long head start. She'd driven without lights, slowly and quietly, then parked behind tall reeds. Her little VW bug was easy to conceal.

Rap took a taste. Coke passed from plastic bag to finger to nose.

Jan knew a drug deal when she saw one. She'd been right. Rap was getting paid. Not in this to save the refugees, he did moonlight business on his own. Business that just might interest the feds enough to put an informer in the group.

Business that he'd kill to protect.

The question was, what was Jan going to do about it?

Rap ordered the men onto the boat. They walked with heavy landlubbers' steps across the powdery sand. Rap held the boat steady as one, then the other lumbered on board.

She was a good boat, the *Layla*, a lithe craft with all the speed and unpredictability of a panther. She was small for the families, who had to crouch under the cabin roof on the daylight runs, but she was a perfect night boat.

The lake was quiet; miniature whitecaps lapped the shore. Beach grass grew on the dunes; marshy areas ringed the clearing where Rap had built his short pier. The water was fresh, not salt, so trees hid the beach from the road. It was a perfect launching area for illicit operations.

The nameless man stumbled as the boat lurched. He fell heavily against the side, cursing in gutter Spanish. Rap smiled under cover of night, ducking his head under the hull. He loved it when these macho monsters acted like sissies, cowering as each wave slapped the sides of the boat.

He gunned the motor softly, muffling the sound as best he could. Noise during daylight was okay, a pleasure boater's shout of pride. At night it called too much attention. Rap's wake was as low and his engine as quiet as even Dana could have wanted as he guided the boat out of the inlet onto the lake.

She glided over the wavecrests like a paper plane held aloft by wind eddies. A sweet craft, the *Layla*, the best money he'd ever spent. Rap let the spray of lake water hit his face, tasting its musk. There was an undertone of corruption in Lake Erie's depths; pollution halted but not erased. It smelled of industry, of dead fish, of rotten weeds, of nature dying without hope of rebirth.

Rap let the flavor linger on his lips, then licked it off. He loved the stink of the lake, loved its corrupt depths, savored its taste. He was one with its dirty, silvery, sweet-sour essence.

A clear night. Rap preferred fog, even rain. Not a storm; that might bring the Coast Guard. But this limpid evening when the moon was bright as a streetlamp had its own dangers. He shrugged; at least he'd see an approaching craft in advance.

Plenty of smugglers had made this trip. Prohibition was a prosperous time for the small boat owners of Port Clinton and Put-In-Bay. A quick trip to Canada, and you came home with hundreds of dollars' worth of good booze. No grain alcohol—name brands from England. And who could patrol an entire Great Lake? Only the main docks were watched, and those sporadically. Even now, marijuana made its way across the lake, into Canada from the United States. Rap had done a couple of those runs himself, until he'd come to see that grass was kid stuff compared to the Spanish gold he carried now.

After twenty minutes of wave-bumping, spray-in-the-face motorboating, the Snake leaned over the side and threw up his dinner. He said nothing, not even to his companion, just slid his cookies into Lake Erie and sat up straight, as though nothing had happened. His face was green in the pale moonlight, but there was no expression on it.

Rap had deliberately done the number with the boat; these Latinos were inlanders, not used to the water, and he liked to take the starch out of them by showing them what he could handle that they couldn't. It equalized the fact that he'd never put electrodes on a guy's balls—and they had.

Jan waited till the boat was out of sight of land before she turned on her flashlight. Even with Rap far away, on the boat, she hadn't dared risk a light he might glimpse and remember. She had no illusions about her safety if Rap knew she'd spied on him.

She let the flashlight make a tiny second moon on the path, following its erratic course back to her car. She'd hidden it in deep reeds, where it wasn't visible from the main drive. As she walked toward it, her feet sloshed into marshland. She hoped the car was all right; she hadn't realized the tide was rising.

By the time she reached the car, panic had set in. The wheels were deep in mud. What if she couldn't get the car out before Rap came back? What if he caught her? God, it would be so easy to dump a body out here in the reeds.

She opened the car door with sweaty hands that shook as she put her key in the ignition. What if the noise of the car starting carried across the lake? What if—

No, that was stupid. The *Layla* would be making her own engine noise. Rap couldn't hear or see her car, if she got it out before he came back. If she didn't get stuck in eight inches of merciless Lake Erie mud.

The engine started with a grinding sound. "Okay, here goes," she said to herself. "The acid test." She shifted from park into reverse and found herself literally spinning her wheels. Mud flew from under the rear tires; she felt the car sink deeper into black ooze.

Rap could come back any time; he wasn't necessarily meeting the *Esmeralda* at the daylight rendezvous point. If he came back and found her, what would he—

She knew all too well what he'd do, what he'd have to do. She had to get the hell out—and fast.

She stepped out of the car and turned on her flashlight, aiming the beam at the rear tires.

The flashlight startled Dale Krepke. Who else was out here? And how had anyone managed to get so close without him seeing? He left his dirt bike and crept through the brush toward the source of the light.

The sound of a car starting guided him closer to the spot. He grinned as the unmistakable whine of wheels spinning in mud greeted his ears. Whoever was out here was stuck like a fly in a spiderweb. And he was going to be the spider.

"How long?" The Snake's accent turned the *h* into a *j*. It was an accent Rap could, and did, mimic with comic effect.

But the voice was a harsh rasp, used to being obeyed. Nothing funny about the voice; it had all the cold-blooded menace of the man's nickname.

Rap shrugged, then shouted above the motor's roar. "Not long. We should see the *Esmeralda* in five or ten minutes." Abruptly he cut the engine and sat back on the lake-soaked seat.

"Why we stop?"

"We wait," Rap answered. He pulled a pack of soggy cigarettes from his pocket. "Smoke?"

They all smoked. Rap didn't inhale anymore, just lit the thing and held it in his hand to show how friendly he was. An act of solidarity. First the henchman, then the Snake lit up. The moonlight and the boat lights were joined by three tiny red circles in the silvery darkness.

When he'd had five puffs, Rap tossed his butt into the lake. It hissed as the lit end hit cool water. Then he pulled the Luger from under the control panel, savoring the hard swish of metal on metal as he pulled back the clip. The sound echoed across the water; the passengers jumped at a noise they knew as well as the babble of their own children.

Rap had one second to enjoy the stark terror in the Snake's eyes before he pulled the trigger. The man fell backwards into the lake. That was the beauty of a thin boat like the *Layla*; there was only one place to fall and that was off. Over the side. Man overboard.

The henchman jumped up and rushed Rap, huge ham fists making for Rap's neck. Two shots this time, both in the heart. Blood to spare, some of it on the seats, some on Rap's windbreaker. Shit! He liked things neat, but sometimes a mess couldn't be helped.

Rap hefted the man's bulk over the side and watched him float next to his boss.

He swabbed fresh blood from the deck with a mop and pail, turned the engine back on, and headed for the Ohio shore.

Jan was up to her rear bumper in mud; the only good news was that it was fairly wet. She needed something to put under her wheels, something to give a little traction. She reached into the back seat and stared down at a towel exactly like the one that had been wrapped around Ron's legs during the ride to Crane Creek. Exactly like the one she'd held against Miguel's bleeding stomach.

She couldn't think about that. She couldn't think about the fact that what she'd done to help people could also result in death.

She lifted the towel and placed it under her right front tire. Wedged it under, so the wheel would have purchase when she next turned the engine over. She had to get out before Rap came back.

As she squished her way back to the driver's seat, the sound of a boat engine cut across the night sounds of bird and wave.

Was it the *Layla* returning, so soon?

How could Rap have met the *Esmeralda* in such a short time? It wasn't possible—or did Rap have another rendezvous point, a second contact in Canada? Her thoughts tumbled over one another and she fumbled with the ignition key, her fingers messy with Lake Erie mud.

I have got to get out of here.

Rap pulled the throttle back and let her roar like a lion. He opened his mouth wide, eating lake water, howling like Coyote. His cargo was dead. He was alive. He had a hard-on the size of Michigan between his legs. Before he took the boat into her slip, he cut the engine, unzipped his jeans, and jerked off, his come shooting into the lake, mingling its musk with the smell of corruption.

The car bounced backwards, fell into the hole again. Jan put the gear into drive and rocked forward, then gunned back into reverse.

One towel wasn't enough. The rear wheels dug deeper into the mud. Jan turned off the motor and rested her head on the steering wheel. What the hell was she going to do?

Rap buttoned his fly hastily, the car noise jolting him into sobriety after his danger high. The cops? Feds? Who was out here in the middle of nowhere? Whoever it was could only be after one thing.

Him.

He jumped off the boat and stumbled through the weeds until he found a break in the bushes.

There was a woman standing next to a shadow that might have been a car. Rap squinted; his binoculars were on the boat.

The woman bent down and he saw the movement of hair.

Long hair. Not Dana, then.

Jan. Jan out here spying. On him.

How much had she seen? And what would she do about it?

No, that wasn't the question. What would he do about her? And how soon?

The second watcher knew what he was going to do about it. Dale Krepke had returned to his bike, binoculars at his eyes. He hadn't bothered following Rap out to the dunes; he'd just staked out the place where the *Layla* was moored.

The fact that Joel Rapaport hadn't even bothered to move the boat confirmed Dale's suspicion that the dealer was paying off the people who were supposed to enforce the law.

And now he had proof that someone else was involved as well. He trained his lenses on the little car trapped in the dune and memorized its license number. He'd run the plate back at the office. And no matter what anybody said, he was going to be the guy who finally brought Joel Alan Rapaport to justice.

Jan took off her jacket and placed it under the other wheel. She hopped back in the driver's seat and rocked the car back and forth, jerking the stick and pumping the clutch in a frenzy of fear. God, please, she prayed, don't let Rap find me.

At last, the car lurched forward and promptly stalled. But it was no longer mired. She started it again and roared out of her hiding place, no longer concerned about the noise. Rap must have heard the car; the only thing she could count on now was that he had no idea who was driving.

CHAPTER NINETEEN

I woke up feeling like hell. Like I was in hell, to be exact. I hadn't turned up the air conditioning when I came home and fell into bed wearing just a pair of panties. The sweat-soaked sheets were tangled around my legs, and to make matters worse, there was a persistent knocking at the door.

It was late morning. That much I could tell by the amount and brightness of the sunlight trying to force its way in through the slats in the mauve blinds.

"Coming," I called in a voice that could have sung the baritone part in a light opera. I felt as if I'd smoked a pack of cigarettes. My head pounded and I was afraid I was going to be sick before I reached the door to stop that horrible knocking.

I stumbled to the closet and slipped on an oversized T-shirt, then veered toward the door. "What?" I asked, opening the door on Zack, who stood in the doorway with a look of exaggerated patience on his face—and, more to the point, a thermal pitcher of coffee in one hand, a mug in the other.

"Bless you," I said with feeling, opening the door wide.

"No problem," he replied. He made for the tiny table next to the television cabinet. "I've been where you are a few times myself."

"Hey, don't get the wrong idea." I padded toward the table.

"I don't get drunk like this every night. It was the pressure of the situation. I got a little carried away." Actually, I'd gotten very carried away, staying in the bar with Rap and talking over old times until I got sloppy and maudlin. We'd covered everything from the Fourth of July tornado to Sunday evening band concerts at the Toledo Zoo, with lions and peacocks adding new notes to the Gershwin tunes.

"Using alcohol to push away feelings is one of the warning signs of alcoholism," Zack replied. There was a fanatic's gleam in his eyes; I was in for the lecture all reformed drinkers seem obliged to deliver to anyone who has more than three in a row.

"Do tell me the others," I muttered. I could forgive this man almost anything for bringing the coffee, but gratitude could go only so far.

Irony was lost on this guy. He started ticking them off on his blunt fingers. "One is drinking alone. Another is having blackouts, not remembering things that happened while you were drunk."

"I know what a blackout is."

"Have you ever had one?"

"Once or twice. Not for a long time. In college, you know how that is."

"If you're admitting to one or two," he said quietly, "then there were probably four or five. And not as long ago as you'd like me to believe, either."

I swallowed the coffee black and hot, letting it scald my tongue. I used the time to think. There were two options here: I could throw Zack out of my room and give him hell for insinuating that I had anything in common with a self-professed drunk—or I could admit that I scared myself sometimes with my dependence on alcohol.

The truth was, I'd gone out with Rap determined to stay in control, to limit my drinks so I could keep my head and use the opportunity to interrogate the man I suspected of keeping so many secrets. Instead, I'd had too many rum-and-Cokes, I'd fallen apart, I'd been brought home and deposited in my room like a sack of potatoes by the guy I'd hoped to put on the defensive.

But I wasn't ready to share all this with a missionary from AA.

"I need to get dressed," I said, not looking at the big biker. "Could you please give me some privacy?"

"Sure," he replied. He reached over and took my hand in his huge one. I took quick note that the hand belonged to the "Jesus Saves" arm. "If you ever want to talk, you know where I am."

I nodded. *Don't call me, I'll call you.*

He left. I stood alone in the disheveled room, noting for the first time that I'd left my clothes in a pile on the floor, my purse overturned on the chair next to the little table.

I had no memory of coming back to this room. No memory of undressing.

No memory of Rap bringing me home.

Blackout.

For all I knew, Rap had thrown me on the bed and—

But who would want to? Who would want a motionless, sodden lump of drunken womanhood underneath him?

Bile rose in my throat. Tears started in my eyes.

I'd get a cab, head to the airport, get on a plane, and go back to Brooklyn.

I couldn't face Rap again, not after last night.

I couldn't face Zack again, not after the pitying look in his eyes.

And if Zack knew, then Ron knew.

I lifted the cup to my trembling lips and tried to stop my tears with lukewarm coffee.

It didn't work; I was sobbing when I put down the cup and ran to the bathroom.

I ran a seriously hot shower and stood in the tub with my face directly under the nozzle. Hot water mingled with tears and mucus until the crying stopped. By the time I stepped out, I was rosy-red and a little more clearheaded. I ran cold water and downed three aspirin. While I was toweling myself off, the phone rang.

It was Luke Stoddard. "I think you and I should talk about this new development," he said in his dark-chocolate voice.

For one wild, panicky moment, I thought he was referring to my drunken night with Rap. Then I guessed the real reason for his call.

"By new development," I replied, after clearing my throat, "I take it you mean the fact that your prime defendant is in a coma."

It was a tremendous relief to talk about something unrelated to my use of alcohol.

"Well, if I've only got one defendant," Stoddard said, "then I'll have to make my best case against him."

"Or find out if he knows the things you thought Jan knew," I replied, hoping to hell I'd made sense. I poured another cup of coffee and lifted it to my lips.

"I could take you to lunch," the prosecutor offered.

I grabbed a glance at the bedside clock: 10:45. "Make it brunch in about twenty minutes and you're on."

"I'll pick you up at your hotel."

I surveyed that portion of my limited wardrobe that wasn't lying in a rumpled heap on the floor. Linen and silk, I decided. Even if we weren't going to court, it was important that I maintain the image of New York lawyer, big-city hotshot. I turned on the air conditioner and sat in front of it as I slid my last pair of clean panty hose over my legs.

Thinking of my former life in New York brought a sharp memory of old Pops, standing in the corridor of the Kings County Supreme Court, begging me not to abandon him.

I was due in Harry the Toop's courtroom an hour ago. My head pounded and my stomach wouldn't remain still. But I had to call and make my apologies. And hope poor old Pops wasn't either warming a cell or fleeing a bench warrant.

It took several minutes and more than one operator to get me connected to the judge's chambers. I explained the situation to the law secretary, who took the opportunity to read me the riot act for waiting until the last minute—no, an hour after the last minute—to make the call.

Pops was in the courtroom, sitting in the second row, hat

in hand. That more than anything else was what got me the adjournment. He'd had the guts to show up, knowing he might be tossed in the can.

The irony struck me as I put the receiver down. When I'd first come to Toledo, I'd have given anything for an excuse to get on the next plane to Brooklyn, and now I'd begged for the chance to stay.

I knocked on Ron's door to tell him where I was going. He and Zack were on their way out to the hospital to see Jan. "I hope she's better," I said, not meeting the eyes of either.

Stoddard drove a white Cadillac. I walked around to the passenger side before he had time to step out and open the door for me. I slid in, running my hand appreciatively over the dark red leather.

"What are you in the mood for?" he asked as he maneuvered the long car out of the parking lot.

I'd always considered eggs a good hangover remedy. And they were even better with hot peppers. "Do you know where we can get huevos rancheros?"

"There's a great Mexican place out by the airport."

"Okay." I hoped he wouldn't talk business before we started eating. I needed food and more caffeine if I was going to hold my own in a negotiation.

But what were we going to negotiate? Did Ron know things he could trade for his freedom?

If he did, he hadn't told me about them. But that was nothing new; he hadn't told me he and Jan were married either.

Perhaps my best tactic would be to act as if Ron had information Stoddard would want—so long as that information wouldn't hurt Jan, if and when she woke up.

We passed neatly manicured suburban streets and shopping centers, movie theaters and fast-food joints. A blue sign with a plane on it gave the only clue that we were heading in the direction of the airport.

Had it only been two days ago that I'd landed at that tiny airport in the commuter plane from Cleveland? My head started to pound again.

Stoddard followed the blue airplane signs and finally took

a right turn into a gravel parking lot next to a sprawling white clapboard restaurant. The name, Loma Linda's, promised Tex-Mex, as did the spicy smell in the air. I perked up just getting out of the car.

The place was unpretentious; wooden tables and yellowing posters of Mexico on the walls. We ordered. Stoddard asked for a margarita, but I opted for more coffee. I dipped a tortilla chip into the salsa and smiled as my taste buds came alive.

While we waited for our food, I organized my thoughts. I liked taking the offensive with my opponents. I searched my brain for something I could say that would send a message to the U.S. attorney that I wasn't here to be bullied, that I had weapons of my own.

But did I?

Before I had a chance to come up with one, Stoddard took away my initiative. "I told you I wanted Jan Gebhardt," he said, "but I should have explained that I wanted her as a witness. I didn't think she'd turn state's evidence voluntarily, not with Harve Sobel turning her arrest into a crusade, so I was hoping you and your brother could persuade her to tell me what I need to know."

"What you need to know about what?" A young woman in a Mexican peasant blouse and ruffled skirt set a plate of eggs, beans, rice, and soft tortillas in front of me. I nodded my gratitude and picked up a fork, grateful both for the food and for the chance to think.

Was he talking about Rap's drug dealing? And what if anything did Ron know about whatever Rap was up to?

The refried beans were creamy and topped with melted cheese. I rolled them around in my mouth and let the rich, earthy flavor sink in. I lifted a forkful of egg and savored the hot chili peppers. A few more bites, and the fog lifted ever so slightly.

"Some of your friends were using the sanctuary movement, and the refugees, as a cover for making counterfeit airplane parts."

"I know." I forked another piece of egg and assumed a

bland air that said nothing Stoddard told me was going to be a surprise. "Dana Sobel told me."

The deep-sea smile showed white, even teeth in his dark face. "Did she also tell you she made a deal with Walt Koeppler back in 1982?"

One positive benefit of a hangover is that your reactions are dulled. This can pass for calm indifference if you play it right. I tried to play it right, looking into Stoddard's brown eyes and asking, "So why wasn't Rap prosecuted at the time?"

It was the right question. The smile left Stoddard's face. "Because that was then and this is now."

I forked another bite of egg as I deciphered this remark. "Nineteen eighty-two," I murmured. "Reagan in the White House. Not exactly the most favorable climate for government regulation. So faulty parts in airplanes mostly flown overseas didn't merit a full-scale prosecution."

"The word came down from on high. Bury the whole thing. No negative publicity about plane crashes. Sawicki was called in and told in no uncertain terms that novice U.S. attorneys didn't prosecute cases that belonged to the FAA."

"And of course the FAA put the whole thing in the dumper," I finished. "It's only now, with a Democrat in charge and a few plane crashes that there's a big flap in Washington about airline safety. So that's why this has surfaced again."

The deep-sea smile was back. "And guess who happens to be the investigator general over at the National Transportation Safety Board?"

I remembered now that I'd seen Catherine Sawicki on television. A fortyish blond with a taste for navy suits with white piping. A midwestern girl playing hardball with the big boys. And now she wanted vindication on the charges she'd tried to bring fourteen years ago.

"Who quashed the investigation? Who asked Sawicki to lay off?" I knew the answer. Rap, of course. Rap with his little deals and his secrets and his dirty money. I just wanted to see whether or not Stoddard would say the name out loud.

Now the smile threatened to eat me like the little fish I was in this particular pool. "A congressman named John Wesley Tannock."

I tried and failed to dismiss Stoddard's assertion. Wes and Tarky had made a point of reminding us that they weren't involved in the sanctuary movement, but that didn't mean Wes couldn't have done a favor for a constituent. But would he really have been stupid enough to cover up for Rap?

I would definitely follow up on Stoddard's information—after I went back to my room and lay down with an icebag on my head for several hours.

And never again, not in the history of time, would I take another drink.

But when Stoddard dropped me at the motel, Ted Havlicek was waiting for me in the lobby. "I've been thinking," he said, "about that notebook Kenny was keeping."

My head still pounded, but this was too promising a line of inquiry to be cut off. "Do you know where it is?"

He shook his head. "But I know where mine are. And maybe I wrote down something that might help us."

"I thought reporters never kept their notes, in case some lawyer comes along and subpoenas them." I was half teasing, but I also didn't want to waste my time on a wild-goose chase when I could be sleeping off the rest of my hangover.

Ted gave me the crooked smile I remembered. He'd capped his teeth, but they were still engagingly off-kilter. "I was a kid, Cass. Those were my first-ever real reporter notebooks. I'd be willing to bet they're in my mom's attic."

He walked me to his rented Honda and opened the door to the passenger's side. He drove along city streets, refusing to take the expressway. We passed dilapidated storefront blocks that were a sharp contrast to the spiffed-up downtown. Finally he turned on a street of large duplex houses and pulled up behind a pickup truck parked at the curb.

The senior Havliceks were out; a note on the kitchen table informed Ted that they were at the movies. Ted got a stepladder and removed the hatch to the attic, which was filled with table lamps, ceramic figurines, a bowling ball in a powder blue case, and several years' worth of children's outgrown clothes.

It took us over an hour, but finally I opened a cardboard box that had Central Catholic High School yearbooks on top. I lifted them off, resisting an impulse to find a particularly geeky picture of young Ted. Underneath, stacked neatly in two piles, were tan-colored steno pads.

"Bingo!" I cried, lifting one pile in the air and waving it at Ted, who sat on the other side of the room rummaging through a second carton. He raised himself to his feet and walked over to where I knelt. He took the stack from my hand and opened the top one. "Yeah," he said, "these are from '69, all right."

I reached for the second pile. The top one contained an interview with Abrahan Murillo, leader of the migrant union. I flipped through it and set it aside.

The second one had Kenny Gebhardt's name in pencil on the cover.

My breath felt trapped in my chest. Sweat congealed on my skin and a shiver shook me. This notebook was Kenny's. That poor doomed kid wrote in this thing the very week he died.

"Ted," I said, my voice sounding strange even to myself, "I think this one's Kenny's."

He put down the stack of notebooks in his hand and leaned over my shoulder. "How did that get here? He never gave it to me."

"Maybe he just shoved it into your desk at the Amigos Unidos office. Maybe he figured nobody would notice it there."

I lifted the cardboard cover. This was the moment of truth. The moment when Kenny Gebhardt, dead almost twice as long as he'd been alive, would name his own killer.

The pages inside held words, scrawled in a boyish hand, but the notes were lacking one very important element. Instead of names, Kenny had used symbols. Symbols I didn't recognize. Symbols I couldn't relate to any of the people I'd known that summer.

I showed the page to Ted. He shook his head. "I don't know

what the hell this means,'' he said, his voice edged with frustration. ''Here we found the damn thing, and we can't read it. It might as well have stayed in this stupid box for all the good it's going to do us.''

CHAPTER
TWENTY

July 17, 1982

Walt Koeppler wore a beige shirt, beige pants, tan desert boots. Even his eyeglass rims were the exact tint of flesh-colored Band-Aids. He looked like a Thurber cartoon, all roundness and paunch and balding forehead.

He scared the hell out of her.

But the last thing Dana Sobel ever did was let people know she was scared. She'd perfected the art as a serious little girl with more brains than beauty, honing her skills in chess tournaments that took her to the state championships. Winning through intimidation: the best gift her father ever gave her.

She sat in the INS office in the green and white federal building in downtown Toledo with her feet firmly planted on the floor, glaring into the face of the man behind the desk, daring him to scare her.

Which he did with a single question. "You have a son named Dylan Rapaport?" The voice was as deceptively bland as the rest of the man, quiet, flat, midwestern.

Dana nodded. Dylan was twelve now, tall and gangly like Rap but with her dark hair and eyes. He was a great kid, and hearing his name on this man's lips was deeply troubling.

"What about him?" Belligerence was her only ally; her tone was brusque.

"You tell me," Walt Koeppler replied. "He's been seen

near the church, near the trailers where the illegals were hidden. How much does he know about what you and your husband were doing?''

"Ex-husband," Dana corrected automatically. As if it mattered. Her deep voice rose slightly as she said, "He rides his dirt bike out there. That's all. He doesn't know a thing about the refugees."

"He does now," Koeppler countered. "He must know why Jan Gebhardt and Ron Jameson were arrested."

"He does now," she agreed. "The whole county knows now. But he didn't before." Dana clamped her mouth shut on the pleading tone she heard in her voice.

It was not the way to win chess games. *You don't have to take this shit*, she told herself. *Move your queen in and crowd him.* Staring straight into the man's strange beige eyes, she said, "This whole conversation is out of line and you know it. I have a lawyer; you can't talk to me without him being here."

He smiled a thin beige smile, waved a soft hand with tiny red hairs on it at the phone and said, "By all means, Ms. Sobel, call your father. I'm sure he cares as much about his grandson as you do."

Check. Queen taken by opponent's knight. He knew what she knew: that Harve Sobel didn't lose cases, wouldn't back down no matter whose freedom was on the line. Not even his grandson's. He'd give Dylan the best defense he could, then punch the boy on the shoulder and tell him how proud he was as Dylan marched off to the youth farm to do time for something he hadn't done. Dana had been very careful not to let Dylan get too close.

But had Rap been as careful? That was the hidden piece on this chessboard, the queened pawn waiting to pounce. How much had Rap let Dylan know?

A jolt of pure fury shot through Dana. *If that bastard involved Dylan, I'll—*

She caught herself, pulled back into the hard shell she'd created. Divide and conquer. Oldest trick in the cop book. She had no reason to believe Rap would put Dylan in danger any more than she would. This cop was messing with her head, that was all.

"There's a girl named..." Koeppler pretended to root through papers on his desk, waiting for Dana to fill in the name. She sat silent, making him finish. "...Ysabel Navarro," he went on, bringing out the name like a chessmaster moving his bishop in for the kill. Triumph underneath the flat beige tone of voice.

"Belita," Dana amended. "She's called Belita." She sighed; this little man who looked more like an insurance agent than a law enforcement officer had more pieces on the board than she.

Dylan and Belita. Why shouldn't her son spend some of his summer working at the migrant day care center at Amigos Unidos? Why shouldn't he play ball with migrant kids in the field behind Our Lady of Guadalupe? Why shouldn't he learn early that the privileges his white skin and middle-class upbringing gave him were gifts that had to be paid for?

Because Belita was up to her ears in the sanctuary movement, that's why. Because with his mother, father, and nominal boss involved, how could anyone believe Dylan didn't know what was going on?

Walt Koeppler didn't believe it. "Look," he said, his flat voice going flatter as he stared at her with his colorless eyes. "We can do this the easy way or the hard way. The hard way is you get on your high horse, call your father in and grab the headlines, make a big stink. If that happens, I got no choice; I have to involve your boy." He let the words sink in.

"Or you and I can work a deal. You tell me when and where you're going to move Joaquín Baltasar and I'll not only keep your son out of this, I'll see to it you don't go to jail for obstruction. That boy'll need one parent at home, and it might as well be you."

Dana surveyed the imaginary chessboard in front of her. On her side: a few pawns, a trapped rook maybe. Not much room to maneuver. Arrayed against her: formidable pieces ready to move in from every direction.

A good chess player knew when to quit. She tipped her king over, conceding defeat.

"Tomorrow afternoon," she said, her voice a hoarse whisper. "From the van Wormer place."

Hard folding chairs. Protestant chairs, Jan thought as she arranged them into a haphazard circle. Wednesday noon meetings didn't get many comers. She wouldn't need more than fifteen. No, make it twenty. Nobody should come into an AA meeting and have to unfold their own chair.

If she'd had to do that, if she'd had to tiptoe past the other drunks, trying not to disturb the speaker, conscious of all eyes on her, aware of the whisky still on her breath, if she'd had to lift a chair from the rack and open it without a noise, hands shaking, knees knocking—

Hell, she'd have run out the door and never come back and would probably be lying dead drunk on a bunk in the county jail right this very minute.

You couldn't have too many chairs.

Or too much coffee. Ninety degrees in the shade and she had a pot of coffee perking in the back of the room, a box of donuts next to it, going soft and mushy in the humid heat.

Jan went to the closet and pulled out the scrolls. They were faded, but their gold-edged mottoes still spoke truth, still called the warriors of sobriety to arms with slogans like "One Day at a Time" and "Easy Does It." She carefully positioned them at either side of the room, next to the Twelve Steps and the Twelve Traditions.

Behind the scrolls was a blackboard with words in Spanish and English, the legacy of the ESL class taught by Belita Navarro. The meeting room at Our Lady of Guadalupe had many uses, had seen everything from Spanish bingo games to FLAC meetings to strategy sessions for the sanctuary movement.

Which was why it was bugged. Behind the plywood panel in the closet from which Jan took the banners sat a voice-activated recording device.

Most of the words the little machine recorded were useless. But every now and then one of the cassettes yielded pure gold.

As Jan waited for the designated speaker, her fingers drummed nervously on the battered table that held the literature. It was her job to set up for the meeting and call it to order; if the speaker didn't show, she'd have to choose someone else to give the qualification or do it herself.

She didn't want to. In AA terms, that probably meant she needed to. One of the hardest things about the Program was that it made you do things you didn't want to do, even though you always felt better once you'd done them. So when eight people sat ready for the meeting to begin, and there was no sign of the speaker, Jan began to talk.

"My name's Jan, and I'm a cross-addicted alcoholic." She paused for the ritual "Hi, Jan."

She almost said aloud the words she always wanted to say after introducing herself at a meeting: *It's been twelve years since my last confession.*

"It's really hard for me to remember a time when alcohol wasn't the center of my life. It was always there, like air." Jan took a breath of the humid, heavy air in the badly ventilated room. Sweat beaded her forehead; her hair and cotton dress stuck to her skin. She'd better make this short. Everyone in this room, including her, was thinking of one thing—cold, cold beer.

"When I was really little," she continued, "I thought my Daddy had a friend named Johnnie Walker. I could picture him—a tall man with curly red hair and crinkly eyes who'd sit and color with me instead of breaking all my crayons. My mom bought me new ones later and told me not to blame Daddy because he was drunk and didn't know what he was doing."

Sympathetic nods; a nervous laugh from a woman in white polyester shorts and hightop tennis shoes.

It was strange yet comforting that the most horrendous things you could say about your family always touched a chord in someone else. As though all those years of feeling alone when you were a kid weren't really true because out there all the time were other kids feeling the exact same pain. You'd had friends and you didn't even know it.

"You might think I'd grow up hating booze, but I think now I must have decided whisky was power. It gave Dad the power to do whatever he wanted. Nothing was ever his fault."

An old man with a bright red nose—booze or too much sun or both—hung his head. Her voice grew stronger. Behind the cabinet door, the cassette whirled as it collected sound waves, trapping words like a lobster pot closing on an unlucky crustacean.

Jan twisted her lank hair in her fingers. "Then I discovered pot," she said, and once again her words were greeted by knowing nods. "But drugs weren't like booze," she explained. "They weren't for getting high, but for getting to that field of rye where the Catcher was waiting to stop me, gently and lovingly, from falling off the edge."

She ran thin fingers through her long straight hair, hippie hair, iron-straight, no style, no color job. Just natural hair, the way God made it. She went through the rest of her story almost by rote, ending with her arrest.

"So the first thing I did when I got sober was get into trouble." Her voice was barely audible. She stopped and let the words from the Big Book echo in her brain. *Our stories disclose in a general way what we used to be like, what happened, and what we are like now.*

What was she like now?

Scared.

Was that a natural response to a life suddenly without the cushion of alcohol, or was it a very real response to what was going on in her life?

It didn't matter. All that mattered was that she tell the truth as she knew it.

"I feel scared." Her voice was a tiny sound in the still, hot room. "I wake up every day and wonder if I'll get through it without a drink. I pray that I will, but I don't really know. It's been eighty-one days now, and I wonder if I'll ever know. I'm scared I'll pick up a glass of club soda and it will turn out to be vodka instead and I won't remember pouring it and I'll just drink it down anyway and pour another and then another until I pass out."

She dropped her eyes, her hair falling across her face. "I wonder if I'll always be this scared." The room sat silent, waiting to see whether she had more to say. She liked that about the rooms, liked the way people listened instead of always rushing in with words to fill the empty spaces.

Sometimes you needed empty spaces.

"I don't think it's just the booze," she said at last. The cassette resumed its spinning. "I know these people. People who are doing illegal things."

Her eyes remained fixed on the ancient, scarred table in front of her. She didn't dare raise her head. She didn't dare look into the eyes of the other drunks, knowing that whatever they thought of her would be reflected on their faces. Right now, she couldn't stand to meet other eyes, to deal with what other people thought. She needed to work this out for herself.

"I mean, the thing is, some of the stuff is illegal under the law but it's still the right thing to do. And some of the stuff is really illegal and bad. And it's all mixed up together and people's lives are at stake." She pulled hard on the strand of hair in her finger. Her scalp stung.

"I know how that sounds," she said. "I know it sounds like a soap opera or something, but it's really true. People's lives are at stake, so I have to help. I have to do this even if I get arrested again."

She sighed. "When I was drinking, I knew who my friends were. They were the ones who helped me to keep drinking, who got me drugs when I was sick. I knew who the enemy was. The cops who busted people for selling me drugs, who stopped me for driving drunk. Now," she went on, her hair swinging from side to side as she shook her head, "I don't know anymore. When you're sober, you're supposed to see things more clearly. But I don't."

Tears started in her eyes. Her voice wavered. "And that's how I am today," she finished. "Scared."

Other people started talking, telling their stories of conflicts at work, angry children, temptations to drink with old buddies. Jan tried to listen, but her thoughts were jumbled.

One thought finally pushed out all the others.

There was one person in the world she could trust. One person who would know what to do and help her do it.

Ron.

She was beaming with a newfound peace by the time the meeting ended.

CHAPTER TWENTY-ONE

It was like trying to get into the parking lot just before the Big Game. Cars were backed up to the highway, horns honking, some edging into the mainstream from feeder lanes. I started counting bumper stickers. There were about three Tannocks for every Spurrier. Of course, this was Toledo, always a Democratic stronghold.

When the car reached the lot itself, I was waved toward a space by a T-shirted volunteer wielding a fluorescent wand. The boy's shirt and baseball cap proclaimed, "Team Tannock: Go with a Winner."

On the way from car to entrance, I was stopped by no fewer than six volunteers handing out flyers. Most were Wes's, but I also received brochures from neatly dressed men and women wearing straw hats with red, white, and blue bands that read, "Spurrier Knows What *You* Need." Loud music emanated from the auditorium and minicams hefted onto the shoulders of local television techies filmed the incoming crowd.

It was reminiscent of the circus I'd been taken to when I was eight.

I walked up to one of the volunteers, a dark-skinned woman in her twenties whose Team Tannock T-shirt covered impressive breasts and was complemented by a bright red miniskirt. "I'm supposed to meet Paul Tarkanian," I said, shouting over the music and crowd noise.

"If you're with the press," she shouted back, "you'll have to talk to Ms.—"

"I'm not," I said, stepping close enough so that I could lower my voice. "I'm a personal friend. Tarky invited me to watch the debate with him."

"Oh, okay." She walked, making maximum use of the short, swingy skirt, over to a man in a cream-colored suit. He stepped over, shook my hand, and walked me toward the front of the hall.

It was a huge room, with rows upon rows of comfortable-looking, royal-blue-covered seats. The front four rows were cordoned off, a hand-lettered sign proclaiming "Press Only." On the stage, two identical tables and chairs flanked a podium with the Great Seal of Ohio embossed on the front. An American flag and an Ohio burgee stood on poles behind the twin tables, which were illuminated by pinlights against a royal blue drapery. It was austere, but it would probably look good on television.

The man in the ice-cream suit led me up a small flight of stairs onto the stage, then veered to the right, ducking behind the curtain. I followed, stepping over a snake basket of wires that reminded me of Jan hooked up to her IVs and machines. We passed a huge sound console with lights blinking and flashing. A young man with earphones fiddled with the controls and shook his head as if displeased by the results.

I threaded my way through a maze of cables, feeling a thrill of excitement at being backstage, of seeing the little men behind the Wizard of Oz. My guide opened another curtain and led me down steps and corridor to what I assumed was a green room.

". . . shouldn't parents be able to choose the school best suited to their child's needs?" The voice was Tarky's. I thought it strange that he was asking Wes a question like this twenty minutes before the debate started, but then I realized what he was doing. In law, we call it moot-courting. Helping a colleague prepare for an argument by throwing all the tough questions at him so he could practice the best response.

Wes's rich baritone filled the room. "Giving parents vouchers for private schools is one of those ideas that sounds good on paper." He paused and gave me a nod of recognition. "But in practice it means the abandonment of our public school system. A system that taught generations of children to be good Americans. A system that instills values of citizenship and diversity. A system that—"

"Excuse me, Governor," Tarky cut in, "but if that system is failing, why shouldn't parents be entitled to get the best possible education for their children without regard to whether that school is public or private?"

The smile on Wes's face diminished slightly, but he kept his voice bright. "What we need in this country," he said firmly, "is to strengthen and enhance the public schools, not put them out of business by—"

Tarky shook his head and lifted his hands in a time-out gesture. "No, Wes, I don't like that 'putting the schools out of business' line. I can just hear Spurrier saying that a business that's failing ought to be put out of business."

The aide who'd led me to the room stepped up to Wes and said, "Governor, it's almost time to go for the last-minute prep."

Wes turned to me with a smile of rueful welcome on his tanned face. "He's trying to say it's time for makeup and hair." He shook his head. "Television. Without a little powder, I'd go out there looking like Nixon, and we know what happened to him."

He stepped toward me and put a hand on my shoulder. "I'm glad you're here, Cassie. Not just here in this auditorium, but here in Toledo."

I murmured something completely untrue about being glad to be here. Wes's effusive charm tended to make me feel like a curmudgeon.

"Take the briefing book with you and study the school voucher section." Tarky handed Wes a leather portfolio.

He turned to me. "Let's go to the skybox. I've got a bar in there if you want something to drink."

The thought made me shudder. "Soda's fine," I replied.

The memory of my hangover was still fresh in my aching head.

We took a tiny elevator to a higher level, then walked along a corridor overlooking the audience. The royal-blue seats were filling up. As with the bumper stickers, I counted about three Team Tannock shirts for every one that touted Wes's opponent. Not that everyone wore campaign garb; there were suits and ties, turtlenecks and sweaters, jeans and skirts and one or two work uniforms.

The box was just that, a tiny square room with a glass wall on one side. There were three comfortable chairs, a table with a few bottles and glasses on it, and four television monitors. I settled myself in one of the chairs, let Tarky fix me a soda with ice, and considered the problem of when and how to bring up the matter of Wes's quashing of the investigation into the bogus airplane parts factory.

The band in the downstairs hall swung into a rendition of "Hang On, Sloopy." It sounded truly strange played by a full orchestra. I said as much to Tarky, who barked a laugh. "That is, believe it or not, the state rock song."

"There's a state rock song?"

"There's a state everything. The next time you see the candidate, he'll be wearing a red carnation."

"Don't tell me—the state flower."

"And our worthy opponent is never seen without a cardinal pin."

"I remember that one. State bird."

"I considered telling Wes he ought to wear the state fossil, but he drew the line at commissioning a trilobite tie tack. Said it might piss off the creationists."

Tarky picked up a remote and turned on the televisions. Each showed the stage from a different angle. One camera would focus on Wes, another on Spurrier, a third on both at once, and the fourth would roam the audience for reaction.

"All this for a statewide race?"

"I'm convinced they built this thing in hopes of luring a presidential debate. No luck yet, but with Ohio a big swing state, it just might happen next time."

Down in the hall, ushers herded the audience into seats, pushing people in toward the middle rows, bringing those in the rear up front so as to create a solid phalanx instead of letting empty seats fill the cameras.

Three people stepped onto the stage. One was Wes, wearing his famous smile, the red carnation in his lapel matching the red stripe in his tie. The second was a local newscaster. The third was a tall, slender woman with short-cropped, curly silver hair and glasses that dangled from a silver chain. Her powder-blue suit was softened at the throat with a scarf of pastel blue, pink, and yellow swirls. Sally Spurrier, former mayor of Cincinnati, looked like the firm but kind headmistress of a very exclusive girls' school.

It took a couple more minutes for the crowds to settle and the lights to dim. The newscaster introduced himself and the panel of Ohio reporters who would be allowed to question the candidates. I wondered if Ted would be among them. He wasn't.

The candidates each gave an opening statement, mostly fluff and rhetoric. I glanced at Tarky, who sat in his chair with one leg propped over the other. His pants had ridden up above the sock line, revealing an extremely hairy leg. He bit down on the unlit cigar so hard I was sure it was going to fall into his lap.

I liked Spurrier's voice. It was low, throaty, and she spoke with a slight tinge of the South, reflecting the fact that Kentucky was just across the river from her native city. She had a trick of picking up the glasses dangling from the chain around her neck and holding them as she made a point.

The first question, asked by the Akron *Beacon-Journal*, was the dreaded school voucher question. Spurrier launched into a set speech about choice and parental rights. Tarky leaned forward in his chair like a man following a particularly close football game. He grunted and muttered as Spurrier gave examples of places where voucher systems had worked wonders.

"Propaganda," he said once, and "Elitist bullshit." He took the cigar from his lips and shoved it at the screen. "Tell the truth, Sal," he urged. "Tell the voters you don't want white kids in the same school with blacks. That's what this is really about.''

It was hard to tear my eyes away from the campaign manager, but I glanced at the screen that showed Wes. He sat in classic listener pose, his face as intent as if he were hearing all this for the first time. Once or twice he shook his head slightly, as if registering the tiniest possible dissent. I had no idea which pictures were going out to the viewing audience, and, more to the point, neither did Wes. He was clearly operating on the old political principle that you're always on camera.

''Governor Tannock,'' the reporter droned in a monotone that confirmed his identity as a pencil and not a camera reporter, ''you have consistently opposed the use of school vouchers. What is your rationale for this position?''

Tarky frowned as Wes stood and walked to the podium. ''Give it to 'em,'' he urged. ''Give 'em the red meat, not the pablum.''

''The year,'' Wes began, ''is 1872. A child walks into a school and is introduced to her new classmates. The child is from Ireland and this is the first time she's ever been to school. By the time she graduates, she'll be able to read and write and get a job that lets her send money home to her family.''

''Go, Wesley,'' Tarky said. He lifted a clenched fist to the sky and waved it as if urging a running back to gain yardage.

Wes paused and looked down at the audience, moving his eyes from side to side, taking in the room. ''The year is 1896. This time the new child in class is Jewish, from a tiny village in Russia. By the time he leaves school, he's learned so much he earns a scholarship to college and becomes a doctor.''

A little clichéd, I thought, but the audience was rapt. I noted a few nods on the monitor that showed the first rows.

Wes's voice rose. ''The year is 1958. The child is black, and for the first time in her life, she's able to go to a school with an indoor bathroom and new textbooks. She grows up to become a teacher. The year is 1996, and the child has come to this country from Mexico. He needs the *same* public education, the *same* opportunity, the *same* cultural experience, that this country afforded all its other children. This child, and *all* our children, need public schools. They don't need vouchers that separate them into rich and poor, black and white, Catholic and Jewish and secular. Vouchers separate. Public schools unite."

The audience response clearly favored Wes. While Spurrier had been given a polite smattering of applause and a few raised signs that proclaimed, "School Choice Is a Family Value," people stomped their feet and whistled when Wes finished.

The next question came from the *Blade*. The woman asking the question was young enough to be a student stringer; her voice was high and breathy. But the question was a killer.

"Governor Tannock," she began, "is it true that you received a substantial donation to your 1982 congressional reelection campaign from a political action committee representing airplane parts manufacturers?"

Wes's face, shown up close on the monitor, went blank. No frown, no grimace, no dropped jaw—but the lack of expression showed he was rattled. He opened his mouth to reply, but the reporter raised a restraining hand.

"That was the first part of the question," she said. "The second part is, did you suppress an investigation into the manufacture and sale of bogus airplane parts directly after receiving such a contribution?"

I glanced at Tarky. No camera sat poised to record every nuance of his response. He'd slumped back in his chair, and his face was pale. "Fucking shit. Who the fuck put that bitch up to this? Who the fuck—"

"Luke Stoddard said the same thing to me three hours ago," I said quietly.

"Shut up. I've got to hear this." He leaned forward, clasping his hands in an attitude of what might have been prayer.

"Don't let 'em get you, John Wesley," he begged the man whose face filled the screen.

"I have never," the candidate proclaimed, his voice cracking ever so slightly, "ever allowed any contribution to influence any vote I cast when I had the honor to serve in the

House of Representatives. I have never permitted campaign contributions to dictate or influence my position on the issues. And I strongly deny any innuendo that I had anything to do with putting a stop to any investigation. You have my word that this is the first time I've ever heard anything about bogus airplane parts.''

Tarky drew a huge breath and expelled it in a long whoosh. He settled himself in the chair as if burrowing into a hiding place. Spurrier stood and gave a speech that indicated her staunch belief that bogus airplane parts were the worst thing ever to happen on the face of the earth and she, for one, was never going to be found tolerating them. It was clear she'd never heard of the issue before tonight either, but if there was political hay to be made, she'd be there with her pitchfork.

The next four questions involved taxes. Both candidates were against them. At length. I wanted to talk to Tarky, but I didn't want to be told to shut up again, so I held my fire.

The next tiny bit of fireworks came when the Cincinnati *Enquirer* raised the issue of drug use. Spurrier looked old enough and conservative enough that she could answer honestly that her lips had never wrapped themselves around a joint. But Wes was another matter. I recalled vividly the hemostat roach clip he'd carried in his pocket, and wondered how he'd answer.

"Like many people of my generation," Wes said, a look of rueful apology on his face, "I admit to experimenting with what we used to call soft drugs. One marijuana cigarette, to be exact. I decided," he went on, with a little laugh, "that I didn't like it very much, so I never had another one. And then we learned how dangerous drugs are. We learned that there is no such thing as a soft drug. All drugs are hard. All drugs destroy people. So I say to the next generation: Be smarter than we were. Say no the first time."

"Is this for real?"

Tarky shushed me with a wave of his hand. The debate wound down. On points, it was a clear victory for Wes, but then this was home territory for him. I'd been told Spurrier wiped the floor with him in her native city.

The moderator closed the session and both candidates strode to the aisles to press the flesh. I poured another club soda and waited for Wes to come backstage.

Ten minutes later the door to the skybox opened and a furious John Wesley Tannock entered the room. He pointed a shaking finger at Tarky and said in a low, thrilling voice, "You are so fucking fired. Get your shit out of the office and don't bother showing up tomorrow. You and I are finished. Finished."

CHAPTER
TWENTY-TWO

July 18, 1982

"Do you, Ronald Douglas Jameson, take this woman, Janice Elizabeth Gebhardt, to be your lawful wedded wife?"

For a wild moment, Ron considered answering in the negative. How could he, who would need help putting the ring on Jan's finger, dare to take any woman as his lawful wedded wife? What could he offer her except a lifetime of service to his terrible needs?

What he could offer her was friendship. And love. And respect. And a lot of things that didn't depend on having a whole body. He just hoped they would be enough.

He looked into Father Jerry's serene face and replied, "Yes." Then he smiled at Jan, who held out her left hand. With Father Jerry's help, he slipped the thin gold band over the slender finger. She leaned down and kissed him.

It was done. They were man and wife.

The witnesses were Father Jerry's housekeeper and Ron's home attendant. They all adjourned to the sacristy, where Father Jerry served cheese and crackers and jug wine over ice. The "reception" lasted twenty minutes, after which the bride slipped away to change from her light summer dress into shorts and a T-shirt in preparation for the truly important project of the day: getting Joaquín Baltasar safely out of Lucas County and into Canada.

"You really ought to leave before all this gets started," Father Jerry said.

Ron faced the priest. "I didn't marry Jan so I could let her carry the weight for the sanctuary movement. I did it so I could be there for her. You said the words yourself—'for better or for worse.' That means I don't run away the minute it looks like the worst is coming."

"There's nothing you can do here," the priest said. "I'm sorry to put it that bluntly, but it's the truth. We have everything under control."

Ron's face held a stubborn resolve his sister would have recognized. "Maybe so, but I'm staying."

The priest, dressed in his Roman collar for the wedding, reached up and unbuttoned it from the back. He then released the top buttons of his black shirt and slid it over his shoulders.

"Ron, you married Jan so you could protect her. But she has a need to protect you as well. That's what marriage is about, and that's why I agreed to perform the ceremony even though you're not Catholic."

He stood up and walked over to the closet at the back of the room. He hung the black garment on a hanger and walked over to a dresser, from which he removed a bright green golf shirt. "So, much as I admire your desire to be here for Jan, I also have to respect her desire to protect you. She wants you to go before we start moving Joaquín." The priest's head disappeared inside the green shirt.

"Look," Ron replied, "it's bad enough I'm not part of the plan. The most I can do is sit here and wait until it's over and Jan comes back. So please, Father, let me do that much."

"What if Koeppler charges you as an accessory?"

Ron lifted one shoulder in a shrug. "How can he? All I am is a man who came to a church to get married and stayed for a glass of wine afterwards. I just want to be here when Jan gets back. I want to share as much of her life as I can, and this is part of her life. I don't want her facing this alone."

The priest walked over and placed his hand on Ron's shoulder. He gave a nod and said, "Okay. I promised her I'd do what I could to make you leave, and I've done that. Between you and me, I think you're doing the right thing. Jan's been out there on the edge alone for too long. She needs to learn to lean on someone else for a change.''

His long face broke into a warm smile. ''I'm just glad she found you. I think you two are going to be one of the best marriages I've ever seen. Jan's a passionate woman who needs a strong purpose in life, and you can help her focus that. I don't mean just on your disability, don't get me wrong, although strangely enough, I think Jan's one of the few women in this world who could handle being married to a man as profoundly disabled as you are. She's got a lot of love and a lot of strength—and so do you.''

Ron gave the priest a grateful smile. Jan stepped out of the spare bedroom dressed in khaki shorts and a yellow T-shirt. She'd pulled her hair back in a ponytail held in place by a perky yellow ribbon. If you didn't concentrate on the lines in her face, the scars on her thin arms, she looked about fifteen.

'' 'Chantilly Lace,' '' Ron sang in a mock-bass, '' 'and a purty face. And a ponytail, hangin' down. Wigglin' walk, gigglin' talk, makes the world go round.' ''

Father Jerry took the chorus, holding his hand to his mouth as if singing into a microphone: '' 'There ain't nothin' in the world like a big-eyed girl, makes me spend my money, makes me talk real funny.' ''

Both men trailed off into laughter as they realized they'd come to the end of their musical knowledge. Jan put her hands on her hips and said, ''It's a good thing Dana isn't here. That must be the most sexist song ever recorded.''

She walked toward the wheelchair, ran her hands along Ron's shoulders and said into his ear, '' 'Oh, baby, that's what I like.' '' She stretched the words out in the Big Bopper's provocative tone and added, ''Just hold that thought, hon. I'll be back from this little jaunt before you know it.'' Her face crinkled into the bad-girl grin he liked so much. ''And then it's honeymoon city.'' She leaned down for a last kiss and then dashed out the door, but not before Ron saw the shimmer of tears in her eyes.

• • •

She was meeting Dana behind the van Wormer farm. She drove along the dirt roads and made the proper turns, but all she could think about was coming back to Ron when it was all over.

What could they do in bed? That was the question anybody who saw this marriage would ask. The truth was, she didn't know for certain. There would be kissing, lots and lots of kissing, and she could guide his hands to where her body would appreciate them most. But there was no feeling in his lower body. No way he could react as a man in the physical sense. Still, she looked forward to lying in a double bed with him, caressing and being caressed.

Sex wasn't everything. For a woman who'd been used and who'd let herself be used for more years than she cared to remember, sex wasn't even on the board. Ron could love, and love was what she needed, in every single cell of her body.

She parked next to the trailers and opened the door to the nearest one. Dana and a man wearing a baseball cap were inside; they greeted her with curt nods.

Walt Koeppler handed the binoculars to his second-in-command. "There he is." He pointed to the straw-hatted man in the bright yellow shirt who was emerging from the nearest trailer.

The man was tall and wiry, his long, tanned feet clad in huaraches. The only part of his face that was visible beneath the straw cowboy hat was the jet-black mustache. A cigar, undoubtedly a prime Havana import, protruded from his lips.

"Pretty cocky," the other INS man said. "Anybody who's ever seen a *Newsweek* would recognize him."

He turned back to his boss. "And this is the guy they think they can get out of the country without anyone noticing?"

"They're desperate," Walt replied. "They can't leave him here either. They know we're inspecting all the farms around here that use migrants." He saw no reason to inform his associate that they were staking out the van Wormer place based on inside information.

"So why don't we bust them now?"

"Because I want the boat. We go down now and we get Baltasar and Sobel. Big deal. I want them all, and I want that boat. So we wait until they reach their destination. We follow them and when we have a full house, we round them up."

Dana Sobel drove to the rear of the van Wormer farm and pulled up next to the trailer. The straw-hatted man opened the door and got in. She drove; he sat in the passenger's seat. They sped out of the trailer area toward the highway.

Walt and his companion stepped into their car and followed from a discreet distance. One thing about the long, straight farm roads, you could stay far behind and still see your quarry. Of course the bad part was, your quarry could see you in the rearview. But since Sobel knew he'd be there, he didn't anticipate any problem.

The second man to emerge from the trailer wore a Toledo University Rockets T-shirt, his tanned arms sticking out of the sleeves. His cutoff jeans were ragged and his sockless feet were thrust into ancient boat shoes. A New York Mets cap shielded his face and hid his unruly black hair, which was pulled back into a ponytail like the girl's.

From a distance, he looked just like Joel Alan Rapaport.

But the voice that emerged from the half-hidden face spoke with a Spanish accent.

"Should we go now?"

Jan looked at her watch. Dana had been gone for ten minutes. Time enough to have lured Walt Koeppler far away from the van Wormer farm.

She nodded. She and Joaquín Baltasar walked slowly toward Rap's car. He opened the door and slid into the driver's seat, while Jan walked around to the other side.

As he started the engine, Joaquín rubbed his upper lip. "I shall have a requiem mass for my mustache. It has been with me since I was sixteen. But I suppose it was necessary to remove it."

• • •

Dale Krepke lowered his binoculars. What incredible luck! Not only was the INS out of his hair, following Sobel and Che Guevara, but Rapaport was alone with Gebhardt.

He shook his head. Busted for drugs more than once, supposedly in a recovery program, but here she was sitting next to her favorite dealer. It went to show what he knew already: There was no such thing as an ex-junkie.

He stepped behind the wheel of his Jeep and kept a discreet distance as he followed the vintage Mustang. Fire-engine red. Krepke shook his head; that just showed the kind of balls Rapaport had, driving around the countryside in a car that screamed "drug dealer on the loose."

What do you say to a national hero? Jan sat in the passenger's seat of Rap's beloved Mustang and wondered whether her companion would prefer conversation or silence. Did he want to talk about the newspaper articles he'd written about the Nicaraguan *contra* activity in Honduras?

Finally she could stand the silence no longer. "I read the article about you in *Newsweek*," she said. Her fingers clutched the armrest so tightly they ached. "In fact," she went on, trying for a conversational tone, "a friend of mine wrote it. Ted Havlicek."

Her companion's face broke into a wide smile. *"Sí,"* he said, nodding his head. *"Sí, Teodoro es mi amigo."*

That was about the extent of Jan's Spanish. *Ted is my friend.* Conversation languished. She focused on the plan.

They were supposed to meet another car out on Pickle Road, near the radio station. Joaquín would step into that car and be whisked away toward the New York–Canada border, a new approach they all hoped the INS wouldn't be prepared for. Jan would drive the Mustang back to Our Lady of Guadalupe and start her new life with Ron, her work for the sanctuary movement finished at last.

She took the turn that would lead them toward the radio station. She smiled and then frowned as she remembered the summer of '69 and the Spanish-language program they'd broadcast for the migrants. The smile was for their innocence;

the frown was for the time Kenny took the wrong tape and "Mellow Yellow" went out over the airwaves instead of pro-union speeches.

Rap had been furious, called her cousin a stupid little fuck who played practical jokes with people's lives. But if there was one thing she knew about her long-dead cousin, it was that there wasn't a practical-joking bone in his body. He'd been a totally serious kid, and he'd wanted more than anything to be a real part of their group. He would never have sabotaged the broadcast on purpose.

So someone had slipped him the wrong tape. But who, and when?

Why was easy. Why was so that Kenny would get a repu-tation for screwing up, a reputation that would come in handy when the parathion canister proved to be real instead of fake.

The corn was shoulder-high. Ready to eat. She'd stop at a farm stand on the way back from the rendezvous and buy a dozen ears for dinner. Home-grown tomatoes, too, hand-harvested, not picked by machine for the ketchup factory.

Her mouth watered, but her mind clicked along, remember-ing the tape screwup in vivid detail. Whose job had it been to make the tape in the first place?

Rap's, of course. He was the electronics wizard, the one who knew what dials to turn for the best sound. Abe Murillo made the tapes at the White House, on Rap's equipment, since the station didn't want its facilities used directly for the mi-grant union movement.

So who was to say Rap didn't intentionally bury the real Murillo tape and substitute the Donovan song?

Or maybe Dana, who practically lived in Rap's one-room lair in the White House. She'd been in the forefront of the "lynch Kenny" movement at the time.

Then Ritamae's voice, strong and sure, sounded in her head: *How long the boy been dead? This shit is not where you need to be at right now.*

The other car was a plain white van. It sat in a roadside picnic area, as if its occupants were about to spread a check-ered cloth and enjoy Grandma's cold fried chicken and Aunt Susie's potato salad. But the men in the car didn't look like picnickers.

They didn't look like sanctuary movement people either. They were bulky and big and menacing. They stepped out of the van and stepped over to the Mustang as if about to make an arrest.

Jan's heart stopped. Walt? Had their elaborate deception been a complete bust? Had Walt Koeppler seen at once that the man in the Rockets T-shirt was Joaquín, not Rap?

She was so panicked that she failed to notice the plain tan sedan sliding into the alfalfa field next to the picnic area. She also failed to notice Dale Krepke stepping out of his car and heading toward the rendezvous.

The two men stepped over to the car. Joaquín got out and said, "Is all set? Go to Canada?" He handed a small pack to the man, who took it and tossed it into the back of the car.

The big man in the plaid sport shirt nodded. "Yeah, yeah. All set. Just get in the car, okay?"

Joaquín stepped toward the white van. Krepke ran up, gun drawn, and yelled, "Stop. You're under arrest. I'm a federal officer."

"So are we," the taller of the two men replied. "Put down that gun."

Joaquín reached over and pulled the gun from the waistband of the man in the plaid shirt. He pointed it directly at Dale Krepke and pulled the trigger. The young DEA man grabbed his stomach and fell to the ground, moaning.

Jan stood transfixed. It was just like Miguel. A horrible replay of the day she'd watched Miguel bleed to death in the dust. But who was this guy, and why was he here? And who were the big guys in the white van? They weren't the people she expected to meet, but who—

Joaquín strode toward the dying man, who sobbed and prayed as he clutched his bleeding stomach. He lowered the gun to the man's temple, then fired off two more rounds. The head disappeared, replaced by a huge puddle of blood. The moans ceased.

"You killed him," Jan whispered. She was shaking badly and she wasn't sure whether the moisture on her legs was sweat or urine.

"What the hell—" The plaid-shirted man seemed to realize only belatedly that his gun had just killed a federal officer.

"Get the fuck in the car, you stupid shit," the other man yelled.

Joaquín shrugged. "I do what I have to do," he replied. "In my country such a man could not—"

"In your country, you torture women and children. Get in the fucking car before I forget what I'm supposed to do with you, you piece of—"

It came to Jan that the man she'd known as Joaquín Baltasar didn't talk or act like a refugee from political persecution.

"Who is he?" she asked in a small voice. "He's not Joaquín, is he?"

"Lady," the man replied, "you don't want to know who he is. This whole mess is going to take a hell of a lot of explaining in Washington."

The other man, having stashed "Joaquín" in the van, came over to Jan, a speculative look on his face. "I checked his ID," he said. "DEA. This guy was after drugs, not illegals."

"Drugs," the other man said with a self-satisfied smile. "That'll work. This whole thing can go down as a bad drug bust, Cookie here can take the fall, and we can get *Caña Dulce* out of the country and into—"

"*Caña Dulce?*" The name hit Jan in the stomach. Since going to work for the sanctuary movement, she'd learned more than she'd ever wanted to know about Central American politics. *Caña Dulce*, Sugar Cane, was the ironic nickname of a torturer notorious for his sadism even in a country where cruelty was an everyday occurrence.

So the man they'd thought was Joaquín, the man they'd risked their lives to free, was really a torturer. How in hell had he been slipped into their sanctuary stream? Who had known about it, and how had—

"You say word one about all this, Cookie," the big man said, holding his gun to her chin, "and we—"

''No, Cal,'' the other man cut in. ''We can't rely on her to keep her mouth shut. There's only one thing to do. When the Ohio state cops come out here and find Junior's body over there, they'd better find hers too. Drug deal gone wrong. One dead fed and one dead dealer. Case closed.''

Jan lifted her knee in the classic female defense move she'd learned in sixth grade and took off in a dead run toward Dale Krepke's car. He'd left the motor running and the keys in the ignition. She tore away, tires squealing and gravel flying. She heard gunshots and knew they were aimed at her. But she also knew they'd have to get *Caña Dulce* out of there before any other law enforcement people showed up. They couldn't afford to follow her.

But could she afford to go back to Our Lady of Guadalupe? Could she expect that the truth she'd tell would be believed? Or would the government deny any knowledge of *Caña Dulce*, would the death of the mysterious drug cop be put on her tab?

Anything that would happen to her would happen to Ron as well. They'd pull out their tired old conspiracy laws and wrap all of them up in a nice neat package and send her and Ron and Father Jerry to jail for a hell of a long time.

She couldn't do that to him. She headed the car south, driving along back roads so obscure they had no numbers to identify them. She ditched the car along the side and walked until she reached a gas station in a little town with a civil war memorial in the middle. She cadged a ride to Fremont and spent four hours in the bus station, waiting for the first bus to God-knew-where.

As she sat on the hard bench in the tiny bus station, a tear rolled down her cheek. By now, Ron would know it had all gone sour. By now, he'd know she wasn't coming back.

Honeymoon City was far, far away.

CHAPTER
TWENTY-THREE

I *want my life back.*

She had to pee. It was ten minutes until her break, when Teri from Housewares would step up and take the register. Her left hand swept the merch across the scanner and the green numbers lit up the console over her head.

Anybody could do this job. Hell, they could train monkeys and pay them in ripe bananas. You didn't even have to be able to add or subtract, just read the numbers on the console and make change accordingly.

I want my life back.

It had been so long since she'd had a life. Since she'd even considered the possibility of a life. Fourteen years down the drain and all she had to show for them was a series of low-paying jobs, a lot of drunken nights in cheap motels, and a head of hair destroyed by too many color changes.

Way in the back of the bustle and noise, the chatter of customers, the wail of toddlers, the beeps and pings of machines, the canned music played an old Beatles tune.

> *there are*
> *places*
> *I remember*
> *all my life*

Places like her hometown, which she hadn't seen since that night in 1982 when she ran for her life. Places like Our Lady of Guadalupe, where she'd married Ron Jameson.

She gave the customer a big smile and said, "Thanks for shopping at Wal-Mart." Old Sam Walton would be proud of her.

God, she had to pee. Where was Teri? She glanced up at the big clock behind the register. Five more minutes.

She flashed a smile at the next customer, a wan young woman with a huge pregnant belly and a towheaded toddler in the seat of the wire shopping basket. "What a cute little boy," she said, infusing her voice with an enthusiasm she didn't really feel.

If I'd had a life, would I have had a child?

Not with Ron. Unless they could do some kind of medical miracle thing and extract his sperm and plant it in her belly like they did with cows.

She hummed along with the Beatles.

> *some are dead*
> *and*
> *some*
> *are*
> *living*

Kenny was dead. Ron was living. Or at least she assumed Ron was living. What if she went back only to find that he'd died?

Two more minutes. The speaker's words from last night's AA meeting came back to her in startling clarity, almost as if she could see them on the green console: "We're only as sick as our secrets."

Too many secrets. That was the trouble. That was why she couldn't have her life back.

But what if she told the secrets? What if she stopped running, stopped hiding, and went back? Would she go to jail? Maybe. But maybe not, if she told all the truth, all the secrets.

A hand tapped her shoulder. She froze, then turned to see

Teri holding her money tray, ready to take register four so Jan could go on break.

Jan flashed a grateful smile and rushed to the Ladies. She used the toilet, then stood in front of the mirror as she washed her hands in the ugly yellow soap.

I want my life back.

She took off her royal-blue smock, laid it carefully on the little bench in the anteroom, and went to her locker. She took her purse and walked out of the store into the Kansas sunshine, taking her first steps homeward.

CHAPTER TWENTY-FOUR

Tarky smiled. It was the hard, bright smile of anger. A smile like a knife, slicing through Wes's hot fury.

Tarky had always been the spider to Wes's glittering butterfly. Tark was the sinister, quiet creature sitting inside the intricate web, waiting for a victim to enmesh itself in sticky strands.

"You know, John Wesley," he said in a tone of total unconcern, "that line's getting a little tired. Every time you hit a bump in the road, you try to fire me. I'm—"

"A bump in the road?" Blood suffused Wes's face; I began to worry that a stroke was on the way. "I just learned that I supposedly took money from people making bogus airplane parts and you call that a bump in the road?"

Tarky held up a hand. "Wait a second, Wes. I can explain."

"I can explain, too, Tark. You ran short of money to pay off the loan sharks so you sold your most valuable possession—my name. You made some goddamn phone call quashing some goddamn investigation I never even heard about, and now I'm going to spend the rest of this campaign explaining it."

Neither man seemed to care that I was in the room. They were both enraged, Wes in a loud and Tarky in a quiet way.

Wes shook his head. "I can't afford this, Tark. I was kicked out of the state house, remember? This is my last big chance. If I lose this one, the party won't even bother putting me up for city council.'' He ran his fingers through his carefully moussed and sprayed hair.

''I gotta cut you loose, Tark. The only thing that's going to give me any credibility is standing up there and saying I didn't know what my campaign manager was doing. The voters may not believe it, and the press sure as hell won't believe it, but it's all I've got. I mean it this time, Tark.''

''No, you don't.'' The cigar shifted from one side of Tarky's mouth to the other. I caught a glimpse of brown-stained lower teeth. ''You don't mean it, Wes. You and I have been together too long. You need me.''

Wes let out a long sigh. He reached up and loosened his tie, letting it hang from his neck like a striped noose. He shook his head. ''No,'' he said in a soft, deadly tone. ''No, I don't. Not anymore. I know all I need to know about winning elections. I can hire another campaign manager. What I can't do is keep you on and win this election.''

Tarky sat absolutely still. He seemed to shrink into the chair. In the dim light of the skybox, his dark skin looked sallow.

''Wes, you know nobody's ever going to hire me if you let me go.'' The tone was uninflected, but there was a great sadness underneath it precisely because Tarky was trying so hard not to beg.

''You've got more to worry about than that, Tark. If you used campaign contributions to pay off gambling debts, you could face indictment.'' Wes's tone was apologetic, as though he was pointing out that his friend had egg on his tie.

The words were so low I barely heard them. They were so unexpected that I couldn't process them. ''So could you.''

''What did you say?''

''I said, so could you.'' Tarky's face was turned toward the television sets, which still showed the stage, empty now, on which the candidates had faced one another.

''And just what do you mean by that?'' Now Wes was as quiet, as dangerously patient, as Tarky had seemed earlier.

"I've got the hemo."

"The what?"

"Oh, my God." I put my hand to my mouth to recall the words, but it was too late. Both men turned and stared at me as though aware for the first time that there was another person in the room.

Wes pointed a finger in my face and said, "Nothing said in this room goes out of this room, understood?"

"I can't agree to that," I replied. "What Tarky's talking about is the weapon that killed Kenny."

Wes turned his attention back to Tarky. "What hemo?"

Tarky shook his head. "Give it up, Wes. You know what this is about. Everyone thinks Ron and Cass discovered Kenny's body under the weeping beech tree." He pulled the cold cigar out of his mouth and pointed it at his heart.

"But that's not true. I found Kenny. I found Kenny lying dead and I found your hemostat, the one you used as a roach clip, next to his hand. I picked it up and kept it all these years. So," he continued, putting the cigar back between his lips, "I'd reconsider that firing if I were you."

But the man who'd just demonstrated his ability to think on his feet smiled. "The old magic twanger. I wondered what happened to it."

"That's pretty lame, Wes."

"No, Tark. If you give this thing even one minute's thought, you'd see that I didn't kill Kenny. If I had, why would I leave the magic twanger?" Wes's face wore the same self-satisfied smile he'd used on Sally Spurrier. "It would be like signing my name to the murder. Which means it must have been left by someone else in order to implicate me."

Tarky pursed his lips. "It might be interesting," he said, "to produce the hemo and see how it squares with your little speech about smoking just one joint in your whole—"

Wes made for the door. Over his shoulder, he called out, "Fuck you, Tark. Have your shit out of the office by ten tomorrow."

Tarky forced his lips into a smile that contrasted with his gray face. "He doesn't mean it," he said. "He'll call me first thing in the morning and ask where he's supposed to be when and what the focus group said about the debate. You'll see.''

"Maybe.'' It was as far as I could go in encouraging Tarky's optimism. "But if and when he finds out that the person who gave you that so-called political contribution was Rap, I—''

"Go away, Cassie,'' the former campaign manager said. "Please do me a favor and go the fuck away.''

I considered Tarky's story as I drove to the hospital to check on Jan and see Ron. We'd learned at the time that Kenny had inhaled parathion, but it wasn't clear how, since there had been none found at the crime scene. Now the pieces came together with startling vividness: poor Kenny accepting a joint from a person he considered a friend, and then dropping dead when it turned out to be laced with an extremely potent poison.

Wes had a point. If he'd been the one handing the marijuana to Kenny, why wouldn't he have taken the hemo with him? Which meant that the killer's plan to incriminate Wes had been derailed by Tarky's unexpected appearance on the scene.

And what was Tarky thinking when he removed the magic twanger? Did he believe his future candidate had killed a six-teen-year-old boy—and did he deliberately suppress that fact so he and Wes could go on to political glory together? His pathetic attempt at blackmail seemed to have failed, but Wes was facing a tough fight. Questions about a long-ago murder, a sixties act of defiant radicalism, and contributions from a drug-dealing bogus airplane parts seller were likely to bury his political career for good.

I closed my mental file on the subject as I slipped my rental car into a space in the Toledo Hospital parking lot.

Jan lay in the intensive care tent, tubes and pipes and machines surrounding her. I could see her chest rise and fall, but how much of that was her doing and how much was the work of the respirator, I didn't know.

Death would be easier.

Wouldn't it?

Wouldn't Ron be—well, not happier, but more at peace if

we had a nice funeral, Father Jerry presiding, and put Jan in the ground? Shed the tears, say the prayers, and move on.

Hard to move on, though, without knowing who wanted Jan dead so much that he slammed her skull five or six times with a baseball bat.

Zack and Ron had gone for a coffee break. I was alone with the woman who had been my sister-in-law without my knowing it for fourteen years.

Could people in a coma hear you if you talked to them? It all depended on which segments of *Oprah* you'd seen.

But what could I say to her?

I sighed. It all boiled down to one thing. One thing I hated like hell to have to say to anybody, let alone the woman who'd stolen my brother.

"I'm sorry, Jan," I whispered.

As long as I live, I will never believe that what happened next had anything to do with my words.

The eyelids fluttered, like the wings of a fly trapped in a spiderweb.

I held my breath.

More fluttering. The fly was in serious trouble.

At last I saw blue. Jan's eyes were open. She stared straight at me and gave a strangled croak. Her lips moved and sounds came out, but none of it made sense.

She was conscious—but how much of her brain still worked?

And what was I supposed to do about this? Call a doctor or try to communicate with her?

I ran for the door and called out, "Someone help. Quick."

Then I ran back to the bed. "Jan, it's me. Cassie. Can you talk? Do you recognize me?"

The bruised, swollen face was incapable of registering emotion. She looked like a beefsteak pounded into submission by a French cook. More strangled sounds emerged from her mouth, but nothing I recognized.

Where the hell were the doctors? On TV, there would be six of them surrounding this bed. I patted Jan's limp hand and said, "I'll be back. I've got to tell somebody you're awake."

Before I made it to the door, a nurse rushed past me and lifted Jan's hand for a pulse reading. She leaned down and moved Jan's eyelids, nodding at whatever it was she saw. She put a blood pressure cuff on Jan's arm.

I couldn't stand it any longer. "Is she conscious? Can she understand what we're saying? Will she be all right?"

"We don't know that yet," the woman replied, her voice heavily accented with the rhythms of the West Indies. "I'll go get Dr. Singh. He can tell you more than I can, but I doubt that even he will have a prognosis at this early stage."

When she'd bustled out the door, I stepped over to the bed. "Well, at least you've got a prognosis," I said. "That's an improvement, you know. Yesterday I heard Ron talking to Father Jerry about your funeral, and tonight you've got a prognosis."

I stroked the limp hand, which reminded me of Ron's. "I hate funerals. I'm kind of glad I won't have to go to yours. I'd be even gladder if I knew you could understand a word I'm saying, but I guess you can't have everything."

The limp hand moved and grabbed mine with a sudden strength. The head lifted off the pillow and the face screwed itself into an expression of intense purpose. The swollen mouth opened and sounds that might almost have been words came out.

"Gaaaaaa," she said. She broke off in frustration as the realization hit her that whatever was in her injured brain wasn't coming out of her mouth the way she'd intended. She tried again. "Caaaaaaaa Daaaaa."

"Canada!" A rush of elation hit me. She was making sense. "Yes," I shouted. "You were trying to get refugees to Canada."

"Ooohhhh," she grunted. Her neck muscles bunched as she tried in vain to move her head from side to side. I gathered she was trying to say no.

I reached for her bandaged head. "You can't move," I said firmly. "You'll rattle what's left of your brains."

"This is correct," a precise voice behind me agreed. Dr. Singh stepped up and gently took my hands away. He put his stethoscope on Jan's chest and nodded at whatever he heard through the long black tubes. He took a penlight from his white coat pocket and shone it into each eye, lifting the lids just as the nurse had done. I could have sworn a look of deep annoyance gleamed from those blue orbs. Warmth swept over me; whatever Jan's problems communicating, it seemed there was still an active intelligence inside the battered head.

Sudden tears stung my eyes. Was it possible that my brother was actually going to have a living, breathing wife?

The whirr of Ron's wheelchair sounded behind me. He came into the room under his own power, with Zack following. "What happened? I heard someone at the nurse's station say she was conscious."

"She is," I replied. I stepped out of the way to let him roll closer to the bed.

"Jan, honey," he said in a tone of voice I'd never heard him use. He lifted his hand, slowly and deliberately, toward hers. She saw him and her mouth twisted into what might have been a smile. She tried to lift her own hand to reach his, but it jerked like a gaffed fish instead of moving in his direction.

Ron's hand was steady if slow. Finally he connected with her white fingers and clenched his own fingers around hers. She stopped trying to move and gazed at him the way a baby fixes on its mother.

Another person entered the room. Dr. Singh frowned. "There can be no more visitors," he said sternly. "There are too many people in this room as it is."

Then he saw who the newcomer was. "Oh, it is you, Father. Well, if you are here for religious purposes, I suppose I cannot ask you to leave. But it would be better for the patient if there were fewer stimuli." He turned his critical eyes on me.

I saw his point. Ron was the husband, Zack was here for Ron, and Father Jerry was a man of the cloth. Which left me as the superfluous visitor.

When Jan saw Father Jerry, her neck muscles bulged and her eyes widened. She made more sounds. "Caaaaaaa Daaaaaaaa Saaay." Her hand left Ron's, flying up like a startled gull.

The priest stepped closer to the bed, standing next to Ron and placing a hand on Jan's shoulder. "Stay calm," he said in a mellow, soothing voice. "We promise not to leave until we understand what you're trying to say. So take your time."

"Uuuud." Her head fell back, and her neck relaxed.

"Does that mean 'good'?" I asked. She didn't look in my direction, but her head moved slightly up and down.

"Blink twice if it means good," I ordered. All those *Ben Casey* reruns were finally paying off.

She blinked twice.

Then she ruined the effect by going into a series of ticlike blinks, clearly uncontrolled. The limp hand clenched into a limp fist. She pounded the fist on her thigh.

Father Jerry stopped the hand, holding it in his own brown fingers. "We said we'd stay and we will. There's no hurry."

"What I want to know," Ron said slowly, "is who hit you? Who did this to you?"

This time there was no sound, no blinking. Jan lay on her slab as if stunned. No expression on her face, no light in the blue eyes. She seemed to be staring deep within herself. At last she opened her mouth. "Oohhnn Memmmmmmmerrr."

"You don't remember," Ron translated. Then he added, "Blink twice for yes."

She blinked twice. The blue eyes filled as she added, "Ooorrree."

Ron smiled and took her hand once more. "Don't be sorry. We're just glad you're back this far."

Tears slid out of the corners of her eyes onto the pillows. She turned again to the priest. "Naaaaaakeeen," she moaned. "Caaaaaaanaaaaaa Daaaaaaa Saaaay."

Father Jerry shook his head. "I don't understand. What are you trying to say?"

Dr. Singh edged Father Jerry aside and leaned over the bed. "I have some questions I must ask," he said. "Can you tell me your name?"

Jan's eyes lit up; she tried to nod, but her head was locked in a fixed position. "Aaaaaaaan Eeeeehaaaaa," she managed to say. She tried again and this time there was at least one more consonant.

"Knows who she is," the doctor remarked, making a note on his clipboard chart. "What year is this?" He raised his voice when he addressed Jan, as if testing her hearing as well as her comprehension.

Jan's face wore an expression of pride as she replied, enunciating each syllable, "Nnnniiiiiiinnnnnteeeee." She stopped for a breath. "Aaaaaaaaaay Dooooooo."

By no stretch of the imagination could her reply be translated into "Nineteen ninety-six."

Dr. Singh confirmed my growing suspicion when he asked his next question. "Can you tell me the name of the president of these United States?"

"Ooooooooonal Aygaaaaaaa."

Right. The year was 1982 and the president was Ronald Reagan. Jan was alive and conscious, but she hadn't come back to this decade.

CHAPTER
TWENTY-FIVE

I ran into Ted on the way out of the hospital. I told him the good and bad news about Jan and saved him a trip by telling him there was no way Dr. Singh was going to let him into her room.

"Meanwhile, how are you coming with Kenny's notebook?" I stepped up my pace to keep up with Ted's long legs. "Any breakthroughs I should know about?"

He shook his head. We were in the parking lot now and the light from the overhead lamps made silver streaks in his hair.

Kenny's notebook. We had to figure out what Kenny's symbols meant. Nothing in the notes would make sense until we did that.

"I need coffee," I said.

Ted nodded. Five minutes later, we were sitting at a table in the hospital cafeteria, a thermos pitcher of coffee between us, and Kenny's notebook open to the first page.

"Who could L be?" I asked, not really expecting an answer. "Libby Altschuler?" She'd been Wes's girlfriend, later his wife, still later his ex-wife. But she hadn't really been one of us, so I doubted she'd have appeared in Kenny's notes as often as the person designated as L showed up.

"This one is like the symbol for a man," Ted said, pointing. It was the classic circle with an arrow pointing upward on the right side.

"Well, that doesn't narrow it down very . . ." I began, then turned the page and put my finger on another design. "And here's the female symbol." The familiar circle with a cross underneath adorned several T-shirts and posters in my possession.

"Not exactly," Ted corrected. "It's like the female symbol with little horns on top of the circle."

I smiled. "So maybe it stands for a she-devil."

We both said it at once: "Dana!" The resulting laughter made me feel almost as good as the hot coffee warming my throat.

"I know this one," Ted said. His finger rested on a design that was a cross between a 2 and a 4.

"What does it mean?"

"I don't know. But I've seen it before. It's like a planet or something. Astrology."

"You believe in astrology? A just-the-facts-ma'am reporter type like you?" It was fun teasing Ted. It made me feel like the teenager I'd been when we dated.

"Not me," he replied. "It was my ex who was into all that stuff. Horoscopes, tarot cards, crystals—the whole bit. Drove me crazy after a while. There was nothing that she didn't relate to the stars. So all I know is, I've seen this before. I just don't know what it means."

I considered asking Ted about his marriage and divorce. Did he have kids? Were they still friendly? Was he seeing anyone?

I decided to stick to business. "Well, okay. That gives us one masculine symbol, one feminine symbol with horns, one unknown planet. And here's a circle with a dot in the middle."

We found three more symbols. Three variations on one symbol, really. It was a letter P with a dot in the middle, and each of them had a subscripted number underneath. There was a P_1, a P_2, and a P_3.

We wrote down all the symbols and tried to match symbols with people, and came up dry every time. There was just no clue, no matrix, to help us decipher Kenny's notes.

Sixteen years old, and he'd created a puzzle we couldn't solve.

"He was just a kid," I said. "A kid who spent his spare time reading comic books when he wasn't—"

"Comic books." Ted stopped cold. "That reminds me of something. Some damn comic book he used to read. What the hell was that thing called?"

"Superman had kryptonite," I said, doubt in my voice. The symbols looked scientific to me. Scientific or astrological; my friend Dorinda back in Brooklyn wore a strange symbol around her neck, signifying what she called her sun sign. Although as I recalled, she was more impressed with the fact that her moon was in Pisces.

Ted flashed a quick smile at me. "I doubt that you'll find kryptonite on the periodic table," he said. "These are real designations for certain metals, of that I'm—"

He broke off, enlightenment flooding his face with an energy that made him almost handsome. "I remember," he said simply. "*Metal Men.*"

"There's a comic book about metal men?" I hated to rain on his parade, but—"Like robots?" There had to be forty comic books about robots.

"No, no. Superheroes, sort of. Made out of metal. They had the periodic table symbols on their heads."

"Yeah." But my scorn was half-kidding. He looked certain. He looked positive. He looked sexy.

"Okay, so we get a copy of this comic book," I said. "Or we find a twelve-year-old boy."

Which made me remember, really remember, Kenny Gebhardt. A kid. A kid with a lot of years ahead of him. Sure, I'd been upset by his death when it happened. But now that almost thirty years had passed, thirty years during which I'd lived and loved, I felt the real tragedy of Kenny's passing.

What kind of man would he have been? What would he have done with his astonishing intelligence? Would he have fathered children, made love to a wife?

Someone had deliberately stolen all those years from him. And it looked as if the same someone had tried to steal the rest of Jan's life from her.

"Let's go on a comic book hunt," Ted said, rising from his chair.

"It's after ten," I pointed out. "Are the stores going to be open?"

"We can start with drugstores. They stay open late." Ted made for the door. I followed, keeping up with difficulty.

The first two drugstores we hit were a bust. I started waxing nostalgic, picking up an *Archie* and saying, "Gee, I didn't know they were still publishing these. I always liked Veronica. Betty was such a goody two-shoes."

Ted had a *Spider-Man* in his hand. "This guy was my hero," he said. "I liked the way he climbed up buildings with his suction-cup hands."

But no *Metal Men*.

At the third store, we found out why. "Those are out-of-print," the man behind the counter said. "You'll have to go to a specialty store. There's a guy down on Tenth Street, near the library, sells old comics. Maybe he'll have what you're looking for."

A place on Tenth Street near the library. I wasn't the Toledoan; I waited for Ted to find the place, driving slowly up and down the dilapidated street with its bail-bondsmen and pawnshops. Nothing was open. "Maybe we should come back tomorrow," I said.

Ted just kept driving. Finally we came to a lit storefront with a huge Green Lantern poster in the window. It was next to a plastic model of the starship *Enterprise*.

"This must be the place," Ted said. He maneuvered his car into the nearest parking space.

The guy behind the desk reminded me of Zack. A Zack who'd never worked out, who weighed about ninety pounds less. But he had the leather and he had the tattoos. And he had the attitude.

"You look like Trekkies," the guy said. "Baby-boomers usually want *Star Trek* stuff."

Next to the door stood a huge standup of Worf, the Klingon, holding a phaser in his hand. Pasted to his shoulder was a hand-lettered sign that read, "Shoplifters will be nuked back to the Stone Age."

"Under ordinary circumstances," Ted replied, a smile in his voice, "we'd be happy to buy a life-size cutout of Jean-Luc Picard, but right now we're looking for a *Metal Men* comic book."

"I thought you'd prefer the Counselor," I murmured. The *zaftig* Betazoid stood in front of me, wearing her lavender jumpsuit and radiating sexuality even though she was made of cardboard. "I didn't know your taste ran to bald guys."

"*Metal Men*?" Our host wrinkled his nose. "That's a toy comic," he said. "Strictly for kids." Then he brightened. "That's it, right? You two want it for your kid?"

Ted leaned toward the guy and said in a low voice, as if we were surrounded by listening ears, "We think someone used the Metal Men as a kind of code. We need a copy of the comic so we can translate the symbolism."

"Wow," the leather dude said, giving a long whistle. "That's heavy stuff. Like a Captain Midnight decoder ring, or something."

Like this kid was old enough to remember Captain Midnight. Another Gen-X nostalgia-tripper. It would have been a nice shot in return for his baby-boomer crack, but I didn't say it. The poor guy couldn't help it that he was born twenty years too late.

We had easily risen to the top of his pyramid of customers, almost up there with people who knew obscure Japanese comic artists.

"So do you have a *Metal Men*, or what?" My patience was gone; I went into New York City mode.

It didn't faze the shopkeeper. "Yeah, back here," he said, waving at a long table with cardboard boxes filled with comic books laid out on top. Each box was labeled in black marker. We found the one marked "Metal Men" and picked one out.

"Does it matter what year?" the guy asked.

"No," Ted replied. "I guess any one will do. We just want to compare the symbols with this notebook." To my surprise, he pulled Kenny's steno pad out of his windbreaker pouch pocket.

I wasn't sure why we were involving this flake in our business, but I followed Ted and Mr. Leather to the front counter. Ted opened the comic book and the notebook and set them next to one another.

"Here's a page identifying each of the Metal Men," he said, pointing to the brightly colored illustrations.

Ted had been right. Each of the Metal Men—and one Metal Woman—bore a symbol on his forehead.

He looked carefully at each metal head, then at Kenny's notebook. Suddenly he broke into a delighted laugh.

"What?" I was looking just as closely, but—

"Look at Mercury."

The character of Mercury was red; he had sharp features. The symbol on his forehead was the one usually associated with the female: a circle with a cross underneath. And little horns on top of the circle. The one we'd called the she-devil.

"That Mercury's a sarcastic dude," the owner cut in. He was apparently more familiar with this "toy comic" than he'd wanted us to know.

It was his remark more than the picture itself that tipped me off. "You think Mercury is Rap?"

Ted nodded. "Yeah. And it fits. Mercury is quicksilver. It's changeable, it's hard to put your finger on."

"That's Rap all right," I agreed. "I always thought he was like a chameleon, except that instead of changing his color, he changes your color to his."

My pulse quickened. We were actually getting somewhere. Ted had his own spiral notebook open; he made the mercury symbol and wrote "Mercury = RAP" on the blank page.

I looked more closely at the Gold Metal Man. His symbol was a circle with a dot inside. "Wes," I said firmly. "He was the golden boy. I think he's Gold."

Ted nodded. "I like it." He wrote "Gold = WES" in the notebook and made the symbol mark next to it.

"There are only six Metal Men," I pointed out. "But there were, what, nine of us?"

"And there's only one woman," Ted agreed. He glanced at Kenny's book. "But he's got those P_1, P_2, P_3—I think P with the dot in the middle stands for Platinum. Since we had more than one woman in our group, he called each female Platinum, but designated them as One, Two, and Three."

"Oh, great," I said. "Now all we have to do is figure out which of us is which."

"My guess is that Jan's P_1. She was his cousin, so she'd be the First Female in his mind."

"Makes sense. Although I guess I always thought of Dana as the strongest woman in the group."

"We can figure it out more clearly when we translate the code. Kenny made notes on what people said or did on specific dates. All we have to do is figure out who was actually where and then we'll know which person he's referring to."

"I'll pretend I understood that," I replied. "Now who's Lead?"

The symbol for Lead was the letter L. Which helped a lot, since we'd earlier thought the letter L was an initial.

"Lead's heavy," Ted said in a musing tone.

"Tark."

Ted nodded. "Yeah, I'll buy Tarky as Lead." He made a note in his steno book. "Although I think the Lead character is a little slow, which certainly isn't Tark the Shark."

"Tarky could be Iron," I pointed out.

"We've got Tarky, Ron, and, I suppose, me," Ted said, "to figure out. There's a skinny little guy called Tin. Seems to be like a mascot. That could be Kenny himself."

"I wonder why he didn't differentiate between the women." The question answered itself as soon as it left my lips. "Because he didn't see us as important enough to have separate identities. We were 'the chicks.' He was sure none of us was a threat."

"He was a kid," Ted reminded me. "He was sixteen."

I shook my head. "Thanks for trying to soften the blow, but he was just acting out what all you guys thought. Dana's right. We rolled the joints and brewed the herbal tea, but we weren't players. Not really."

Ted wrote the name "RON" in his notebook and then laughed again. I was getting attached to that laugh; it was the delighted cry of a kid making a discovery. Before Ron's name he wrote the letter *I*.

"I get it. 'I RON' equals Iron." Then it was my turn to laugh.

"Which makes *you* Tin," I finished. "Think about it. Why would he need a symbol for himself? There's only one Metal Man left, and it looks like you're him."

"Tin's kind of a wimp," the leather dude contributed.

The crestfallen look on Ted's face prompted me to say, "Maybe Kenny meant you in your Clark Kent mode. Mild-mannered reporter."

"Thanks," Ted replied with a wry smile. But he wrote it in his notebook. "Tin = TED." He made the symbol and closed the comic book.

"How much?" he asked the proprietor.

"Six bucks."

"Six bucks for a lousy comic book?" But he took out his wallet and handed over the cash.

As we walked toward the door, the dude asked, "You sure you guys don't want a 'My Other Car Is a Federation Starship' bumper sticker?"

I shook my head, but then halfway to the door, I turned around and bought it for Ron's van.

It was late, but there was no way either of us was going to be able to sleep. We needed a place to sit in peace and cull through the notebook, decoding Kenny's observations. I suggested my motel room, not without a slight quiver of curiosity as to whether we might do more than read comic books.

An hour later, we'd learned some interesting things about our friends. We'd learned that Dana and Rap had a knockdown fight the night before the county fair. We found out that Kenny knew all about Ted and me making out under the weeping beech. We read Kenny's account of following the FBI man into the art museum and confirmed what he'd told us: that he never saw the person the FBI man met in the Swiss room.

There was a full account of the parathion switch. After he

and Jan were finished, they'd driven back to his house, where he'd left the canister in his dad's garage. Unlocked.

But no smoking gun. We followed Kenny's story to the end, but there was nothing we didn't already know.

I flipped through the blank pages, stopping myself when I realized they weren't all blank. In the middle of Kenny's steno book there was one page with a note dated the morning of his death.

"Give me the translation sheet," I said. "There's one more entry we haven't done."

Ted handed me his code-breaker.

"It says here," I said slowly, "that Iron was in contact with the FBI."

"Wait a minute." Ted leapt up from his chair and hovered over my shoulder. "I thought Iron was Ron."

"So did I. But there is no way on God's earth," I said, hitting the little table with my fist, "that I'm going to believe my brother was the one who sold us out."

CHAPTER
TWENTY-SIX

The next morning, I met Harve Sobel in the rear booth at Posner's Deli. The place smelled almost like Junior's back in Brooklyn. I considered getting a bagel with lox and cream cheese, then decided that was asking too much of Toledo. I picked up coffee and a bialy and slid into a straight chair across from the old warhorse.

"So are we going to do anything today, or is this just a meaningless appearance?" I took a sip of weak coffee. "I mean, what can you do if your defendant is in intensive care?"

"Well, for one thing," Harve said, "I can tell you what my daughter finally decided to tell me."

That remark did more to open my eyes than the coffee. "But I talked to Dana."

"She didn't tell you everything." Harve's voice was heavy with phlegm. He hawked and spat into a cloth handkerchief.

I waited with barely concealed impatience. "She did say something about Rap being involved in something dangerous."

Harve shook his head. Long strands of gray, stiff hair were stretched over his balding scalp. It curled slightly at the ends, which were yellowed like the pages of an old book. "This wasn't about Rap. This was about her and Walt Koeppler."

I choked on my coffee. "Luke Stoddard said something

about Dana making a deal with Walt, but I thought he was putting me on. Don't tell me she really—''

"No," he said, holding up a meaty hand. "This was actually pretty clever, although I wish she'd told me about it at the time."

"Harve, please put me out of my misery and tell me what you're talking about."

"She pretended to sell out. She told Koeppler when and where they were going to move this Joaquín Baltasar. And then they pulled a switch. This Joaquín shaved off his world-famous mustache and put on Rap's T-shirt and baseball cap, and Rap got a stage mustache and a cigar and pretended to be Joaquín. So Walt Koeppler followed the wrong couple. He stopped Dana and Rap just this side of the Michigan border, while Jan and the real Joaquín went in the opposite direction."

"Only to be stopped by the DEA," I said slowly. I was thinking aloud. I was also wondering why Ron hadn't told me about the switch.

"That's why the whole thing was dropped at the time," Harve said. "The feds screwed up big-time. They were looking to nab this Joaquín fella and he gets away. The DEA agent thinks he's busting Rap on drugs and instead . . ." Harve trailed off and raised his hands in a you-know-what-happened-next gesture.

But I didn't know what happened next. "Let's think that out a little bit," I invited. "The DEA guy stops Jan and Joaquín, thinking he's Rap. And then somebody shoots the poor guy dead and leaves him in the road. Joaquín disappears into the ozone and is never heard from again, and Jan runs away and hides for fourteen years. But why? Who shot Krepke? Jan or Joaquín? And how did Joaquín get out of the country?"

Harve rubbed his chin. His basset hound face looked grave as he replied, "They must have intended to meet somebody else. Somebody who was going to get Joaquín into Canada. Rap used to meet a Canadian boat called the *Esmeralda*."

"So maybe Jan did shoot Krepke," I mused aloud. "Or maybe Joaquín did it, thinking Krepke was with the Border

Patrol. Or maybe the people they were meeting lost their heads and started shooting."

"Whatever happened out on that road, it was bad news for Koeppler." Harve mopped his forehead with a handkerchief I hoped wasn't the same one he'd just used. "The *Blade* came down pretty hard on him at the time, and Cathy Sawicki over at the U.S. attorney's office quit her job and left town."

"She's in Washington, D.C. now," I said. I filled Harve in on my conversation with Stoddard. "It seems her new crusade is nailing your former son-in-law for making and selling counterfeit airplane parts."

"I wish her luck," the old man replied. He lifted his empty coffee cup as if offering a toast. "Go get the *mamzer*," he said to the invisible U.S. attorney.

"I imagine she'd appreciate a little help." I didn't dare look the veteran defender in the eye. "If Dana wanted to turn state's evidence, she could probably cut a deal."

He raised his eyebrows, a thicket of gray hairs that went well beyond bushy. "I didn't raise my daughter," he said, "to be an informer."

"Unless of course she's lying to the police," I murmured.

The old man's only response was a grin that wavered between innocence and cunning. Whatever Dana thought of her father, she was his daughter through and through.

In court, Harve explained in detail what Judge Noble must have known from the news reports. He agreed to a longer adjournment and then turned to Luke Stoddard. "Can you turn over discovery material at this time?"

The U.S. attorney handed Harve a pile of documents and a manila envelope. I leaned over and whispered, "Where's mine?"

Stoddard answered by declaiming, "The United States wishes at this time to move for dismissal of all charges against Ronald Jameson."

The judge raised the same eyebrow I was considering elevating. "Is there any condition attached to this motion, Counselor? Does this dismissal depend upon Mr. Jameson's testifying for the government at Ms. Gebhardt's trial?"

"No, Your Honor," the prosecutor replied, his deep voice ringing through the courtroom. "There are no conditions. Which is not to say that Mr. Jameson might not be subpoenaed at the proper time, but he is under no obligation beyond that of any citizen to testify truthfully."

The judge banged a gavel and stood up to leave the bench. I wanted to say something, to ask why, but there was no precedent for a defense lawyer objecting to a dismissal. I was, in the court's view, getting a gigantic Christmas present in October, and mine was not to reason why.

But I wanted to know.

Stoddard picked up his file folder and moved for the door. I stepped after him, tripping over my own feet in my anxiety that he might disappear without an explanation.

"Luke," I called. He turned, an expression of angelic innocence on his shiny black face.

"Yes, Counselor? What else can I do for you, having already given you more than you could possibly have hoped for?"

"You can tell me why. You can tell me what game this is. You can tell me—"

The deep-sea smile split his face. "You can't think of a reason? You can't see that maybe I didn't like the idea of trying a man in a wheelchair? Or of forcing that man to testify against his own wife?"

The answer was no. No, I didn't think for one minute that this decision was prompted by charity, or even by the publicity factor. Something else was going on, and I was at a grave disadvantage not knowing what it was. But before I could formulate a question, Stoddard opened the door behind the judge's bench and disappeared into the back corridors of the courthouse.

He left me standing in the courtroom, suddenly and powerfully aware of one simple fact: I was free.

I could go home. Ron didn't need me anymore. Not as his lawyer. Maybe as his sister. But that was only a maybe, and my role as his legal representative had been solid, real.

Without that role, what was I doing here?

I looked around for Harve, as if he could offer me guidance. But he was gone. He'd scooped up the massive pile of discovery documents and hustled to the next courtroom, the next case.

I walked slowly out of the massive marble building onto the busy downtown street. There was a formal garden, filled with yellow and bronze chrysanthemums, surrounding a statue of William McKinley, one of Ohio's contributions to the presidency. A maple tree with half green and half rusty-orange leaves waved in the brisk breeze. The sky was a bright postcard blue, with little white cloud masses scudding along.

Nature. I was actually noticing nature for the first time since I'd stepped off the plane. The hard knot of fear in my stomach was beginning to melt. Ron was not going to jail. Ron was safe.

But Jan wasn't. Jan wasn't safe from Luke Stoddard, and she wasn't safe from whoever had tried to batter her to death.

And now she was conscious. Now she was aware. And the closer she came to regaining her memory, the greater would be her danger.

I wasn't going anywhere. Not until I knew who had attacked Jan and who had killed Kenny and what really happened to Dale Krepke out on that lonely road.

I got into the little red rental car and drove toward the hospital. As I waited for a light to change on Monroe Street, I realized why I'd been so insistent on making Luke Stoddard explain his sudden dismissal of the charges against Ron.

I wanted him to tell me, in no uncertain terms, that it wasn't because Ron had made a deal with the feds back in the summer of 1969.

The light changed. I surged forward in the jackrabbit style favored by those who have driven the streets of New York City.

Ron hadn't wanted to get involved with the parathion demo. Not really. He'd done it because I was going to do it come hell or high water, and he wasn't the kind of older brother who'd let me do it alone.

Had he arranged for us to be arrested before any real damage could be done? Had he called the cops on us?

For our own good, of course. More to the point, for my own good.

I didn't believe it. I didn't want to believe it. But it wasn't as completely impossible as I'd insisted to Ted.

What was impossible was that Ron would have handed a poisoned joint to a sixteen-year-old kid.

I parked the car and took the familiar path through the lobby to the elevator leading to the ICU.

Jan was awake, propped up in bed by pillows, her head still held in place by a brace. Ron's chair sat as close as possible to the bed and his hand rested on her bare arm. The expression on her face was meant to be a smile, but one side of her mouth drooped and saliva drooled down her chin.

"How is she?" I supposed I was talking to Ron, but Jan herself said, "O-ay."

Since she couldn't turn her head, I conveyed my skepticism to Ron with a facial expression. His almost imperceptible nod reassured me.

I mouthed the words *What year is it?*

Now Ron frowned slightly. So it was still 1982.

Which might not be all bad. Maybe Jan couldn't tell us who'd hit her on the head two nights ago, but she ought to be able to fill in a blank or two regarding the death of Dale Krepke.

I pulled a chair over to Ron's side of the bed and placed it in what I took to be Jan's line of sight.

Some of the swelling in her face had gone down, but there were railroad-track stitches along her shaved scalp and the bruises had turned yellow and purple. I swallowed hard and worked at treating her like an intelligent adult in spite of her obvious limitations.

"You were taking Joaquín Baltasar to—"

She tried to shake her head. Since she couldn't move, her neck muscles bulged. She flailed her arms and moaned, "Noooooo."

"No, you weren't? But Harve said—"

"Nnnnn-aaaaaakeeeen. Caaaaaaa-daaaaaa-saaay." Jan's

face wore an intent expression that begged me to understand.

"Yeah, you wanted to get Joaquín to Canada," I said. "We know that part."

More frantic hand-shaking. Ron lifted his hand and caught one of hers. "Relax, Jan. Please."

"Maaaaaa. Naaaaaaa. Waaaaakeeee." Now her tone was purely annoyed, as though she couldn't believe she was talking to people who were this dense.

"Does Waaa-keee mean Joaquín?" Ron asked.

Jan's face relaxed into a relieved smile. "Eeeeess."

At this rate, it would take us three weeks to figure out what Jan was trying to say. I opened my mouth to try another question when my beeper vibrated.

"Back in a minute," I said. In truth, I hoped that Ron would have more luck than I and that I'd come back to find him in full possession of Jan's message.

"Law offices of Harvey Sobel," a deep female voice said after three rings.

"Dana?"

"Who is—oh, Cassie. Harve's right here."

"Wait, I—" But the clank of receiver on desk top told me to save my breath.

Harve's rich, phlegmy baritone greeted me. "Cassie. Two things I thought you should know. One: Koeppler had a wire-tap warrant in '82. Planted a bug at Our Lady of Guadalupe. Two: Stoddard dropped the case against Ron after he got a call from bigwigs in Washington."

"FBI?"

"I don't know. All I do know is that he was told to make this whole thing go away. He called to offer me a very sweet deal for Jan. As soon as she's able to talk, I'll tell her about it."

"Actually, she's doing pretty well for somebody who thinks Ronald Reagan is still president."

The old lawyer rumbled a laugh. "Poor kid," he said. "I wouldn't wish that on my worst enemy."

When I got back to Jan's room, Father Jerry had joined the team. He sat in the chair I'd vacated, asking Jan more or less the same questions I had. With, it seemed, little better luck. Jan's face was screwed into an expression of frustrated urgency. Whatever she was trying to say, it was of vital importance in her battered mind.

"Caaaaaa," she said and paused. Then she opened her mouth again. "Neeeeyaaaa." Another pause. "Daaaaaa." She fixed Father Jerry with pleading eyes. "Saaaaaay."

He repeated her sounds, one by one. "Ca. Neeya. Da. Say."

"Essss. Naaaa. Waaakeeeen."

"You were taking Joaquín—"

"Naaaaaattt. Keeeen." She struck at her hips with her flailing fists, willing us to understand.

"Sounds like she's saying 'not Joaquín,' " Ron pointed out.

Jan's face melted into delighted agreement. "Essss. Essss. Yeeee-essss."

"Now all we need is the other part," I said.

"I'm not sure," the priest began, "but maybe—" He leaned closer to Jan. "I think she's saying 'Caña Dulce.' "

Tears started in the blue eyes and spilled unheeded down her cheeks. "Essss. Esssss. Caaaa Daaaa Saay."

"Sugar cane?" I turned to the priest. "But why would she be talking about—"

"It's a name." Father Jerry looked at Ron. "Remember?" Ron nodded. His face was grim.

"Will somebody tell me what's going on?"

"Caña Dulce was listed with Amnesty International as one of the worst torturers in Guatemala," the priest said. His face wore a troubled expression. "He killed three Jesuit priests. The sad thing," he continued, shaking his head, "is that our own CIA trained him."

"So Jan's saying—"

Ron finished my thought. "That the man we thought was Joaquín Baltasar was really Caña Dulce."

I flashed back to Dana's account of the extra refugees, the ones who carried guns. She'd said Rap made night trips; what if he was ferrying the death squad torturers to Canada?

And what if the federal agency that pressured Stoddard into settling Jan's case wasn't the FBI but the CIA?

Which raised another, very pressing, question: Assuming any of this was true, who could we tell? Who could we trust?

CHAPTER
TWENTY-SEVEN

Who could we trust? If Harve was right, this conspiracy went all the way to Washington. So it was unlikely that Ohio state troopers or lower court federal judges or the county sheriff was going to be able to help. Assuming, that is, that they'd even listen to wild talk about CIA operatives spiriting a Central American priest killer across the border.

When I returned to Jan's room, she was asleep. Worn out from the ordeal of making us understand.

I wheeled Ron's chair into the hall and told him what I'd learned. "We might try Wes," I said tentatively. "He'd know the right people."

The look on Ron's face convinced me that I was grasping at straws. He pursed his lips and said, "Well, there's always the press."

I nodded. Memories of Watergate flooded my mind. When all else fails, there's Woodward and Bernstein. "I'll try to get Ted on the phone."

Ron raised a single eyebrow. "You think the *Plain Dealer* has enough clout to—"

"I don't know," I called over my shoulder as I made for the phones, "but he's the only reporter we know."

I called the number Ted had given me. From the background noise, I deduced he was talking from his car phone. I explained what I'd learned and concluded, "It's got to be Rap, doesn't it? He probably got caught running drugs back in '68 or '69 and cut a deal with the feds." I felt oddly disappointed. For all his dangerous ruthlessness, Rap had been tender with me the night I got drunk and maudlin.

"Listen," Ted said when I finished, "there's a guy I consider the best political editor in the Midwest. He's got contacts in Washington. Let's lay this whole thing on him and see if he has any suggestions."

"I don't know," I replied. Now that I had Ted's attention, I wasn't sure this was the best way to handle things. I was beginning to feel like one of those people in science fiction movies trying to warn everyone about the pods.

"Where are you?"

"At the hospital."

"I'll be there in ten minutes."

He made it in seven. Ron and I were in the hall outside Jan's room. Father Jerry was on another floor, visiting a parishioner who'd suffered a stroke.

Ted strode up to us. "I called my friend on the car phone. He's at the Bayview Yacht Club. I thought we could meet there. It's as good a place as any to talk."

I picked my bag up and prepared to leave. Ron said, "I'll go with you."

I wanted to object. I wanted to protect my brother from whatever was going on. But I saw the stubborn set of his jaw, the glint in his eye. He wasn't going to listen. "Okay," I said. "Let's get Zack and—"

Ron shook his head. "We don't need Zack. I gave him the afternoon off, since I expected to be here with Jan. But since she's sleeping, she doesn't need me."

"But how will we get you in the van?" *And what if there's something else you need, something I don't know how to do?*

"Cass, the van has electric controls. You push a button and I'm inside. No big deal. I'll walk you through it."

The van Ron called the Quadmobile was parked in the nearest handicap spot. I noted that Zack had affixed the Star Trek bumper sticker next to the one from the Disabled American Vets.

"The keys are in my pouch," Ron said. I reached into the fanny pack strapped around his waist, took them out and opened the door. I slid into the driver's seat and pulled the lever that opened the rear doors. Then I hit the red button that lowered the platform.

It whirred as it stretched from the back of the van, then slid down to the pavement. I wheeled the chair onto the platform and locked Ron in place with the oversized seat belt, following Ron's instructions. Then I went back and raised the platform.

I gave the keys to Ted. "Since you know where we're going, you might as well drive." I walked around to the passenger's side and hoisted myself up onto the seat.

The yacht club was located on Maumee Bay, which connected the Maumee River with Lake Erie. As we approached, a breeze blew off the water, carrying the musky smell I associated with Lake Erie. Ron and I had grown up on the other side of the lake, but it was the same smell.

Across the bay stood the gasworks, their flames flickering like St. Elmo's fire in the overcast gray day. It was an odd contrast: the golf green, the yacht harbor, the accoutrements of wealth and privilege, and in the distance a reminder of the industrial base that made it all possible.

We passed green and white signs marked Bayview. "Hey, shouldn't we turn here?" The park was green and inviting; I glimpsed masts and a big white building on the shoreline.

"Rap lives near here," Ted replied. "I thought we might go to his place and check out a few things."

"Are you crazy?" I inclined my head toward Ron, strapped into the back of the van. "You want to take Ron and me out to a killer's house just so you can get a story?"

"He's not there," Ted replied. "Dana said he went to Michigan last night."

"Ted, turn this damn van around and take us to the yacht club. This is too dangerous." I pounded on the dashboard like a kid demanding an ice cream cone.

"We'll just drive past his house," Ted said. "If his car's there, I'll come back. I promise."

I glanced back at Ron. His face wore a worried look that matched my mood exactly.

"Ted," Ron said, "turn around."

"We're almost there," Ted replied. We turned onto a street lined with white clapboard houses and headed north. "He lives on the Lost Peninsula."

Ted's conversational tone relaxed me a little, although I was angry at him for not obeying Ron. "That's an odd name," I said.

"It's called that because the state line between Ohio and Michigan runs through it. So whenever a tornado hits," Ted said, "each state claims it belongs to the other, so it takes forever for anything to get fixed."

I was beginning to picture Rap's house as a smuggler's cave, but the houses stayed normal-looking, except that the backyards ended at water's edge and boats were as common as cars. And it was the last house on its street, a good quarter mile from its next door neighbor. But then, I reasoned, Rap was Coyote, and he could blend in when it suited him. Even to the point of having a white picket fence around his lair.

There was no car in the driveway, which reassured me slightly. Maybe Rap really was in Michigan.

Something Harve had said on the phone was trying to break through to me. Something that changed everything.

We passed the last house.

"Ted, there aren't any more houses," I said, my voice quavering.

"He lives just up the road," Ted replied.

Wiretaps. Walt Koeppler had wiretapped the church. He'd bugged the sanctuary movement.

Which meant he hadn't needed an inside informer to find out what was going on.

And if he'd had an inside informer already, why would he have made a deal with Dana?

More than that, if he'd had someone inside the movement, he'd have known that Dana was setting him up when she told him when they'd be moving the man they'd known as Joaquín Baltasar.

There was no informer in 1982.

I'd narrowed my suspects to those members of our 1969 group who'd been in northwest Ohio in 1982 on the theory that the same informer who'd betrayed us and killed Kenny was active in the sanctuary movement, but that no longer had to be the case.

Which left the one member of the group I'd never really considered.

And, I realized, stealing a sidelong glance at Ted, that person was also the last American journalist to interview Joaquín Baltasar.

His article in *Newsweek* established Caña Dulce as Joaquín. From there, the sanctuary movement simply did what it would have done for the real Joaquín.

I leaned my head back on the car seat, trying to remain still, trying not to alert Ted to the fact that tumblers were falling into place in my brain.

Kenny's notebook had named Ron as the 1969 informer, a charge I'd rejected out of hand. But looking back, I realized Ted had orchestrated the entire search for the notebook and the translation of Kenny's code.

There was one more house. A neat little white clapboard Cape Cod with bushes and flowers and lawn. Ted pointed and said, "There it is."

Kenny had trusted his killer. I'd considered Wes in that role, since Kenny had idolized the Golden Boy, but the hemostat had gone a long way toward convincing me that someone other than Wes had left it on the scene. But who else would he have trusted so naively?

Not Rap. If Mercury had appeared under the weeping beech, offering him the magic twanger, Kenny would have run the other way. Tarky, too, would have put the kid on alert.

But Ted, the man who'd given him the steno pad in the first place, was eminently trustable.

After all, hadn't I trusted him? Weren't Ron and I in this situation because Ted was the guy next door?

Cold sweat prickled my skin. I'd been worried about Ted taking Ron and me to Rap's, afraid that he was taking us into Coyote's lair. But the reality was even worse. We were in the hands of a killer, and he'd driven us to Rap's empty house because it was a nice, lonely place far away from help.

Maybe I could keep up a pretense of ignorance. After all, I'd been doing a great imitation of a person who had no idea what was going on. Of course, it was easier to do that when you *were* completely in the dark.

"Well, it looks like Rap isn't here," I said, trying to sound as if I still believed Ted's cover story. "I guess we can go see your friend at the yacht club now."

"Get out of the van, Cassie," Ted said. A hard metal thing prodded me. If it wasn't a gun, it felt enough like one that I opened the door and slid out.

I glanced at Ron. The white plastic medallion was around his neck. I hoped he'd been able to push it. But his hand was moving toward it with agonizing slowness. Could he reach it before Ted saw what he was—

Ted reached in through the rear doors of the van, which he'd opened from the driver's seat. "You won't be needing this," he said. He pulled a Swiss army knife out of his pants pocket. I caught a glimpse of metal in his waistband. He did have a gun.

He opened the knife and used the largest blade to cut the cord on the medallion. Then he slipped the medallion into the pocket along with the knife.

Our best hope of rescue had been cut off.

Ron's limp hand hung from the edge of his chair like an empty glove. He seemed deliberately to drop it. I didn't know what was going on, but I felt it was vital not to draw Ted's attention to it. I fixed my eyes on Ted's bland face and said, "Why?"

"The oldest and stupidest reason in the world," he replied. "I got caught in a drug bust in Texas when I was down visiting my cousins. Do you know what the penalties were for selling marijuana down there in those days?"

''Extremely high, I suppose. And that justified your selling out to the feds?''

I willed myself to keep my eyes away from Ron. But it was hard to look at the plain, honest face of the man who'd handed poison to a sixteen-year-old and bludgeoned Jan with a baseball bat. Forget about the sellouts; this man had killed.

And was going to kill us. There was a look of what might have been regret in his eyes, but it was not tempered by doubt. He might shed a tear or two over Ron and me, but he was going to eliminate us just as soon as possible.

And he was going to do it at Rap's house so that the blame would fall on him. With Rap's drug history and Dana's story about extra refugees and the investigation into bogus airplane parts, a couple of murders could go on Rap's account without much trouble. The cops would be only too happy to pin our deaths on him.

''They told me nobody would get hurt,'' Ted said. ''And they were right. But they were upset that the charges were dropped, even though that wasn't my fault, and they got really pissed when Kenny started snooping around. They said if my cover was blown, the deal was off and I'd go to jail.''

''But you'd convinced Kenny that Ron was the informer.''

The fact that my brother said nothing, even though this was the first time he was hearing this, told me he didn't want to call attention to himself. I kept my eyes locked with Ted's. It was vital to keep him talking.

''How long do you think that would have lasted?'' he asked. ''The best I could hope for was to lull Kenny into trusting me long enough to get close to him.''

''How could you?''

''I was twenty-one years old, Cass. My whole life was ahead of me. You'd have done the same thing.''

I didn't state the obvious, that Kenny Gebhardt had had his whole life ahead of him, too. As to whether or not I'd have done the same thing, I wanted to believe I wouldn't have sold out my friends. But I hadn't been facing thirty years behind bars for using a drug the rest of my generation considered less harmful than the two-martini lunch.

"See, my real value to them was that I was studying journalism. Infiltrating the migrant union was just a trial run. What
they really wanted was a tame reporter." He leaned against
the van as if we were all going to step into the backyard and
go for a sail, as if there was no gun in his waistband.

"So your whole career has been a lie. You were really a
plant for the CIA." I kept my eyes fixed on Ted's face, willing
him to keep his attention on me.

"Cass, whole years went by and I wouldn't hear from them.
Not a word. And then they sent me to Nicaragua, to interview
Joaquín Baltasar." He sighed and shook his head. "It was a
piss-poor masquerade. I knew right away it wasn't Joaquín,
but I did what they wanted. I wrote the article and praised
Joaquín's bravery and took pictures. And then I forgot the
whole thing. I didn't know what it was about, and I didn't
want to know."

Dana had said the same thing about Rap's activities. But
there was a high price to be paid for some kinds of ignorance.

"Then all hell broke loose up here," Ted said. "The papers
were full of Joaquín's escape and how the sanctuary movement helped him. Only I knew the guy wasn't really Joaquín.
I suspected the CIA had used me to get Caña Dulce into the
States, but I didn't ask any questions. I was just grateful that
Jan split. If she'd been caught and tried back in '82, all the
shit would have come out."

"So when she decided to come back and face the music,
you slugged her with a baseball bat."

"If the goddamn priest hadn't knocked at the door, I'd have
finished the job."

"Because by that time, you had Kenny and Dale Krepke
on your conscience."

"No, I don't blame myself for Krepke." Ted shook his
head. "The stupid fuck shouldn't have been there in the first
place. And I didn't shoot him, Caña Dulce did. If the CIA
wanted to protect him after that, so be it."

He was good at rationalizing his own guilt. Better than I,
in fact. I'd felt worse over Kenny's death all these years than
Ted had, and his was the hand that held the poison.

A sound remarkably like a shot rang out. I turned toward it, jerking my head without thinking. A wetness sprayed my arms and chest. I jumped, then looked down. Red blotches. Red and yellow and—

I screamed.

Ted lay on the ground, crumpled like a playing card. His head was—

His head was gone. I screamed again, raising shaking hands to my face and then screaming even louder when I realized they, too, were bloodstained. I jumped back, stumbling over tufts of grass.

The splotches on my skin and blouse were blood. Ted's blood. And his brains.

I retched. I gulped acid, then retched again. I leaned away from the head splattered like a Halloween pumpkin and emptied my stomach contents on the grass.

I became aware of Ron saying something from behind me. I turned. "Oh, God, Ron, he's—"

I swallowed sour, bitter fluid. "He's—his head—"

"Get a grip, Cass." My brother's voice was incredibly calm. His face was pale, but he didn't look faint or sick.

There was an animal bellow. A wild man ran up, a big ugly weapon held aloft in both hands. Zack ran to Ted's body and gave it a vicious kick with his pointed cowboy boots. Then he rolled it over and thrust the gun into Ted's stomach. He poked the body with the barrel six or seven times, jabbing the metal into soft, dead flesh.

"Oh, my God. What's he doing?" I turned to Ron. "Stop him. He's—"

"He's checking the body for booby traps," Ron replied. "In 'Nam, the Cong used to plant bombs in dead bodies."

"He's not in 'Nam!"

But he was. Zack was back in the bad boonies. His eyes were wild; he jerked his head from side to side as if the enemy could be found crouching behind the carefully pruned yew trees.

Suddenly, he gave a deep, animal grunt and shifted on his

feet, bracing himself. He hoisted the gun and pointed it at my chest.

"*Chu hoi,*" he shouted. "*Chu hoi,* you goddamn gook bastard. *Chu hoi.*"

"Cass." My brother's voice was sharp, insistent. "Raise your hands in the air and say *chu hoi.*"

I did. My hands shook, but I lifted my arms. My legs were about to give way, but I managed to stay standing. The gun that had just blown Ted Havlicek's head off was now pointed directly at my heart.

"*Chu hoi,*" I said in a strange, small voice.

Something changed in Zack's eyes. He came back, slowly but visibly, from 'Nam. Clarity settled over his big features. He looked down at the rifle and lifted it high over his head, then threw it as far as he could. He bellowed as it sailed over the bushes, landing in a clearing.

He squatted. He went down on his haunches, the soles of his feet planted squarely on the ground. I'd never seen an American squat like that. He rocked back and forth, mumbling in a language I took to be Vietnamese.

Neighbors were beginning to gather at the houses down the road. What the hell were we going to tell them? One part of my mind tried to work while the other gave way to sheer hysteria. There was no way I could look at the bleeding lump of flesh on Rap's front lawn.

In the distance, a siren sounded. My knees refused to hold me up any longer. I stumbled toward Rap's porch and sank down on the concrete. "How did Zack get here?"

"I signaled him." Ron's tension had melted. He sagged in the chair, only his stiff body brace keeping him from complete collapse.

"But Ted took your medallion."

"I have a phone hooked onto the side of the chair," Ron said. "It's on a business band. All I have to do is press the green button and it sends to base, which is Zack. So I knew he'd come, I just didn't know when."

Zack drew a harsh, ragged breath. It turned into a profound sob, a cry of the soul. I crawled over to him, wrapped my arms around him and cradled his huge bulk in my arms as best I could. He emanated a powerful male animal smell, composed of sweat and fear and adrenaline.

At first, I rocked while he cried, but then my own tears flowed. I cried for Kenny, for Ted, for Ron in his body-prison, for Zack, for the pain of Vietnam. For Jan. Finally for Jan's lost years and Ron's lost marriage. And for me. God knows why, but all tears seem in the end to be for oneself.

Zack's sobs became less animal. I pulled away and wiped my face with a dirty hand. "I need a drink," I muttered.

Zack's huge hand enveloped mine. He squeezed hard and said, "No, you don't."

CHAPTER
TWENTY-EIGHT

"I mean, it was kind of an impulse thing," Ron said. "It seemed right at the time. But, hell, it's been fourteen years. I don't know her anymore." He lowered his eyes, then raised them again, meeting mine with a look of pure anguish. "I'm not sure I knew her then. How can we start over as if the last fourteen years never happened?"

We sat in the hospital cafeteria. Several grueling hours had passed since the police drove up to Rap's house and found a very dead body, a man in a wheelchair, a distraught Vietnam veteran, and a near-hysterical lawyer. Somehow we'd explained enough to get Zack to the V.A. hospital and Ron and me released. It helped a lot that the gun in Ted's waistband hadn't been registered. It helped even more that Luke Stoddard vouched for Ron and me by telephone. The V.A. admitted Zack for observation and Ron would be sleeping at Toledo Hospital until his attendant was released.

I sighed and leaned my elbows on the cold Formica table. I was bone-tired and sick at heart. Sick of blood and violence and betrayal. I wanted to go home.

"She needs you more than you need her," I said, trying to focus on Ron instead of the image that haunted me: Ted's twisted glasses, lying in a pool of blood. "That's not a bad start."

"You mean, now that she's disabled and needs physical therapy." His tone was as bitter as I'd ever heard it. He was usually so upbeat, so unwilling to give in to the darker emotions.

"That is not what I mean and you know it. Or you should know it." My voice was raw. "Jan's been alone so long. She needs a home. She needs a husband." I had a tiny moment's wondering whether I was really talking about Jan. Was there a portion of my feminist, independent soul that would have liked to be loved the way Jan was so obviously loved? It didn't help my mood to realize that the piped music in the cafeteria was playing a particularly saccharine Carpenters tune.

Ron's set, intent face relaxed into a smile. "Well, let's go see my wife." Was it my imagination, or did his voice linger just a little on the last two words? Words he'd probably given up hope of ever saying in public.

We took the oversized elevator, which was crowded with nurses and doctors and visitors and one smiling elderly man walking with his IV. I pushed the chair down gleaming corridors, past the nurses' station and the sunrooms.

Jan was out of the ICU. She was in a regular private room. I had a quick lawyer-thought: Would whatever insurance she had from Wal-Mart cover her now that she was really someone else?

I pushed open the door and saw Father Jerry in one chair, Harve Sobel in another, and Dana sitting on the wide windowsill.

"Better not let Dr. Singh see this," I said. "He'd throw at least three of us out."

"I was just telling Jan," Harve said in his smoker's voice, "that Ronald Reagan is no longer president. She considered it good news."

Jan sat almost upright, her bandaged head propped by pillows instead of braced. Her face was more yellow than purple now, but her cheeks had more color than I'd seen before.

A vase of blood-red roses rested on the wheeled bed table. I cocked my head toward it and raised an eyebrow. "Wes," Dana said with a disdainful wave of her hand.

Father Jerry pointed to the *Blade*. Tomorrow's paper, I was sure, would contain a carefully doctored account of the bizarre shooting on the Lost Peninsula, but today's headline said that Wes Tannock had slipped twelve points in the polls since it was revealed that he'd accepted a campaign contribution from "alleged manufacturers of counterfeit airplane parts."

"Nice of him," I said noncommittally.

"The anemones are from Tarky," Dana said. A smaller vase with a mix of red, purple, and orange flowers rested next to her on the windowsill.

"The *Blade* says he's going to open his own political consulting firm," she went on. "Like anyone's going to hire him after Wes gets through trashing him." She shook her head. "I almost feel sorry for Tark the Shark. I guess I feel sorry for anyone who got taken by my beloved ex-husband."

"Speaking of Rap," I said, "is he really in Michigan? I was afraid for a minute that Ted killed him."

Dana gave a sound somewhere between a grunt and a laugh. "No such luck. He's up in Monroe doing some deal with sound equipment for a political rally."

Father Jerry cleared his throat. "I heard on the news that a group of anthropologists went down to Honduras and dug up a lot of bodies. They think one of them was Joaquín Baltasar."

"Waaa-keeen," Jan echoed. "Ooooor Waaakeeen."

"Yeah. Poor Joaquín." Ron's voice tried to sound sad, but the smile on his face rejoiced in Jan's comprehensibility.

"All she needs is about five more consonants," I murmured.

Dr. Singh swept into the room, followed by a short, dark-skinned woman in a white coat. "I thought since you were so much better," he said to Jan, "that I should introduce you to the best plastic surgeon in this hospital. She will take charge of restoring your face."

The young woman stepped forward, held out her hand, and said, "I'm Dr. Ysabel Navarro."

Belita. Little Belita of the round brown face and laughing eyes. Little Belita, whose solemn child-face I had last seen on a bunch of pastel flyers I was about to distribute at the county fair.

The breath rushed out of my body. I wanted to jump up and hug her, all five feet of her, but then I wondered whether she'd know me. Did she have any memory at all of the Amigos Unidos day care center? I glanced at Father Jerry. He gave a tiny shake of his head. Not now, he seemed to say. Wait.

Sounds drifted in from the corridor. The clanking of meal trays, the chatter of passers-by, the canned music. The tune caught my ear; it was a "lite" version of Simon and Garfunkle's "Bridge over Troubled Water."

The words came back to me as I rested my head against the cool white wall. "When you're weary, feeling down. When evening falls so hard."

Belita was our bridge over the troubled waters of the past. We'd done it for her—or at least we believed we were doing it for her. Calling attention to the fact that one child injured in the fields by deadly poison was one too many. Acting as if she was important, not just a migrant kid who could be thrown away, left to a dead-end future.

And her future hadn't been dead-end. Somehow she'd climbed out of the limitations of her background and gone to medical school. Something good had come out of that summer after all.

I was still shaken by Ted's death. Still fragile. That was the only explanation for the tears that I couldn't seem to stop. They slid silently down my face as Belita took Jan through the steps of her proposed surgical plan.

There were other Belitas out there. I felt it as the song swelled to its climax. "Like a bridge over troubled water, I will lay me down." Other children had made it out of poverty, thanks to Head Start. Other families had found decent housing, thanks to Legal Services. Other kids had been trained for careers thanks to the Job Corps.

We hadn't ended poverty, but we'd made a dent. And even a tiny dent was better than complacent acceptance of the unacceptable.

After Belita and Dr. Singh left the room, Jan turned to Ron.

She held out her hand and grasped his. She murmured something I didn't quite catch, something that sounded like "honeymoon city."

But that didn't make sense.